BORED GAY WEREWOLF

BORED GAY WEREWOLF

TONY SANTORELLA

atlantic · *fiction*

First published in hardback in Great Britain in 2023 by Atlantic Books, an imprint of Atlantic Books Ltd.

Copyright © Tony Santorella, 2023

1 2 3 4 5 6 7 8 9

A CIP catalogue record for this book is available from the British Library.

Hardback ISBN: 9781838957018
Trade paperback ISBN: 9781838957223
E-book ISBN: 9781838957186

Printed and bound in Great Britain by TJ Books Limited, Padstow, Cornwall

Atlantic Books
An imprint of Atlantic Books Ltd
Ormond House
26–27 Boswell Street
London WC1N 3JZ

www.atlantic-books.co.uk

MIX
Paper from
responsible sources
FSC
www.fsc.org   FSC® C013056

For anyone who has ever cried
in a walk-in refrigerator

ONE

The light floods into an austere studio apartment, the industrial windows magnifying the stark midday sun so that it bakes the cinderblock walls and all its contents. Like most revitalized buildings in the neighborhood, the unit is blank and impersonal like a Nordic prison cell, the kind designed for rehabilitation rather than punishment. The particleboard cabinets in the kitchenette hold a menagerie of mismatched glassware, stolen pint glasses and Icelandic yogurt jars repurposed as whiskey tumblers, still tacky to the touch where the labels have been scratched away. Pots and pans overflow from the sink, stacked atop the steel counters amid receipts and flyers from nightclub promoters and street fundraisers. The polished concrete floor is a graveyard of unopened packing boxes, dirty thrift-store T-shirts and stacks of never-read books, through which winds a footpath toward a mattress in the center of the room. The pile under the pilled flannel duvet begins to stir with kicks and elbows, until an outstretched hand shoots from under the blanket. It fumbles across the books, laptop, phone charger, briefly holding and contemplating each until it finds a half-empty Red Bull.

The hand snatches it quickly under the covers like a fresh kill. Brian heaves himself up to sitting, swigs down the flat cotton candy battery acid, crushes the can and throws it across the room. Pushing his messy hair from his eyes, he growls as last night's drinks begin to pound in his head. He squints on either side of him; he didn't bring anyone home with him. That's good. He looks at his hands and pulls up the covers for his feet to peek out at the bottom. He takes a deep breath and lifts the blanket, then slowly exhales upon seeing the outline of his morning erection in his boxer briefs. He's alive and ended the night with the same number of appendages he started out with. Maybe last night wasn't so bad?

For a good thirty seconds longer Brian is in a blissful state of ignorance before his memory kicks in, a stream-of-consciousness slideshow of … wait … ouzo shots? And did he really commandeer the dive bar jukebox to dance alone under the disco lights to Björk's 'Hyperballad', hoping that the bulky tattooed doorman he had been directing weapons-grade flirting at all night would finally look his way?

The pounding quickens and Brian hides under his blanket to begin his well-rehearsed morning recitation of self-loathing. Starting, of course, with the most immediate: *you should have known this would happen.* A couple of drinks is never just a couple of drinks with Brian. He has two speeds for alcohol, on and off. But despite this knowledge, he hasn't been able to rein himself in. *Next time will be different*, he promises his pillow.

But will it? He tells himself that *next time will be different* most weeks, and most weeks … it's not. He didn't think his self-destructive phase would last this long. It would be a blip in the grand scheme of his twenties. But it's been nearly a year now of every night starting as *okay, but just a couple.* He had moved here to get on with his life, but he's barely even unpacked. He still hasn't bought curtains. He holds his hand over his eyes to block the sunlight. At least he got out the bar in time. He managed that much.

He rolls out of bed onto all fours, a wounded animal in boxer briefs and a ratty T-shirt. He follows the trail of clothing leading from his bed to the door. He can smell his jeans before he sees them, the familiar scent of a hundred collective meals from last night's shift combined with about a thousand after-hours cigarettes. He lifts them from a packing box and holds them at arm's length, their blunt odor making his stomach lurch. He pats them down and pulls out a wad of cash and his cracked cell phone. Thirteen missed messages from his group chat with Nik and Darby. He scrolls to the top.

Nik: WHERE DID YOU GO?!

Yep. He made it to the park in time. He skims the rest of the exchange of text bubbles, ending with both of them confirming they are safely at home. They don't seem unduly pissed at him – Brian's friends know he has a penchant for the Irish goodbye. He shoots off a quick apology text, anyway.

Brian: Sorry guys. Had one too many and had to leave IMMEDIATELY. See you tonight tho!

Brian waits and watches for a response. Nik is typing. He wonders vaguely if they suspect anything.

Nik: Just let us know next time! I was worried. BTW you left your bike at the bar. But in the state you were in, it's probably for the best.

Darby: And bitch, you better hydrate. I can't pick up your slack tonight. Have to put on my own face mask before assisting others.

Brian rolls his eyes at Darby and clicks his phone into the charging cable on the floor. One would think with five years of experience and the cyclical nature of the moon, the twenty-five-year-old werewolf wouldn't be caught off guard each month. But plans rarely work out for Brian and take more energy than they're worth. He thinks of his transitions in the same way he does his piles of laundry on the floor – he has never separated lights and colors and, so far, nothing that bad has happened. Okay, sure, there was that one person in the park last month. But, if you average that with all the nights he *hasn't* killed someone, he definitely has a passing grade.

As penance for his bad decision-making, Brian begins to organize the chaos of his apartment. Starting from the front door, a trash bag in one hand, he works outwards, widening the footpath carved through the detritus that links the bed, bathroom and kitchen. He picks up takeout flyers, balled-up tissues and empty packs of cigarettes.

He tosses away a pile of unopened mail (everything is online anyways) and uncovers a long-forgotten plate and fork with the remnants of some hardened spaghetti and marinara sauce. Holding it in one hand, he slowly turns it upside down, but the fork is fused to the plate. He shrugs and throws them both away. He picks up a greasy pizza box and is delighted to hear the rattle of leftovers. He gnaws at a four-day-old pepperoni slice for breakfast while absentmindedly kicking sweaters, socks, T-shirts and jeans across the floor into their respective piles, triaging them from dirty to less dirty. He clears off the steel countertop, surgically unfurling a couple of rolled-up bills that he found next to the microwave. He squints to see if any flecks of coke have dusted the countertop. It's not much, but he dips his index finger in what's left and rubs his gums anyways.

With some space now freed up in the room, he resolves to tackle the packing boxes. He has been avoiding them for months. When he moved in, he only unpacked the essentials – laptop, kitchenware, clothes and lube, unsure if his stint in the city would take. He's spent the last twelve months sliding, stacking and unstacking the neat cardboard boxes into a range of Tetris formations. They've been dinner tables, nightstands and chairs; and during one mushroom-induced trip they were both the walls and the distinguished guests of a tea party in his blanket fort. Their alternate uses protect him from both their contents and the arduous task of having to pack things up quickly if he's ever found out. But he can't live among boxes forever.

Brian takes a deep breath and puts himself to work.

Kneeling before the box labeled 'School', he removes the unused textbooks and stacks them against the wall with the others. The hardcover copies of *Moral Philosophy*, *Historical Sociology*, *Cultural Anthropology*, serve as a strong foundation. He stacks the paperbacks on top, each a variation on the same theme but with the word 'Perspectives' clunkily added to the title. All of which were tools to prepare him for a career in … being hard to talk to. He was two years into his degree when he was turned. It's hard for him to remember the version of himself that got him into university in the first place. The years of studying, volunteer work and struggling to pull his weight on the Mathletics team were all done in the service of a future that now seemed entirely out of reach. He had tried in the beginning to keep going, keep up his studies, to not let his condition hold him back, but he had struggled too much with the hypocrisy of preparing himself for a vocation that would put some good in the world with the murderous tendencies of being something that goes bump in the night. He had left school about a week after he'd eaten the campus cat and hadn't looked at his textbooks since. He thinks to himself that if they're out in the open at least, he may one day have the inclination to pick them back up and jumpstart his motivation to finish his degree. And if that doesn't happen? Well, if he's ever short on cash, they're a sort of millennial nest egg. Textbooks can be sold for a fortune on Amazon.

Once he's emptied out all the books, he crawls over

to another box, pausing at the flap, where his mother has written in marker pen 'beach towels and rugs'. Brian runs a finger over his mother's familiar cursive, a flourishing penmanship beaten into her through years of Catholic school. He didn't even know he owned any rugs. He remembers the day his parents picked him up from college. He was scant on details, only telling them that he was done. The paperwork was submitted, he was leaving. They had never really had a particularly effusive relationship. When they pulled up to meet him outside the student housing, they must have been thinking the worst. Their young, whip-smart son who had quietly exceeded their expectations was a stark contrast to the sallow-cheeked twenty-something stood before them. They must have thought it was drugs. That their gay son was out gaying it up at the first chance he got to get out of the suburbs. That or crushing amphetamines to keep up with the breakneck academic pace he had set for himself.

He stood outside the dormitory as the gray sky misted over, flaring the lights from inside the academic buildings. His mother by his side, with his father diligently packing his things in the hatchback, the other students flowing between classes, giving the family a wide berth.

'Maybe you'll feel ready to go back next term?' his mother said, trying to sound optimistic.

'Uh-huh,' he said from his 10,000-yard stare.

'You know, I never told you this, but your old man was no stranger to parties in my college days. I'm sure if you just buckle down ...'

'It's not that.'

His dad closed the hatchback with a thud. 'Do you want to talk about it?'

'No. No thank you.' The two of them both seemed relieved at that.

They all piled into the car and wordlessly began the two-hour drive back home. Brian slept most of the way. On the occasion he was awoken by passing traffic, he would catch concerned looks from his mother's eyes in the rear-view mirror.

His parents let him sleep for days. They washed his clothes. Left him plates of food and folded laundry at the door of his childhood bedroom. After a week, he worked up the courage to join his mother in the living room during the day. He would lie down on the loveseat, his feet now hanging off the armrest, and watch daytime talk shows and soap operas. She would sit in the armchair beside him, vibrating with unspent energy, using the commercial breaks to take care of housework and bring him apple slices and fruit snacks. It was a second adolescence as he fell into the rhythm of a string of yet-to-be-determined number of sick days home from school. Whenever his mother ran errands, he'd stay home, lest they run into any of his friends from school and alert the cabal of judgmental overachievers. But he did reach out to his old weed dealer, who now managed the liquor store at the end of their street. When he became attuned to the cadence of his mother's errands, he would fire off a quick text and slide his sneakers half on, shuffling up the street on the mashed-up heels of his shoes to the loading area in the back. After a clandestine handoff, he'd hurry back to get high in the garage and tiptoe back to his bedroom to play Super Nintendo till the early morning. Brian gradually felt more like himself and would get more and more courageous with his solo excursions. After a month he had re-downloaded Grindr to peruse the faceless torso pics. When everyone was asleep, he would tiptoe out the door and jump into an idling car a couple houses down for late-night rendezvous with discreet married men within a 5-mile radius. Two steps forward, three steps back.

Brian was used to keeping secrets from his family, forged in the fires of suburban politeness and being in the closet all those years, so being a werewolf fit neatly in the cavity in his mind where things were kept that could never be spoken. They hadn't noticed his late-night hook-ups, so he didn't think much about sneaking out each month for the full moon. He had perfected the craft from meeting his out-of-town boyfriends in high school for romantic midnight drives followed by awkward, passenger-seat hand stuff. This would just be a trial period to get his proverbial shit together before getting back on with his life – he imagined that, when he'd figured out how to have a handle on the whole mythical-beast condition, he'd re-enroll at college, reframe it as a gap year, and continue on the path set before him. And, in truth, the suburbs were a perfect place for Brian to learn to manage his transitions without causing too much collateral damage. He'd go into the huge, sprawling forest, strip down and leave his clothes next to an old beech tree, then spend his night terrorizing the local fauna. But he hadn't accounted for the increased attention paid by middle-class suburbanites to the comings and goings of their only child after suffering an ambiguous breakdown.

Walking back in from the forest one dawn, he had felt particularly relaxed, knowing he was at the furthest point from the next full moon. The soles of his feet had been wet with dew, the sun cresting over the pine trees. For the first time he had thought that perhaps things were going to be all right. With his shoes in his hands, he tiptoed through the kitchen back toward his room. Then the lights turned on behind him in the living room. It was his mother, her robe pulled tightly around her, her hand shaking as she took a drag of her cigarette.

'Where have you been?'

'I was just taking a walk through the woods.' Brian congratulated himself for saying something that was true. She always knew when he was lying.

'I heard you leave around midnight. What were you doing?' Her voice shook. 'Just tell me. Is it drugs? Is that what this is? I know what it smells like, you know. Your poor father thought a skunk was trapped in the garage.'

'No, it's not. It's not that.'

'Then what is it? Something's up. You've been sneaking out at night doing God knows what. You drop out of college without so much as a word. Do you know how much that cost us to send you to school? No, you don't. You just do whatever you want. I just can't believe—'

'Mom! It's fine. I swear!'

'No, it's not fine. You're in our house and you live by our rules. We're trying, Brian, but you're not. You need to straighten up and apply yourself. I just—'

'I'm a werewolf, okay!' Brian yelled, before hushing his voice. 'So now you know.' His mother laughed but stopped when she saw her son's face and knew he wasn't lying. She looked about the room to find her armchair and sat down in silence, her trademark pent-up energy gone. She was completely still. Brian sat across from her on the loveseat and watched as the red ember crept toward the butt of her cigarette. He told her everything he could. But she said nothing in response. He tried to read her face for any emotions – shame, disappointment, fear for herself or even the safety of her only child – anything to confirm that she was listening, that this conversation was actually happening. But as the sunrise began to fill the living room with the morning light, she merely stood up and tightened her robe, and told him to go to bed.

He wasn't sure if she believed him. If she told his father or not. But there were signs. There was the care and attention she took to washing his silverware after he used it. (She must have feared he was contagious, that they could 'catch it' from him.) They stopped having red meat for dinner. They bought a plug-in pet deodorizer. They walked on eggshells around him, careful not to raise his temper. They had just been getting comfortable with Brian after he came out, and they were acclimating to him dropping out of school, but now it turns out he's a werewolf? It all proved too much to handle for them. The effort of avoiding talking about his sexuality, and school, and being a werewolf turned into avoiding talking entirely. There were strings of repetitive lonely days filled with silence, the only virtue of this being that it allowed Brian to concentrate on completing Super Mario Bros. After that, with nothing else to do, Brian decided it was best for everyone if he left and moved to the city.

'You sure? You're welcome to stay as long as you need,' his mom said with zero conviction.

'Yes, we love having you here,' his dad lied.

Within a week, Brian had found a dirt-cheap studio apartment in the city. His parents had driven him over, paid the first month of rent and then left him with the boxes of dishware and old beach towels and rugs, the consolation prize he received for them to wash their hands of his complications.

Brian shakes his head free of the memory, grabs one of the towels and heads to his bathroom. He shucks off his underwear in the cool of the windowless tiled room and turns on the shower to its hottest setting. As the room begins to steam up, he examines himself in the mirror, and the self-loathing picks up right where it left off. *You look exhausted. Do you call that a beard? Make a decision: either grow it out or shave.* He grabs a fold of his belly with both hands. *Look at that gut, you've got to lose weight—*

Suddenly he catches a glimpse of something that wasn't there before. He wipes the mist from the mirror and leans in closer to see four parallel scratch marks starting just under his rib cage. He traces the trail of blood-red lines with his fingers, following them over his love handles to their end point, just above his kidney. That was close, he thinks. Brian's no stranger to the occasional wear and tear that comes with his monthly transitions. The muscle aches, the sounds of his bones creaking back into place, and the joys of passing his werewolf snacks through his very human digestive tract come morning. The scratches and bites typically heal on their own by midday. But these ones are wider and the heat on his hand suggests they went deep. Whatever animal did this could not have survived. House cat? Too small. A big house cat? Forget it, he thinks, there's no time to linger on this now – he's wasted too much time cleaning the apartment and if he's late for his shift, Nik will kill him. He throws himself under the shower head.

Half an hour later, Brian slams the door of his apartment behind him and tries to smuggle his hair under a beanie as he rushes down the fluorescent lit corridor of his old apartment building. He knew it, he's going to be late. Pulling open the door to the outside, he walks out into the cool winter air and cuts across the street, making his way to the nearest bus stop. He pulls on his headphones and cues up New Order on his 'You're running late AGAIN' playlist.

When he moved to the city a year ago, this was the only part of town he could afford. But even in a few short months, the aunties pushing their grocery carts past bodegas and check-cashing shops are being pushed out by thirty-something hipsters on their way to the new farm-to-table 'concept', replete with Edison bulbs and sans serif menus. Brian dodges a group of girls heading into a cocktail bar, walking through a cloud of Santal 33 that stings his nostrils. He inadvertently growls and bares his teeth at the folks ruining his neighborhood. 'Assholes,' he mutters under his breath, before diving into his favorite boutique cafe for a triple-shot oat milk latte, turning up his music so he doesn't have to hear his own hypocrisy.

Brian tries everything he can to avoid public transit. It's top of his list of werewolf nuisances, followed closely by dog walkers, close talkers and, presumably, silver bullets. The combination of his super-lupine sense of smell and a hangover makes the bus unbearable, but with his bike chained up round the back of the bar and his shift starting – he checks his watch – in twenty minutes, he has no choice. He grabs the closest seat to the door and opens the window, trying his best to ignore the sticky-sweet smell of collective humanity. A child whining and screeching in its pram smells of milk burps. A man hanging from one of the hand stirrups forgot to put on deodorant. A woman eating a tuna melt on the backseat should be exiled for her lack of common decency. Brian thinks about how his childhood dog used to stick his head out the window on car rides and how he wishes he could do that now. Instead, he pulls his hoodie up over his nose and stares out into the early evening, the sun lowering in the sky, the cityscape changing from bustling bars and nightlife to rowhomes and tree-lined streets.

The Romanesco is nestled in a quiet, suburban part of town. Look at it long enough and you can see the owner's painstaking effort to reach the nexus of bohemian cafe and utilitarian diner. The large, paneled windows overlook a patio of chattering two-top tables that inch closer into the sidewalk as each guest leaves. Inside, the stained-glass pendant lamps and early 90s peach-colored walls warm groups of diners at the walnut tables and the marble-topped wraparound bar. With its proximity to Thousand Acre Park and a handful of hotels, they cater to a mix of older locals and rotating hordes of tourists and conference-goers. Once it was built and profitable, the owner quickly moved on, allowing his managers to run the shop. The food is a mix of serviceable classics designed to neither offend nor wow any palate. Notably absent is any actual Romanesco, but anyone can find something in their five-page laminated menu. Brian likes the place. It's easy work in a quiet part of town and he figures himself lucky to have got it. He was trawling a local Facebook page for jobs and saw an ad for a new waiter. He turned up the next day, was quizzed on whether he had a police record, and when he said no, they gave him an apron. While the food is cheap and so the individual tips low, he can always rely on volume, and turning over tables quickly means he can guarantee at least $150 a night. Plus, they close early to prevent conflicts with the homeowners, which affords Brian time to transition after hours, chase down nature in the nearby park, and then sleep all day whenever he wants, or as his hangover requires.

By the time Brian's bus pulls up, the dinner rush has already started. He weaves through the customers crowding around the host stand, and angles to the end of the bar to grab his server apron. Behind the bar, a mid-thirties, heavy-set Filipina prima ballerina in Crocs and a messy bun dances from customer to customer, whipping up cocktails as she moves down the line. She glides down the length of the bar toward him. 'Here,' Nik orders, handing Brian a pink fizzing drink with a straw.

'What is this?' Brian asks, but Nik is already at the other end of the bar, cocktail shaker in hand, having dropped a pair of maraschino cherries in two Manhattans as she passed.

'Soda water and angostura bitters,' she shouts back, pouring the drink into a martini glass, garnishing it with a deft curl of lemon rind and placing it on an order ticket. 'It was always my go to. With the state you were in last night, I thought it could help.'

Brian takes a sip. 'Tastes medicinal,' he says with suspicion.

Nik pops the fridge and retrieves a bottle of white wine. With her back to him she begins to pour it out into glasses, reciting the body's internal processes for breaking down alcohol at the same time. 'Once alcohol is ingested, a small amount is absorbed directly by the tongue and the mucosal lining of the mouth. On its way down to the stomach, the tissue lining ...' Brian tunes out at the mention of 'pyloric valve' and catches the open physiology textbook by the cash register as she drones on about enzymes and metabolism. Bartending at night and nursing school during the day means Nik is always finding creative ways to apply her coursework.

'And this,' she says, coming back over and slapping a newspaper down on the bar in front of him, 'is why you need to always let us know you've made it home.' She's already gone again, picking up a bottle of gin from the row of liquors. 'And hurry up,' she yells back at him. 'You're late.'

Brian glances down at the newspaper, then freezes. It's folded open to the Metro section, *Jogger Killed in Apparent Animal Attack*. Time slows down and the noise and light from the restaurant recede; all he can see are phrases jumping out of the report. *Park officials are stunned ... Second attack in two months ...* He reaches under his hoodie and touches the scratches on his side. His eyes widen. 'Oops,' he says to himself. He scolds himself to be more careful, but another part of him thinks it's *fine* – the idea of a werewolf running rampant through the city would be so preposterous that whoever reported it would sooner be visited by a social worker than a detective. Still, the last thing he needs is anyone hunting him, or worse, capturing him. Imagine all the questions he'd get when the caged hell-beast became a chubby naked hipster come morning. What would they even do after they caught him? Execute him, experiment on him or draft him into the military? Seems like the first option is best – same outcome, but with a lot fewer steps in between.

'So, who was he?'

'Huh?' Time speeds up again and the clatter and conversation of the restaurant comes back to full volume. Darby's leaning over Brian's shoulder, seemingly out of nowhere. 'Who? I mean, what? Nobody,' he says, flipping the paper over. How this blond/e, white, *Neon Demon* femby can sneak up on an actual werewolf is beyond him. It's like they were designed in a lab expressly for eavesdropping.

Darby wanders around to the other side of the bar to face Brian. 'The guy you left us for last night,' they say, looking down and tying their apron. 'The doorman.' Darby cinches their apron strings quickly around their waist and peers up at him. 'I'm assuming …?'

'It's nobody.'

Darby cocks an eyebrow, clearly intrigued.

'I mean, there wasn't anybody,' Brian corrects himself.

'Sure,' says Darby, unconvinced. 'Well, whatever he or it was, I hope it was worth it. You missed a good time. The manager had to reset the jukebox after you turned into a Nordic yodeling torture device. Surprised they didn't call in the bomb squad to sort that one out.'

Darby peers down at Brian's newspaper. 'Oof, gruesome. You know, I heard it was one of our customers.'

'How would you know that?'

'I have my sources. Couldn't be anyone too well liked

or I'd notice them missing. But I'll get to the bottom of this. I got a nose for the news and the heels to go get it.'

The shift is the same as it always is. Working consistently together, they have fallen into a natural rhythm, and thanks to Nik making the schedule, she gets to keep it this way. Darby makes small talk with the patrons, aiming for quality of interactions rather than quantity – they take care to recognize the regulars, remember their orders, their kids' names, and other personal details Brian finds extraneous. But this care and attention is always reflected in their tips. Brian opts for efficiency and volume to get folks fed and on their way with limited back and forth, showing no interest, and sometimes even hostility, when parents slow him down so their children can practice ordering for themselves. Nik lands somewhere in the middle, knowing when to turn on the charm at her bar, which is equal parts confessional booth and therapist's couch. At the end of the night, they all take home about the same amount of money. But who worked harder for it depends on your definition of labor.

After the dinner rush, the restaurant empties out but for a few scattered customers. Nik reads a physiology textbook in between putting away glassware, while Brian sits at the end of the bar, waiting for his final customers to leave and trying not to go so heavy on himself for last night's homicide. Is it even murder, he thinks to himself, if he's technically not a human when he commits it?

Murder's a moral category, and animals don't have moral agency. So *surely* it could be argued that what he did last night was simply … nature?

His last table is a straight couple on their third date. They linger over their shared slice of flourless chocolate cake and playfully flirt with one another in hushed conversation. Brian, listening in from across the restaurant, ruefully stares at the happy couple, hoping they'll wrap it up and go fuck already. He always found the werewolf hearing as more of a bug than a feature, especially when you consider how mundane the average conversation is. 'He's left you on read for three days after your second date. I'm sure he's just super busy.' 'Yes, you are the smartest person at your job, and no one recognizes that.' Unsubscribe.

Brian pricks up his super-hearing ears when he hears the gentleman suggest a nightcap at his place. Fiiiiinally. The man holds up a finger to get his attention, but Brian is already printing out their check. He drops it on their table with a hollow smile and his signature *here-thanks-have-a-good-night*, which has all the warmth and sincerity of an airport security agent. As he walks back toward Nik, only yards from his first drink of the night, Darby intercepts.

'It brings me no pleasure to tell you this,' they say, taking a lot of pleasure in saying it, 'but you have a new table.'

'No … really? Why don't you take them? I've just closed these guys out.'

'I would, but he requested your section specifically,' Darby says, nodding in the direction of the blond guy taking a seat at a table in the back of the restaurant.

The clean-cut, thirty-something stranger is dressed in the management-consulting uniform: gingham shirt, performance fleece vest, khakis and a messenger bag. 'And you said there wasn't a guy last night,' Darby lowers their voice, leaning against the bar. 'Got to say though, he's a bit strait-laced to be your type.'

'There wasn't a guy! And what would you know about my type? What's your type?'

Nik, who previously wasn't paying attention, closes her textbook. 'This should be fun.'

Darby purses their lips and scans the remaining customers. 'Hmm … Oh, I don't know … I guess, oh yes, *that* would do quite nicely.'

Brian turns to see a tall older man with a neatly trimmed handlebar mustache and horn-rimmed glasses decked out in an all-black three-piece suit walking toward them. A modern dandy in a bow tie and trench coat. He grabs a stool, fishes out a pocket-sized journal and opens it on the bar.

'*Him?!*'

'Shh!' says Nik, glowering at Brian and then heading to the far end of the bar to take the man's order.

Brian looks back and forth between Darby and the man. The difference between them couldn't be more apparent: Darby dresses like a woodland nymph at a rave. They were a performance artist and gender was another one of their mediums – even hungover, they showed up to their shift today with a shimmery lavender eye and a nude lip.

'He looks like the oldest school shooter in the world,' says Brian. Nik stifles a laugh, already back over to fetch a particularly expensive bottle of Bordeaux.

'Pssh, he's tall, dark and handsome.' Darby grabs the wine out of Nik's hand. 'Don't worry, I can take this one. And don't *you* have somewhere to be?' they say, nodding at Brian's new table.

Brian rolls his eyes, cursing under his breath. People should have the decency not to come in within a half-hour of closing. He trudges the length of the restaurant over to the blond stranger. He's sitting at their largest table, his knees spread far apart. Brian sniffs the air surreptitiously. He can smell a mix of leather and pine. He looks down and fiddles around with his apron pockets as he approaches the table – after all, the moment you make eye contact is when the customer service begins.

'Hi, I'm Tyler,' chirps the customer. 'What about you?'

It's ancient hospitality lore that customers who ask for your name are the first ones to complain. Brian knows he's in for it when he looks up to see an outstretched hand. 'Brian,' he monotones, grabbing his pen and notepad to avoid the handshake. Even at a strip club you can't touch the girls. 'What can I get you?'

Tyler leans back in his chair and casually looks around the emptied-out restaurant. 'It's a cute little spot you all have,' he says. 'I grew up around here but never really made the time to go east of the park. But every time I do, I always find these hidden treasures. I keep telling myself I have to do it more, but you know how it is. You just get stuck in these routines and getting across town is such a *pain*.'

Brian stares blankly and clicks his pen. 'So ... something to drink?'

'Straight to business with you, huh!' Tyler says with a chuckle. 'All right, all right, I know how it is. I'll have a coffee. Now I bet you're thinking, "Who drinks coffee this late?", am I right?'

Wrong. Brian is actually thinking how long it will take to brew a new pot versus risking Nik's wrath if she catches him reheating stale coffee from the day shift again.

'But really, it's true what they say: "You're always working when you're working for yourself." Burning that midnight oil.' He reaches into his messenger bag. Brian's eyes widen as he gulps in anticipation – if it's a laptop, he's here for another hour, minimum. 'Hard to get the recommended eight hours of sleep every night. Some nights more than others. But you'd know all about that, wouldn't you?' Brian sees, to his relief, that Tyler has only pulled out an iPad, but then he registers the vague insinuation.

'What are you talking about?'

'Come on ... it's just us,' he chuckles. 'I thought for sure you would've remembered me,' he says with a wink.

Brian is confused. He has no idea who this guy is. He looks intently at the architecture of Tyler's face. Darby is right, he's not Brian's type. Too classically attractive, with Disney Prince undertones. Surely, he'd remember if he had fucked a cartoon?

'Listen, I'm sorry. You know, I work in the service industry, and I drink a ton ... so, if we've ever ...' Brian exhales before crudely miming sex by tapping his index fingers together.

'What?! No, I'm not … I mean, not that there's anything *wrong* with that. Also, is that even how you … never mind.' Tyler's face is pink. He spins the iPad to Brian; it's open to the article on the jogger, and he taps it and points to Brian's side in what may go down as the first game of mystical gay-panic charades.

Brian's heart stops. He puts a hand over the still-unhealed claw marks, feeling their familiar heat through his shirt. He stows the pen and notepad and scans the restaurant. There's no one nearby. 'Who are you? What do you want?'

'Hey now, no need to fear. I come in peace!' Tyler says, putting his hands up. 'You moved to the city what … a year ago? I've been looking for you for a while and I'm so happy we finally got to connect. Though I wish it were under better circumstances.'

Brian leans in. 'Listen, I don't know what you're implying, but—'

Tyler cuts him off. The charades continue. He slowly rolls up his gingham sleeve to show a faint pink bite mark the length of his forearm. He taps his finger to his nose and then holds it to his closed lips.

'You're a … You're like me?'

Tyler parries. 'Anyways, I'm sure it's hard to start fresh in a new place and *find your pack*, so to speak. After our little scuffle last night, I wanted to come by and introduce myself to make sure we don't get off on the wrong foot.

I'm putting together a group of *like-minded* individuals, and thought you might be interested. It'd be great to grab a coffee sometime and I can tell you all about it.'

Brian's heart has just about restarted. He's never met another werewolf. And this guy is saying there are more out there. Can this be for real? Regardless, he has to shut him up before anyone else hears. 'Yeah, sure,' he says, as cool as he can muster. He scans the restaurant again to see if anyone was in earshot. Nik is disdainfully drying glassware with her eyes on a four-top of drunk suits that still all have their conference lanyards looped around their necks, and Darby's too busy flirting with Mr. Tall, Dark and Handsome at the other end of the bar to notice, but it's best to be safe. 'Now's not a good time, though.'

'Hey, sure. I get it,' says Tyler, handing him his business card. 'Feel free to reach out and we can set something up.'

Brian grabs the card and backs away. 'Oh, and the coffee? How do you take it?'

'Black. And better make that to go. I should head out. I think we're good here.'

Brian hurries behind the bar, avoiding Nik's inquisitive stare. 'Who's that?' she murmurs. Brian shrugs as he fills a to-go cup of stale coffee. She calls after him, 'Wait – you're not going to serve that, are you?' Ignoring her, he turns back to the table but Tyler's already at the entrance, peering at his iPhone.

'Here,' Brian says, handing him his cup.

'Thanks. Money is on the table. Let's link up soon. Really. Don't be shy.'

Brian nods and watches Tyler go out into the night air, his breath misting in the cold. He climbs into a waiting car – an Uber Black, very fancy. Once the car has pulled away, Brian takes the card from his apron, feeling its expensive heft in his hand he flips it over. *Tyler Gainsborough – Entrepreneur and Life Coach.* He shakes his shoulders to release the tension and lumbers over to the now vacant table to grab the cash. It's just enough to cover the coffee. He hastily stuffs it in the back pocket of his jeans, thankful he never rang it in.

TWO

Tyler's business card is the only thing on Brian's refrigerator, pinned there with a single alphabet-letter magnet left by the previous tenant. It stares at him in every corner of his apartment. It's been a week since their encounter, and each time he meets its gaze he tells himself, *okay, Brian. Pick up the phone. Call.* But for a week he has failed to follow through with this, slipping into his inertia like a warm bath. When he wakes up at midday, he tells himself Tyler's likely busy or working. When he comes home at 2 a.m., it's too late to call, or he's too drunk to compose a text with one eye open. Plus, Tyler seems like the type to call rather than text, to use his phone as a power move, and the last thing Brian wants to do right now is chit-chat. *I'll do it in the morning*, he promises himself, knowing that he'll sleep through the whole morning.

Since dropping out of college, Brian's threshold for effort has bottomed out. His werewolf powers allow him to push his self-neglect to new heights. These can be small acts, like grabbing searing hot plates in the restaurant rather than walking to the other end of the line for a cloth or

27

tray to protect himself. Others would send a shiver down the spine of even the flintiest mental health professional. On more than one occasion when he's broke, tired or doesn't feel like riding his bike, there's his proclivity for throwing himself in front of cars to score a free ride home. The frantic drivers scream as they hit the brakes, Brian bouncing over their hood. He'll pop his shoulder back into its socket, brush off the gravel, and slur them assurances that there's no need to get the cops involved if they could just take him across town. Because of this, the tasks without any werewolf workarounds – taking out the trash, doing the dishes, sending his mother a birthday card – are all Herculean efforts that take a level of resolve that Brian cannot muster. Exploring his connection with Tyler sounds like another one of those boring quotidian tasks for Brian's non-existent to-do list. First off, this guy seems entirely too well adjusted, which makes Brian immediately suspicious. Second, Brian has never had any close relationships with straight guys. Performing butch, palatable gay is such a chore. Add to that the issue of Tyler accusing him of murder and maiming him in battle and it all sounds like … a lot.

And besides, Brian's surprisingly busy given his hostility to doing things. Moving through the din of the city, the crowded restaurants and bars, he is constantly surrounded by people. He rides their tide, pushing him from home, to work, then drinks, then home again. He hates his days off; they always feel like he's in a sad airport lounge where he's arrived for his flight twenty-four hours early. He lazes about his apartment, propped up in bed, draining a series of beverages to correct his hangover and switching between the screens of his computer and phone to watch Netflix and endlessly scroll the same three websites. This day off is not unlike the rest of them. But it's hard for him to ignore the tacit obligation from the business card. He *really* should call, he thinks, as he levers himself up off his mattress, puts on his headphones and heads to his cafe to drink cappuccinos and doom-scroll Twitter. When he comes back, the card is still there. 'What do you want from me!' he yells at it, before turning his back on it and throwing himself back down on his bed. He lies about for the rest of the day, opting to start the multi-season odyssey of *Love Island* (which he convinces himself he is enjoying ironically), reading the Wikipedia plot summaries of horror movies he's too scared to see alone, and following the internet to its inevitable conclusion: Pornhub. He quickly loads up some intrepid DILFS fixing a muscle car, puts his hand into his boxers and is about to jerk off but then … feels awkward doing it with the business card there. 'Fine,' he shouts at it, grabs his phone and opens up Grindr. After perusing the faceless, shirtless guys in his neighborhood, he rapid-fires 'hey handsome' texts till one of them bites. He grabs his headphones, jacket and keys, spins around at the front door to raise a middle finger to the card, and then he hits the street.

A quick run-jog down the bustling main street as bus after bus unloads the commuter class, Brian weaving his way through them as they stare down at their phones, and then he's there, outside the modern apartment building of DiscreteDaddy. The steel and glass architecture juts out from rustic brick storefronts on either side of it, individually separate and distinct like the typo in the Grindr profile suggests. He's about to hit the intercom, but instead sneaks in behind a couple of tech bros in performance fleece returning from work. He climbs the stairs to the third floor, knocks on the guy's door and hears a yipping dog followed by a gruff, 'Just a second.' DiscreteDaddy answers the door, a business-casual bear, heavy-set, shaved head and a thick beard. He examines Brian from his beanie to his filthy Chuck All Stars. With a face of subdued satisfaction, he unbuttons the top of his collared shirt.

'You're not 6 foot,' he says matter-of-factly as he walks deeper into the apartment, picking up his miniature Pomeranian on the way and placing it in its crate.

Brian follows. 'Uh, no, I also didn't say I was.' Brian is 5 foot 11 and three quarters. That quarter-inch is such a dealbreaker. 'You didn't say you had a dog.' Brian loves dogs, having grown up with them all his life, but since becoming a werewolf, they haven't seen eye to eye.

The man stops. 'Is that going to be a problem?'

'Uh, no. It's fine. Allergies. Mild, though.'

'Okay, well, this has to be quick. My husband is coming home soon,' he says, somehow taking off his pants while not breaking stride to the bedroom. Brian wordlessly follows him in. DiscreteDaddy is already naked on all fours, perched at the edge of the bed, asshole akimbo. Time is clearly of the essence. Brian wastes none of it, unbuttoning his jeans and pulling them down just enough to free his hard-on. He enters him and he moans. They fuck in silence. It's too quiet, like a Marina Abramovic piece begging the viewer to contemplate the carnality of the act in silent solemnity. Though Brian has never liked the performance of dirty talk, he feels like he should say something.

'You like this dick?' he hears himself ask wanly and cringes; the delivery is akin to checking if one of his tables needed ketchup.

'We don't need to talk,' replies DiscreteDaddy.

Brian shrugs it off and does as he's told. After five passionless minutes of thrusting and grunting, he's finally rewarded by a low growl. 'Yeah, you like that?' Brian gamely tries again, but then he realizes the low growl came ... from behind him. The miniature Pomeranian is out of its cage, staring at the 5 foot 11 and three quarters werewolf pounding his dad doggy style.

'Psst – go away.' Brian takes his hands off the man's hips to try and shoo it away, but it's no use, the toy dog starts barking aggressively. Brian's presence has activated its fight or flight response, and this dog is a fighter. 'Ignore him,' DiscreteDaddy mutters, and pulls Brian deeper. The dog latches onto Brian's leg and bites down hard.

'AGH! FUCK!' Brian kicks the dog across the room, bouncing it off the built-in wardrobe.

'Yeah, that's right. You like this bussy?'

Bussy? 'Uh, sure.' *Sure? SURE? What the fuck, Brian?!*

He continues to fuck while looking at the poofball of a Pomeranian lying on the floor. It's still breathing, thank God. It gets woozily back up and shakes its head, jingling its collar. It looks back at Brian and growls, then runs across the room to sink its teeth into Brian's leg again. DiscreteDaddy is close, he moans over the growl of the Pomeranian, blissfully unaware of the animal attack at the other end of him. Brian tries rapidly shaking his leg, trying to break the dog loose, but it's no use. Whatever, it's clearly working for DiscreteDaddy, who's working up to a noisy climax. Brian finally looks down at the dog, his eyes turn red, and he lets out a devastating, wolverine growl that vibrates the room. 'Oh, yes, pound this bussy!' DiscreteDaddy yells as he comes. The dog releases its grip and yips out the room, its paws click-clacking down the hallway.

Brian holsters his hard-on in his boxers. DiscreteDaddy turns over and grabs a towel to clean himself off. He stands in front of Brian and dabs the sweat from Brian's forehead. 'You really went for it at the end there, bud.'

'Uh, yeah, you were great, really,' he says, pulling up his pants. 'Um, I should probably go.' Brian peers out the bedroom to see the Pomeranian cowering in the corner of its cage. After some perfunctory conversation and even a 'thank you' that Brian will remember saying for the rest of his life, he dashes out of the apartment as quickly as he possibly can.

Brian trudges back to his apartment with his tail between his legs. The sun has gone down, and the nightlife of his neighborhood is waking up. He pulls on his headphones, turns on The Cure and shoegazes his way back past the busy bars and all the people inside. He stops on the sidewalk in front of another new, crowded restaurant with a monosyllabic name, then walks through the people passing on the street to get to the window where he can see a group of twenty-somethings, pulling each other into hugs and smiling as they take their seats. Brian makes a little story for them: they're friends from college who just moved to the city; they're happy to finally see one another again; it's been too long. Now that they're all in the same city they'll feng shui their respective friendship groups so they can snuggly fit each other in, dinner parties and double dates, a whole new, extended community. Brian comes a little closer to the window. It's been so long since he's fully trusted himself with other people. After he was turned, he cut his nascent college friendships dead and refused to look up any of his old school friends who might still have been around when he moved back in with his parents. There were Nik and Darby, sure, but no matter how much he liked them, he'd always have to hold them at arm's length – although he didn't know whether that was because he was protecting them or protecting himself.

One of the men in the restaurant says something and everyone else at the table laughs, heads thrown back. *That used to be me*, Brian thinks. He knows he'd never be welcome, but he wonders if he just stands there long enough whether he could gain some of that warmth, enough to light a candle. If he did, and he kept it close to his chest, his free hand cradling the flame, could it last through the night or would it go out just as he turns the corner to his apartment? It's then that the happy couples notice him staring. They all stop laughing. One of the women frowns and gestures over at a waiter, pointing to Brian. Brian shakes his head and darts into the adjacent liquor store, opting for the synthetic warmth of a bottle of bourbon instead.

Opening the door to his apartment, Tyler's business card welcomes him back. Brian shrugs off his jacket, beelines for the fridge, grabs the card and fires off a quick text. Hey – it's Brian. Are you free to meet up tomorrow? Seconds pass before Brian sees Tyler's ellipsis bubble up to the surface. Brian drops his phone on the counter and peers at it nervously.

Tyler: Great to hear from you. Yes, let's touch base tomorrow.

It's always the tasks that you avoid the longest that are resolved the quickest. He spends a brief moment basking in the glow of productivity, then he thumbs the lid from the whiskey bottle, takes a long pull, grabs his laptop and jerks off.

Three p.m. is either too early or too late to do anything, so Brian was surprised when Tyler agreed to meet him at this time, especially on a weekday. Shouldn't he be somewhere analyzing a flow chart or something? The

Romanesco is quiet during this twilight hour, a post-lunch, pre-dinner no man's land made for teleworkers and the underemployed. He scans the restaurant and spots Tyler, emerging from the reeds of diners bent over their laptops to wave him over to his table in the back. Brian hurries over and plops himself into the seat. 'Hey.'

'Hey there! So glad we got to meet up,' Tyler says cheerfully. 'I've already ordered, but I can flag our girl down if you want to order something.' He throws his hand up without waiting for an answer. Brian winces at the term 'our girl', but lets it go. At least he didn't snap for her attention. Snappers are the worst.

The server is a variation on a hipster theme, split-dyed black and blonde hair, septum piercing and neon eye make-up; the type of employee the owner hires because he thinks it imbues The Romanesco with a Noah Baumbach-movie vibe, despite the complete lack of arthouse aesthetic in the quiet, residential neighborhood. Brian tries to place her, but he doesn't know the day-shift staff but for the complaints they lodge anonymously with management on how he, Nik and Darby close the restaurant. They're always complaining about something, like the tables being slightly too close together after Brian mopped, or Nik shelving the wine glasses in front of the champagne flutes when *we all know* that the brunch shift needs them front and center for mimosas. Never one to take things lying down, Darby found artful ways to get back at them. They would occasionally hide the tip jar at the counter, leaving behind a series of playfully threatening clues for the morning barista to follow, like a service industry *Saw* trap. There was one night when the three of them were rolling silverware in napkins. Darby wrote 'You win! See manager for details!' in a handful of them. The vague suggestion of a prize resulted in an anarchic brunch shift that led to one server tearfully quitting on the spot.

Brian orders a coffee from her, and she sighs and turns on her heel toward the bar. Tyler fills the silence with small talk about the Brazilian jiu-jitsu belt he's training for until the server's back and giving Brian his coffee as if she's wearing a heavy coat, a load too great to bear. Brian notices she forgot the milk, but keeps it to himself. Once she's out of earshot, he cuts Tyler off just as he's describing the finer techniques of a back-mount chokehold. 'So, what's your deal? What do you want from me?'

'Whoa! So direct. It's refreshing, really.' Tyler takes a sip of his coffee and leans back in his chair, puffing out his chest. 'Where should I begin?'

Brian hunches in. 'Who are you?'

'Wow, that's a tough one. I'm a lot of things. An entrepreneur is a good catch-all term, albeit reductive. I'm also a philosopher, a searcher, a life-long learner, a coach and mentor, a writer, some could say an influencer—'

'I can't help but notice one glaring omission from that list.'

'What? Werewolf?' As easy as Tyler has thrown the word away, it startles Brian. 'Yes, that's part of me, but it's not what defines me.'

36

'How long have you, you know …' Brian mimes claws and a hushed roar.

'You can say it. I mean, who would even believe you?' Despite this, Brian still can't think of the last time he's said it out loud. He's never really had to.

'Maybe it would be easiest if I just start at the beginning?' says Tyler. Brian nods, grateful not to have to talk about himself, and Tyler nods in response, grateful for the opportunity to talk about himself. First, he takes Brian on a journey through his pedigree and qualifications, starting with his idyllic childhood in suburbs just outside the city. His father is an executive at a financial services firm in the city, his mother, a homemaker. He tries to make time to visit them – his mother makes the *best* Sunday roast – but it's difficult with his busy work schedule. A by-product of being an only child raised by two Hobbesian helicopter parents with means, Tyler seems to have been training for college applications his entire life.

'I spent the summers in Brittany for French camp. Immersion is the only way to truly learn. I've been learning Mandarin since I could walk, but those were all private tutors. It was the only way it could fit in with fencing and polo.'

'Speedo or horsey?'

Tyler stifles a chuckle. 'Both.'

Second, Tyler's professional résumé. After graduating from his top-tier university, where both of his parents are alumni, and then spending a gap year bumming around ashrams in India, he spent some time in finance (almost certainly at his father's firm, Brian suspects) and then at several prestige companies across the city.

'You know the kind,' Tyler says casually, resting his forearm on the back of his chair. 'Billion-dollar fund management, oil futures, that kind of boring *old-world* stuff. But you and I know, the future is tech. So, I did a pivot. Called in a few favors and did my time at Google. Really cutting-edge stuff. But I still felt confined. Stifled. It was then that I understood the industry was not going to allow me to realize all the goals I had for myself. So, I left the rat race behind to pursue my diverse interests as an entrepreneur.'

Brian sips his coffee and examines Tyler. He hears a lot of words, but they are light on meaning. He manages businesses, he consults, innovates, disrupts. He moves fast and breaks things. Recently, he's taken to coaching, looking for opportunities to share the lessons he's learned throughout his career that have contributed to his success. While Brian still has zero idea what Tyler actually does, his delivery is effective, reminding Brian of a politician, one that his mom would say she voted for because 'he has a kind smile'. He wonders if people are just born with this innate confidence and a silver tongue for bullshit or if it comes through years of conditioning. If being consistently told you are exceptional means that when you say it yourself, it's less subjective and more a statement of fact. How freeing it must be to feel you belong in any room, without the compulsory prologue of gratitude just for being invited in.

Brian suddenly realizes that Tyler has stopped speaking. When did he stop paying attention? Did Tyler ask him a question? Brian studies the Disney face for clues: he seems to be waiting for a response of some kind.

'Yeeesss?' Brian tries tentatively, assuming he can't go too wrong with agreement. He's rewarded with a beam. Brian doubles down and goes for confidence. 'I, um, think the *exact* same thing.'

'I knew you would,' Tyler says. 'I knew it.'

To cover up the fact that he has no idea what he has just agreed with or to, Brian changes the subject. 'This feels like an awkward first date when you eventually bring up your coming-out story.'

Tyler laughs awkwardly. 'So, let's have it out. How did you become one of us?'

'Honestly, it's anticlimactic.'

'Somehow I doubt that.'

Brian lets out a deep sigh. 'Ugh, fine. It was in my second year of university. I was back at my parents' for Christmas break. Heading to the mall in my mom's car to do some last-minute Christmas shopping. It was dark out and the snow was coming down. The road was slick, I wasn't paying attention and I sort of, kind of, *barely* hit this old lady while I was pulling into the parking lot.'

Tyler frowns. 'The old lady was a werewolf?'

'No, wait. I jumped right out of the car to help her up. I remember looking down and seeing her wrinkled hand with all these rings on. Just one hand lying in a heap of black and purple fabric. I was terrified. I thought, "Did

I just kill this woman? I need to get help." So, I got my phone and start dialing an ambulance—'

'Ah, the paramedic was a werewolf—'

'No! Still no. Because before I called, she shot right up to her feet. It was so fast, especially for her age. No lie, she must have been 100 years old. She got in close and was just screaming at me in some language I couldn't understand. Right in my face. So close I could count all the fillings in her teeth. I tried to apologize. I really did. But she wouldn't stop, so ... I put up my hands to get her away from me. The *tiniest* of nudges. And, well, I think that was the last straw.'

Tyler's face is expressionless, but Brian suspects he is being judged.

'I know, I know. Anyway, she didn't like that. The next thing you know, she throws up what *I* thought were gang signs, yells some Latin at me, spits on the ground and disappears into the night. I didn't think anything of it. I was just happy it was over, that she seemed fine, and we didn't have to get the police involved. Nothing happened until the next month when I was at a college party and started to feel sick. I thought it was just the pot brownie, so I left and walked back to my dorm – only of course I never got there. I woke up naked in the football field, covered in blood, with a squirrel tail hanging out of my mouth. And then, well, I guess the rest is history.'

Tyler stares at him blankly. 'Wait. So, who was the werewolf again?'

'That's what I'm saying! There was no werewolf.'

'You've never been bitten.'

'Nope. Just the old "witch's blood curse" situation. See, I told you it was anticlimactic.' Tyler nods slowly, taking it in. 'I'm sorry, man. That's. Not cool. Literally, that's the least cool werewolf story I've ever heard.' He starts laughing. 'A blood curse? Wow. I have not heard that one before.'

'Yeah, yeah, hilarious. So, if yours is so good, what happened to you?'

Tyler demurs, suddenly reluctant.

'I showed you mine, now you show me yours,' Brian cajoles.

'Okay. So, there was this storm ...' What follows is a twenty-minute hero's tale, in which a fifteen-year-old Tyler was the sole survivor of an attack on his scout troop, fighting off the beast with nothing but an ax and a Swiss Army knife, only ending when Tyler – bitten and losing blood – drove the little horseshoe blade that no one ever uses on a Swiss Army knife straight through the werewolf's eye and into its brain. Once distracted, he summoned all his remaining fury to decapitate the beast. Each additional detail makes Brian feel more humiliated.

'And as I lay there, bleeding, surrounded by the bodies of my friends, their blood reflecting the full moonlight, slowly losing consciousness, you know what I thought? I thought, "You're a survivor, Tyler. If you get out of here, you're going to inspire other survivors too",' Tyler finishes, his gaze set in the middle distance, as if waiting for applause. Brian shuffles in his chair and reaches for his phone.

'Well, it was all over the news. The media span it as a bear attack, but it was a werewolf. I'll forward you the article.'

'That's all right,' says Brian without looking up, brooding over Tyler's reaction to his blood-curse story. 'Anyway, what's with this support group you're putting together?'

'Ah, yes!' Tyler claps his hands. 'My "passion project". Well, I've been in the wolf game for a while. I've learned so much through the process. You know as well as I, werewolves have this inner animus, an aggression that drives us. We need to be the alpha and take what's ours in both our personal and professional lives.'

'Uh-huh.'

'And the success of a wolf in the wild depends on harnessing this power, to dominate, gain status and win the respect of others. Now, what does this sound like to you?' Tyler asks.

'A men's rights blog?'

'Business,' corrects Tyler. 'All of a sudden it hit me that I need to explore these synergies. Integrating lupine insights with my professional life and then lending my mentorship and business acumen to the mystical. There are all these lessons I've learned on my way: how to "harness the best within" through strength training; the importance of communing with nature; repeating regular affirmations to control your emotions and manage your monthly transition. If I could just formalize this into an offering, I could break this market wide open.'

'Wait. The werewolf market?' This is, thus far, the dumbest thing Brian has ever heard and he can't resist the opportunity to parrot it back.

'Yes, the werewolf market. How long do you think that we can keep ourselves a secret? If your recent antics are any indication, it's only a matter of time until this whole thing goes public. And when it does, and the villagers grab their torches and their pitchforks, there's going to be a need for leadership.'

Brian realizes he's entertained Tyler's machinations for too long and grasps for the words he'll need to mount his escape. 'Okay, all right. Well, thanks so much for thinking of me,' he says, standing up from the table. 'It's a really interesting proposal, and I'm definitely excited ... for you. But I don't think this is a good fit.' He turns, but Tyler grabs his wrist.

'I'm trying to make something here. Something exciting that people would want to be a part of. All wolves need a pack. A lone wolf is only a wolf that is searching for community. We succeed in groups; we struggle when we are alone.'

Brian suddenly feels weightless, inert.

'You know what I'm talking about, don't you, Brian? Not belonging anywhere? To anyone?'

He stands for a moment, and then lets Tyler pull him back down to his chair. 'What are you proposing?'

'I'm saying, join me. Let's build something! You would be getting in on the ground floor. I am already identifying possibilities for recruitment and scale.'

'Then what is this?' asks Brian, pointing accusingly between the two of them.

'Well, for now, you can think of me as your sponsor. We'll just check in from time to time. You can let me know how things are going and I can find ways to support you. It'll be a good way for me to refine the framework, develop some training modules and for you to get some experience in a fast-paced start-up environment – think of it like an internship.'

'Yeah, cool, but specifically, what about the *murders*?' Brian whispers. 'What does our special relationship mean for them?'

'Murder,' Tyler scoffs. 'Murder's such a loaded term. It's unfortunate, yes. But look, what can you do? It's in your nature. Wolves will be wolves. You're new to town, I'm sure you're missing the networks you once had. But, if you stick with me, I can promise you that this won't happen again. That's the model, here. Everything I put into this I'll teach you personally. How you can take that energy, that determination, that aggression and *master* it; help you and, later, thousands of men like us channel it into their professional lives, their families, sports, even sex. Can you imagine if we could teach men to unleash the beast in a controlled way in the bedroom? On the football field? In the boardroom? Think how *big* this could be, Brian.'

It's been a long time since anyone has described Brian as having anything like energy or determination, and he thinks Tyler the #BoyBoss and his proposal sounds like trouble, but at least this guy seems to have his life together. There's no question that it has been difficult these past couple of years. If Tyler has a way to get Brian out of his funk and gain greater control over his condition, he might as well explore it. It'll give him something to do on those quiet, empty days off. He looks around the restaurant that's started to swell with diners and inadvertently makes direct eye contact with Nik, who has just come in for her shift. Her eyes go wide. He turns away. 'Fine, sure. Let's try it out. I've got nothing else going on.'

Tyler is ecstatic, or at least Brian thinks he's ecstatic – it's hard to tell with someone who's always smiling. They make plans to meet the following week, same time, same place, and Tyler leaves Brian with some homework.

'Exercise and daily mantras? Are you serious?' Brian asks as the waitress drops the check. He grabs it to confirm it includes his employee discount.

'Trust me, let's just start here and see how you like it,' says Tyler, grabbing the check out of his hand and dropping cash in the book. 'I'm heading out of town tonight, but I'll see you next week.'

He watches the crowd part as Tyler strides through the restaurant and out onto the street. There's another Uber Black waiting at the curb. Brian sighs and opens his billfold then, crinkling his nose to do some quick math, throws a couple of crumpled-up bills on top. Looking up from the check, he sees Nik staring at him from behind the bar. He avoids her to clock in for his shift, but she drifts over to meet him.

'I see you. Two dates in a week with that business-casual Übermensch. What's that all about?'

'I'm trying to figure that out myself,' Brian says out of the side of his mouth as he clocks in. When he turns around, he sees Darby leaning over the bar, animatedly telling some story to Mr. Tall, Dark and Handsome. The man smiles over his notebook; his wine glass is empty. 'When did the school shooter get here?'

'Stop it. I think Darby came in early to meet up with him.' Brian is shocked to hear 'Darby' and 'early' in the same sentence. 'His name is Abe, by the way. He runs the flower shop down the block, hence the ...' Nik gestures to her lapel and then nods to Darby. Brian looks across and notices a cream carnation jauntily threaded through Darby's top buttonhole. Brian rolls his eyes.

'Be nice. After all, maybe opposites do attract?' she says, shooting him a look that he ignores.

THREE

Brian and Darby huddle in the cold on one of the benches flanking the entrance of The Romanesco. They are typically reserved for throngs of diners as they wait for their name to be called, but after 10 p.m. the neighborhood goes quiet, all the residents safely asleep in their four-bed, three-bath houses with conservatory and garden. Under the glow of the streetlights, wrapped up in jackets and scarves, they share a ritual post-shift cigarette, Darby bitching about their most entitled tables, Brian only half listening, staring up at the bright crescent moon in the sky and thinking about his conversation earlier with Tyler. Could it be possible to control his impulses? To live again without the constant threat of exposure or the nagging guilt of multiple homicide?

'... and then he asked me whether the fettuccine alfredo was, and I quote, "the same taste over and over again". What does that mean?! It's a pasta dish. So, of course it is. But is that a bad thing? This is going to haunt me for the rest of my life.' Darby took a pull on the cigarette and then handed it to Brian. 'I mean, if you're desperate for variety in the taste of a dish, you can probably do better than fettuccine alfredo.'

'What about the turkey club? There's a lot of layers there,' Brian asks.

Darby cocks their head to think. 'I feel like sandwiches are categorically out.'

'Meatloaf?'

'Brian,' Darby takes a drag. 'Listen to yourself. Are you even trying?'

'The salmon?'

'Maybe, but the problem with salmon is that the glaze gets over all the sides. What about Cobb salad?'

Brian laughs, the sound of it bouncing across the empty forecourt. 'Cobb salad? Perfect! Because you get to build each individual bite!'

'Exactly! Very modular. The bespoke dining experience we're known for here at The Romanesco,' laughs Darby.

The restaurant lights flicker off behind them and they both turn on the bench. Nik pushes through the French doors, her arm deep in her purse, searching for her keys. 'Those things will kill you, you know,' she says, kneeling to lock the deadbolts. 'What are you two laughing about, anyway?'

Darby explains and poses her the question. She jingles the keys and ponders silently for a moment. 'Cobb salad.' Brian and Darby descend into a fit of laughter. She rolls her eyes. 'C'mon, children,' she says, heading into the slush of the sidewalk, hands buried in her pockets.

Their after-hours dive bar is on the cusp of the sleepy, wealthier neighborhood of The Romanesco and the adjacent strip of bars and nightclubs. It exists in a nowhere place between the two neighborhoods, due in large part to the bridge that keeps the uneasy peace between the two. Their spot used to have a name, back when it served as a DIY performance space in the 90s, but now the only signifier is a neon sign aptly reading 'bar'. Branding aside, the bar is fit for purpose, a port of call for weary service workers to exchange the day's tips for alcohol. It provides them with quick service, cold beer, good music and kitschy décor, and it protects them from rich assholes and less experienced binge drinkers.

Entering the bar, stamping ice off their shoes, they are delighted to see the dimly lit dive is empty but for a skeleton staff and the dregs of a karaoke night. Darby squeals in excitement and heads straight to the stage, while Nik and Brian beeline to the bar.

'Usual?' Nik says as they settle on stools.

'Sure.'

Nik exchanges pleasantries with Dan the bartender, an intimidating tattooed older guy who, in another time, would be better placed slaying Vikings on a battlefield than pouring gin and tonics. No matter who's on shift, Nik seems to know and take an interest in them, an intimacy rewarded by free drinks. Brian doesn't really bother trying. They are all her friends, compatriots, brothers in arms. He's just there visiting, he tells himself, unsure if these people would even know who he is without Nik as a context clue. He wonders how long Nik and the bartender have known each other, how many iterations of Brian and Darby he has seen with Nik at the bar over the years. Brian waits quietly as she gets round to ordering their drinks: a Boilermaker for Brian; a Dirty Shirley for Darby; a cheap beer, shot of Grand Marnier and a Diet Coke for herself.

'I can't believe you still drink this,' grunts the bartender, placing the trio of drinks in front of her.

'Listen, I know what I like,' she says, downing the shot and quickly chasing it with the Diet Coke. 'And I'm not afraid to ask for it.'

'Darby, you want this now?' Brian half shouts over to the stage, holding up the fizzy pink pint glass.

Darby grabs the mic and holds their hand flat above their brow to block the stage lights. 'How many cherries are in there?'

Brian counts. 'Just the one.'

'Try again. Honestly, Dan. You act like they're coming out of your paycheck.' Darby walks the stage and stretches like an Olympic breaststroke hopeful as the guitar strings pluck away to Cyndi Lauper's 'Time After Time'.

'Oh God,' says Nik, draining her beer. 'It's going to be a long one.'

Brian is aware that Darby is musical – they're always humming little songs as they work – but tonight is the first time Brian's been able to see it in full, phenomenal effect. Their strong, confident pop voice skates and glides over the synth, sometimes harmonizing with the instruments, other times willfully and effortlessly sowing in small, dazzling moments of discord. Even the servers stop to watch. As they reach the end of the song, Darby vamps, eschewing the sotto voce repetition of the chorus at the end of the song, and arpeggios their way up close to a Mariah Carey top C and then the room breaks out into scattered applause.

'Damn, I had no idea they could do *that*,' Brian says to Nik, as Darby bows like an opera singer being bombarded with flowers.

She shrugs as if it were self-evident. 'Same again?' she says, while Darby begins limbering up for their next track.

Brian and Nik spend the evening talking at the far end of the bar, pausing between beers and ballads to applaud for Darby. At some point, the bartender locks the doors and turns off the neon 'bar' light, making the place feel like home; all the entitled customers and bad tippers from earlier that night seem miles away. Brian always enjoys spending time with Nik. In the year since she hired him, they have got as close as Brian will let her. She feels familiar, safe somehow, like a high school English teacher that recognizes your potential despite your grades. He appreciates being able to talk to someone who feels like much more of an adult than he is, one without any skin in the game. Although Nik was the one to train him, they didn't really speak that much for the first month or two of working together. She had her friends already, and Brian was wary around new people. But one night, after a particularly brutal shift, he noticed Nik struggling to restock the bar with one hand, while at the same time balancing a pile of flashcards in the other.

'You all right there?' he asked, on his way out the door.

'No. Yes.' She sighed. 'Mid-terms coming up and I just … I'm never going to get this done.'

Brian went over to the bar, leaned across it, and took the cards gently from her hand.

'What are the clinical manifestations for diabetes insipidus?' he asked, settling down onto a stool. 'Am I saying that right?'

After that, he regularly ended his shift by staying behind and quizzing Nik on her flashcards while she closed up. Without the customers and the other staff – Darby often had various gigs to go to – the two could talk together uninterrupted, further delaying the inevitable bike ride home to his silent apartment. They soon realized they had the same taste in teen romps, campy horror flicks and the emotional singer-songwriter ladies of the 90s. Slowly, he filled in her backstory through bits and pieces of conversation – that she moved to the city ostensibly for college, but in reality, the punk scene; that as first-generation Filipino parents, the Bacaycays had plotted out every aspect of their daughter's life in exacting detail, wanting her to have all the opportunities they never had; that because they were both doctors, they had assumed their daughter would become one too. When she had dropped out of college – in favor of spending her twenties and a good part of her thirties partying and dating the wrong men – they had barely spoken to her for years. Now, though, she wanted a career, and as her financial situation removed the possibility of med school, she opted for nursing – and felt fully confident now that it was truly her decision.

From there, she started inviting him to the bar, along with Darby, and then recently she surprised Brian by calling him on his day off. 'You doing anything?' she asked, which led to them meeting up at a little noodle spot in the middle of the afternoon, eating pho tái before going together to watch an abomination of a rom-com where they put glasses on Noah Centineo to convince you he's a nerd. It was the closest Brian had got to friendship in a long time, but when she called again a couple of weeks later, he made an excuse. He didn't want to get *too* close to her in case she started asking questions that might lead to answers she wouldn't like.

Still, he, Darby and Nik have become a trio at work, and more often than not, a trio at this very bar. Brian watches Darby hit a deeply impressive near-inaudible note on an interpretive performance of Erasure's 'A Little Respect' and then turns back to Nik. Maybe it's the four drinks and counting or just fatigue from the shift, but whatever is in the air tonight has loosened her tongue. 'You know, I remember when you walked into The Romanesco for your interview,' she says, pink-cheeked.

'Oh yeah? How did I do?'

'Terrible. You said it was "the onus of the individual" with a severe nut allergy to understand they're "taking their own life in their hands" when they go to a restaurant. But I couldn't help myself. It was funny. You were sweet. My maternal instinct, I guess.' She laughs and swigs her beer. It's a joke only Nik is allowed to make about herself: lord help anyone who asks her if she wants kids. 'I know, you think no one sees you, Brian. But I do. That day you walked in it was all over your face. You can still see it there now.'

'Oh? And what is that?'

'Your whole lone wolf vibe. No one can tell you anything. But underneath, you're scared that you don't know what's next.'

Brian is about to deflect, to contradict her, to ask her who *she* thinks she is to tell him anything, but he realizes that would just further prove her point. He drinks instead, draining his beer.

'I know it well,' she continues. 'My parents lost their minds after I dropped out. Those years when we weren't speaking, I thought, "I can do it myself." I know how hard that is, to try and make it on your own. So, when you came in that day, I saw that exact same thing in you. I wasn't sure you would be a good fit. I mean, nothing about you really screamed "customer service oriented". But I figured, if you were anything like me, you just needed some time to figure it out. Brian?'

'I love this song. They can really move, huh?' he says, pointing with his chin to where Darby is using the instrumental break in New Order 'Age of Consent' to do what looks like aerial yoga on stage.

'Brian,' Nik says again. 'You're changing the subject.'

He sighs. 'Fine. You're not wrong. I went through a similar experience with my parents. Though not so much as an abrupt cut-off. More of a WASPy "conscious uncoupling".' He starts shredding the beer-bottle label on the bar.

'I just … I spent so long trying to fulfill the expectations that others had of me. To get good grades, get into a good school. But then, all of a sudden, it became too much. Dropping out was only part of it. A symptom of a greater illness, I guess. I thought if I moved here, if I got space from it all, I could start over, take time to figure out what's next. Something more authentic. But now …' He shrugs. 'I've still not figured anything out. I just work, get drunk, go home, watch TV, rinse and repeat. And somehow, I'm even more confused than before.'

Nik places her hand on his shoulder, squeezes a little. He's taken aback, remembers his promise to himself not to get too close to anyone, but her hand feels good there. He can't help but relax into it.

'When did you know what you wanted? When did you know who you wanted to be?'

'Any day now,' she says, holding a finger up to the barman for another round. 'But I'll tell you, it's a whole lot easier to figure out if you're not alone. You know you can talk to me and Darby, right? We're here for you. I've seen the bags under your eyes, the torn clothes, the ether of booze that surrounds you. Whatever you're going through, we can help. And if we can't help, at least we can listen.'

Brian doesn't know how to answer, but he's saved by Darby appearing between them like a trickster satyr who must acquire 100 secrets before they can ascend Mount Olympus.

'Ooh, shots,' they say, scooping up the Grand Mariner that the barman has just brought over.

'Hey, that's mine,' Nik grouses, while Darby wrinkles up their nose at the taste.

'Jesus Christ. That is *viscous*. Anyway, it's your turn to sing, *tita*.'

'Absolutely not. Under no circumstance am I getting up—'

'There's a full karaoke album of The Slits up there.'

'Wait, really? *Cut*?'

'No, *Return of the Giant Slits*.'

Nik downs her beer, puts a hand on Darby's chest and pushes them to the side. 'Stand back,' she says, before cracking her neck and heading over to the stage.

'Yes ma'am,' Darby says with a salute, then plops themself down on Nik's stool.

'So, what are we talking about?'

'Origin stories and what's next, generally,' says Brian.

'Then we'll need more drinks.'

Darby trained Brian at the restaurant. Nik must have thought that by pairing them together Darby would pull him out of his shell. And it worked, up to a point. Darby made Brian laugh with their devil-may-care attitude to the hospitality industry. Over post-shift cigarettes, bitching about customers and nights out at the bar, a bond had formed. Brian liked hanging out with Darby but was unsure if their friendship extended beyond the confines of The Romanesco. Luckily, Darby took the first step. They would send him GPS coordinates for warehouse parties, drag shows and late-night supper clubs. Brian never actually *went* to any of these, of course, but the gesture meant more to him than he wanted to admit. Still, Darby remains a mystery to him, in part because they're another person Brian can't trust himself to get too close to, and in part because Darby seems to cultivate intrigue as a character trait.

'So, where should we begin? Where are you from?'

'Boring,' says Darby, sipping their vodka soda.

'I thought we were doing origin stories?'

'Ugh, fine. I just don't think it's relevant. You've got to look forward, Brian. Not dwell on the past. But if you must know, it's your classic story. I was a big fish in a small, homophobic pond. I got out as soon as I could. Didn't take too kindly to the gays and the theys in those parts. No one knew what to make of me. So, I had to make something of myself. And here I am. Next question.'

'All right, so what's next for Darby?'

Darby's eyes go wide. 'Woof. How did you answer this one?'

'My answer, in summary, was "I have no idea".'

'And why should you?! Honestly, people these days are obsessed with progressing down this narrow path that was given to them. I never understood that.'

'So, what do you want to be when you grow up?'

They look up to the ceiling and think for a moment. 'A traveling bard.'

'A what?'

'You know, a traveling bard.' They mime playing a lute. 'Unfortunately, the days where you could make decent money as a traveling bard are long gone. But that would be a great gig. Could you imagine?'

Brian could imagine. It was entirely plausible for them. Darby was what you would call a professional dilettante, constantly engaged in a different artistic pursuit, quickly gaining mastery of it before moving on to something new. Working in the restaurant allowed them the flexibility to follow whatever caught their magpie attention. Once upon a time, it was acting – Brian remembers having to find new and creative excuses in response to all their text requests asking for shift coverage for call-backs for plays and TV spots downtown. Over the last few months, it has evolved – there was Darby's stand-up comedy phase, the aerial silks phase, and the magic show. The knife-throwing phase was by far the most terrifying. They insisted on showcasing these talents for Brian after closing the restaurant. After a bottle of peach schnapps for courage and multiple assurances from Darby of their prowess, Brian grabbed a flower from one of the tabletops at The Romanesco and placed it in his mouth. Darby readied themself from 30 feet away and were about to throw when Nik walked up from the office. She saw Darby aiming, then Brian's profile against the wall. 'Our insurance doesn't cover this!' she yelled, stopping Darby in their tracks. Shortly after that incident they started their own cabaret night at a warehouse art space down at the old docks – a monthly demonstration of their rotating flights of fancy, insurance be damned.

'Honestly, I'm jealous.'

'Of what. My bardic ambitions?'

'Yes. No. I don't know. I wish I knew something,

anything I wanted to do. A path forward.'

'I'll stop you right there, my cis-gendered friend. The idea of a single "path" is unrealistic. You see these people making plans for their careers, love lives, etcetera, etcetera. But, let me ask you, how often does anything actually go to plan? Never, Brian. It never does! I don't make plans, I make options. I pursue experiences, places, people. You've got to think bigger. Just cultivate some options. Try new things. And for the love of God, Brian, lighten up a little. It's not that serious. Look at Nik, for example.'

Brian glances over to the stage to see Nik red-faced, hunched over, screaming into the microphone. He smiles. 'I guess,' he says. He lifts his glass for a toast. 'To Cobb salad.'

Darby laughs and lifts their drink to his. 'The dynamic diner diva that is *anything* but the same taste over and over again.'

FOUR

Brian: I look like a well-fed zombie. This is embarrassing.

The first step of this self-actualizing journey was to get a before picture for the eventual blog. Brian felt odd sending an underwear pic to someone he had no intention of sleeping with, but he shared it anyway. Since this one was going to be public, eventually, he cleaned up his bathroom so the viewer could direct their pity to his body and not the *mise en scène* of his livelihood. He snapped a couple of pics, uploading some of the artful ones to his Grindr profile directly. He cringed as he sent the straight-to-camera picture, the absence of the flattering angles that he used to hide or minimize parts of himself that he didn't like leaving him feeling fully exposed. This wouldn't be Brian's first 'before' picture, either. His camera roll was littered with them. The result of multiple aborted 'I'm getting my shit together' resolutions since his transformation, which, when showed in succession, illustrate the steady decline of someone getting larger, tired and more battle-scarred.

Tyler: I don't think your hair looks that bad. A spray tan hides all manner of sins. I can send you some people.

Brian reads the text and places his phone down on the sink. He wets his hair and spends the next fifteen minutes parting, patting, slicking it down with a comb that was left by the previous owner. I look like a featured extra in Grease, he replies, then tussles his hair back into its signature mop.

Though Brian was incredulous that endurance and strength training could quell his more murderous tendencies, it had to be more likely to work than the mantras – sent to him by Tyler as a bunch of hyperlinks to various tweets on the Twitter pages at the nexus of earth mother and TED Talk-er. Still, he had resolved to try and, if nothing else, the exercise would help with the beer belly.

The first run he went on in his neighborhood was also his last. He threw on his headphones, some old gray sweats, and a threadbare Joy Division T-shirt and started trotting from his apartment toward the main thoroughfare. Feeling more confident, he gradually transitioned into a jog. When he reached the house music on his playlist, he went a little faster, eventually speeding up into a sprint. Brian was never particularly athletic, so he had never tested out the enhanced speed thing – the good people of his neighborhood had also never seen a chubby hipster in high-tops shooting down the street like a bullet out of the chamber. After catching a couple of stares from passersby and a near-miss with a grocery cart, he slammed on the brakes, making the lupine muscles in his calves suddenly contract so powerfully, stopping the physics of mass x speed so abruptly, that the concrete lip of the sidewalk cracked in half and his foot disappeared into the rubble.

'Woah,' he whispered to himself. He looked around to see if anyone had noticed he'd just Incredible Hulk-ed a paving slab. People seemed to be ignoring him and getting on with their day, except for a small kid who just stared at him, open-mouthed. Brian retrieved his foot from the hole, shook off the dust, then left the scene of the crime. 'And that, sir,' he growled to the kid as he hurried past him, 'is why you never believe your parents when they tell you exercise is good for you.' He resolved to stick with push-ups and squats at home until he could find a place where he would cause less collateral damage.

The mantras were a harder sell. The first day, he had taken a couple from @yogamama83, settled himself cross-legged on a cushion and then tried them out, only occasionally peering at his phone to make sure he was saying the right thing. It felt ridiculous. Talking is usually a two-person game and, besides, his body architecture was not made for sitting cross-legged. Instead, he tried writing them down on bits of receipt paper and sticking them up on his mirror, so he'd have to confront them when he brushed his teeth in the mornings. 'I am strong,' he would say, through a mouthful of spearmint foam. 'I am in control of myself and how I perceive myself.' 'I am grateful for my body and its strength.' He winced at some of them. 'I am a warrior, not a worrier.' Then: 'I am not a drop in the ocean. I am the ocean in a drop.' What the fuck did that even mean? But at least he was saying them, and he even found that telling himself he was an ocean in a drop of water was at least one way of drowning out the noise of his lively inner critic. And the long dormant optimist that lived inside of him thought that maybe, if he said them enough, he could eventually believe them.

It has been a week since Brian's first meeting with Tyler, and as he rides his bike down the long sweep of road over the park and into the parking lot of The Romanesco for their second session together, he feels surprisingly … good about his progress. He's been able to do a basic HIIT class he found on YouTube most days, though it doesn't feel like he's accomplishing much of anything. He's still struggling with any real enthusiasm for the mantras, and it means that he feels a little like he hasn't done *all* his homework, but if school's any indication, he should be able to talk his way out of it. At the very worst, he can always rely on the old chestnut of 'get fucked, you're not the boss of me!' which worked surprisingly well when his fifth-grade teacher once asked him for his papier mâché volcano that he hadn't done, since he was totally unconvinced that he would ever be around a volcano or that the pedagogical approach of arts and crafts would teach him anything about science.

The restaurant is busier than he expected – there must be another conference in town. The place vibrates with chatter and the clinking of silverware; middle-aged corporate execs in blue suits and nametags on orange lanyards huddle in small groups at the entryway while the waitstaff run around slinging drinks and wiping sweat from their brows. Brian cuts through the suits at the host stand to see Tyler in the back, waving for his attention. He pushes through the customers and dodges the fly-by servers. 'Hey,' he says, as he pulls out a chair and sits down.

'Hey! How are you doing? I already ordered for you. Same as last time. Hope that's all right. Do you know our waitress? She's not as good as our last girl. Took for*ever* to get these.'

Brian rolls his eyes and sips his coffee. 'This is great. Thanks.'

'So, I've got to ask. Have you been doing the work?'

Brian stifles a laugh at 'the work'. This guy must equate his self-care routine to some form of radical praxis, the building blocks of a lupine Gesellschaft. 'You mean the mantras and the exercise? Yeah, I've been working on it.'

'And … How is it going?'

Brian doesn't want to give Tyler the satisfaction, but he relents. 'Honestly, yeah. It's helped a bit.'

Tyler is elated, smiling his ear-to-ear grin. 'That's great to hear!'

'Yeah. I mean, I had been meaning to exercise anyways, so this was as good a reason as any.'

'And the mantras?'

'Yes. The mantras too. Though some of those are a little Goop for me.'

Tyler laughs. 'Always the cynic. I know, it must feel crazy at first. But it really is key to not lose yourself during the transition. Reciting mantras is an ancient practice dating back centuries to focus the mind and body. What we've been given here is an amazing amount of power and the strength, speed and instincts to take what we want. It takes significant focus to harness and control it.'

'Control *it*, or control *me*?' Brian asks pointedly.

'What's the difference?' Tyler counters. 'You're both things, Brian. Do you think you're a different person entirely that one night a month? No, it's just an extension of you. The inner animal of rage and ambition slumbering underneath the surface. With enough training, you can call upon it when you need it, and learn to control it when you don't. Plus, you're an ambassador of this program. We can't have you out there terrorizing the city. It would be a PR nightmare. And to be honest ...' Tyler peers over the edge of the table to look at Brian's ratty sneakers and spies a peek of sock at the baby toe. 'Some mindfulness and discipline could do you good.'

Brian pulls his feet under his chair. His skin prickles with resentment. If these mantras were to be the real power-harnessing deal, he would be reciting Sanskrit rather than lines from *Eat, Pray, Love* every morning. But whatever, he nods anyway.

'You'll keep trying?'

Brian blows out air. 'Yeah. Sure,' he says. 'Got nothing to lose. Anyway, how was your trip? Business or pleasure?'

Tyler smirks and leans in. 'You could say a little of both. It was for this right here,' he says, perching his hand in the middle of the table. 'Our movement. I spotted a similar pattern of animal attacks. Flew out for the week to investigate. Unfortunately, I didn't have any luck. Whoever it is was covering up their tracks. But I'll try again. They can't hide forever.'

The din of the diner makes Brian feel safe. 'Another werewolf?'

'I told you there are more of us out there. And not just werewolves. I mean, look at the headlines. It's just a shame to see these patterns. These wolves are out there uncoordinated with no one to guide them. Rejected by people that fear them. Polite society forces us to hide, to stifle ourselves and our true nature. They're scared of us because we remind them that they too are animals. We're just better at it.'

Brian squints and cocks his head. 'Sure, there's that. But my guess would be that wanton killing of innocent people is their main issue.'

'Yes, yes, of course. What I mean is that these killings can be avoided. There's a way for us to coexist, peacefully, alongside one another. A way where we won't have to continue hiding in the shadows. With leadership and a strong community-based network, these individuals can access the support they need to learn how to control this power, just as you are.'

'This isn't going to turn into a werewolf 4chan, is it? A lupine Mumsnet thing?'

Tyler laughs. 'No, Brian. Think bigger. What we're building here is a community of people like us, who occupy positions from the top to the bottom of society, who we can help to

66

master their instincts and use their transformational power in all aspects of their lives. This will be the first 360-degree lifestyle brand for werewolves. Bringing in tech, social networking and wellness to the mystical. And then? Books, podcasts, conferences, merchandise, advertising, dietary advice, workout routines – the possibilities are limitless.'

'I thought this was about helping people, sort of an AA vibe?'

'Brian, of course it is. That's my mission statement there. To help people like you and me. This isn't some corporate venture. But at the same time, we need to be agile and stay open to opportunities as we build our movement.'

'I see. And does this "movement" have a name?'

Tyler places down his coffee and inhales dramatically. 'I'm so glad you've asked,' he says, as if it's been a secret he's been keeping since the dawn of time. 'I wasn't going to tell you yet; I wanted to be sure. Ready?' Tyler pulls a pad of paper and a pen from his notebook and scribbles. He tears out the sheet and folds it in half before sliding the note to Brian like they're negotiating an acquisition. Brian rolls his eyes and reads 'The Pack™.'

Brian frowns. 'The Pack, TM? Like, trademarked? That sounds pretty corporate.'

'It's just to protect our IP, Brian. But think about it: all wolves need a pack. We'll give them that: a pack of individuals with the skills, networks and influence to ensure that we don't just survive, but thrive. Until then, we need to be careful, deliberate and fly under the radar. We need to play by their rules, which includes absolutely no killing.' Tyler says this last part with an accusatory look in Brian's direction.

'About that. I really don't mean to. Most of the time I just black out and I can't remember anything.'

'Anything?'

'Well, I'm usually drunk.' He reads the judgment on Tyler's face and digs his heels in. 'Okay, first of all, the entire process is disgusting. Shooting coarse thick hair out of every pore. Feeling your fangs grow faster than your mouth can catch up with. And don't get me started on the claws. Don't judge me if that's one Cronenberg film I'd rather experience drunk.'

Tyler rolls his eyes. 'Yeah, yeah, yeah. What do you think happens to me each month?'

'I don't know – you grow an elegant man bun and mantra your way through it?' Brian's sure that Tyler thinks of his monthly transformation as a hot yoga class.

'No, it's tough for me too, but this is what I'm saying. It's about physical and mental conditioning. It's about learning to accept the process. To love the process, even. Now, what's your technique for restraining yourself during the full moon?'

Brian grimaces, knowing he's about to give the wrong answer. 'Yeah, I don't do that.'

'Okaaaaaaay. What *do* you do?'

'I wait in the park at night and transition there.' Brian is underselling what most months is actually a mad dash from the bar to the park when he realizes what time it is. He'll down a shot and throw a wad of cash at Nik and

Darby and bail. 'Most months it's fine. Rack up a body count of racoons, that kind of thing. The *occasional* early-morning jogger, but really, I haven't had too many issues.'

Tyler winces in disapproval.

'Don't give me that face. Don't forget *you* were the one who slashed *me* last month.'

'That was an aberration, a once-in-a-blue-moon necessity to find you. You were really going to town on that guy, I had to get you off him somehow. Plus, the swipe wasn't *that* bad.'

Brian's hand goes instinctively to his side. Though the heat of them is gone, he can still see the long pink streaks in the mirror every morning.

'All right then, go ahead, illuminate me. What's your technique?'

'Well, I had a contractor come in and build a tasteful dungeon in my basement. Reinforced concrete, steel chains, the whole nine yards. I've got a great guy if you need a referral. *Very* discreet. Said he's had a lot of clients ever since *Fifty Shades of Grey*. And I know what you're thinking: it's going to be terrible for my resale value. But you really can't put a price on peace of mind.'

'*You* can't put a price on peace of mind. But I sure can. I can't even hang a picture in my studio apartment without losing my security deposit. That type of preparation is impossible on a waiter's salary.'

'Now that you mention it, waiting tables is an odd career choice for a werewolf.' Tyler's statement sounds like a question.

'It wasn't so much a choice as what was on offer for a twenty-something college drop-out.' Brian can feel his anger bubbling up to the surface.

'No, that I understand entirely. I'm just concerned about managing the temper. How do you do it? Each customer must be a landmine. There are so many opportunities for the anger to take over. Then, next thing you know ...'

'Next thing you know what?'

'You know.' Tyler mimes little claws and a spurt of blood from his neck.

Brian looks blank.

'Oh! You *don't* know. You're not aware of marking? When someone makes us snap in our human form, but somehow it unconsciously registers deep in our wolf bones and then when we transition it all comes out?'

'What do you mean by "all comes out"?'

'Hunt them down. Kill them. Marking is instantaneous. Irreversible. One insult, one slight, and then, on the full moon, you'll stop at nothing to kill them. You must be aware of the anger and aggression that drives us. How it builds and builds the closer we get to our transition.'

'Huh.' Brian is always running at a low-grade level of anxiety and frustration, but his whole world does seem louder, brighter, more irritating the closer he gets to the full moon. That's partly why he drinks: the alcohol helps dull his lycan senses into a more manageable synesthesia. Is this what Tyler is talking about? Could this have been happening for years without him knowing it, that he was marking people and then hunting them? 'Has that ever happened to you?' he asks.

70

Tyler volleys. 'Hasn't it happened to you?'

Brian starts silently taking an inventory: there was the girl who microwaved fish on his dorm floor who mysteriously disappeared. But that was just a coincidence. And then there was a birder back at his mom and dad's who he definitely didn't know but, frankly, who doesn't get mad at birders, and then what about that— Shit, he's just spotted Nik putting on an apron behind the bar. His shift must be starting. 'Tyler, I'm really sorry, I'm going to have to go. What do I do about the marking thing?'

Tyler starts packing up his things. 'Just keep practicing mindfulness. First step here is to recognize your emotions, let them pass through you. Try not to let people get to you. Remember to breathe. If you can control your anger in your human form, you'll have more control in your werewolf form.'

'Thanks,' says Brian, standing up. 'Anything on the workout/mantra stuff?'

'Keep doing them. I'm going to put together a couple of basic martial arts programs maybe; I might test them on you, figure out how they might fit into the app—'

'There's an app?'

'Not yet, but maybe. We need to compile our assets somewhere.'

'Assets?'

Tyler deflects. 'Other than that, just keep with the jogging, keep doing your mantras. It's a big week, so I don't want to overload you. Speaking of which, why don't we do this at my place next Thursday?'

'Big week? Thursday?'

'You're kidding, right? Brian. The full moon is next Thursday.'

'Ha. Yeah, only joking,' says Brian, definitely not joking.

'Let's just get together to prepare your inner temple. We'll get you to the park with a clear head so you can transform with intention. See if we can't spare a couple of racoons.'

That night, Brian is distracted. He can't stop thinking about what Tyler said, about marking, about accidental bloody vengeance. Throughout his shift, as he scoots from table to table, he checks his breathing, tries to let some of the customers' comments bounce off him. When he walks into Darby at the point-of-sales, or waiting for drinks at the end of the bar, he disconnects.

'… and then this white woman had the gall, the sheer audacity, to bring in her own juice and ask me to blend it for her here. Ms. Karen is doing a cleanse, apparently. The entitled brain rot of doing a cleanse and going to *a restaurant* for someone to serve it to you. I told her she can't bring in outside drinks. But then she said she would "pay for the ice" and that I could expect a huge tip – and we *all* know how that goes. She wasn't even going to order anything. Like, ma'am, I will not be a party to your eating disorder in the guise of wellness … Brian. Brian, are you even listening? If you ignore me anymore, I'm going to fall in love with you …'

As the dinner rush begins to slow, he goes behind the bar and asks Nik to teach him how to check his pulse. With her fingers on his neck, she stares at the clock.

'Everything all right?' she asks. He deflects, telling her he just wanted to know now that he's started working out again. Great save.

At the end of the night, the last customers hustled out, the chairs stacked and the tables wiped down, the three of them sit at the bar and count their tips.

'All right, kids. Dive bar tonight? Mama Nik is buying. Darby?'

'No can do. Promised Abe I'd meet up with him. He just got back from a work trip.'

'What kind of work is there out of town for a florist?' Nik asks.

Darby shrugs and continues counting.

'Awfully late for someone his age,' Brian chimes in without looking up from his phone.

'Forsooth, he speaks! Where the hell have you been all night anyways?' asks Darby. 'I haven't been able to get a word out of you.'

'Hey now, play nice or you're going in time out,' Nik says in her manager's voice. 'What about you, Brian? Want to grab a drink?'

Brian isn't listening. After the anxiety spiral he's been on during his shift, he's finally been reunited with his phone. Nik wasn't above confiscating them if they ever broke her 'no phones on the floor' rule. He pores over the Google results for animal attacks around his

university, his parents' house, and now Thousand Acre
Park.

'Whatcha looking at?' Darby appears directly over his
shoulder.

'Jesus Christ. How do you do that?'

'Oh, the animal attack. Shit, I never told you guys
but … I know who it iiissss …' Darby tauntingly sings
this last line. Brian's heart stops as he stares at Darby, who
continues to dance jauntily until Nik finally looks up from
her book bag behind the bar. They confirm that all eyes
are on them before speaking.

'Jonathan. Ainsley.'

'Oof. That prick,' says Nik.

'I know, right?'

'Who?' Brian's still confused. He doesn't make a habit
of learning any customers' names, but Darby remembers
this one.

'You know him. He was that old entitled white guy
who came in and would snap whenever he wanted our
attention.'

'*The Snapper*,' Nik says, binding her flashcards in
elastics.

Then it all comes rushing back in an instant. Brian's
stomach sinks. He remembers everything about him. The
shaggy gray eyebrows, the slicked-back box-dyed black
hair. He smelled like cigar smoke and fall leaves.

'I was wondering where that asshole had been. He knew
better than to sit at my bar. It has to have been over a
month.'

74

'Two months, actually. It was when that bridge tournament was in town. It was like the *Night of the Living Dead* here for a week. All these elderly card players came in en masse and never tipped.'

'Oh God, I remember that week. But it's all a blur of white wine with ice cubes from my end.'

'Yeah, you were slammed. We all were. Everyone was just so needy, as if each table were having their last meal on Earth – everything had to be perfect. Anyways, that night he snapped and, well, I did too! I dragged his ass for filth in front of everyone. Then he started spouting some bullshit and got up in my face.'

'Jesus! I'm sorry, babe. I should have been there.'

'Oh, please, I had him handled. Then Brian jumped in between us. So masc.' Darby feigns a swoon. 'Anyways, he called us both faggots. Said he would never come back, that we lost ourselves a customer. And oh, the delicious irony of how true that was. He's super dead now. Good riddance if you ask me.'

Brian remembers the very instant. Watching him walk away in what seemed like slow motion. It felt like his skin was on fire and, for a brief moment, he saw literal red. His entire body tensed to keep him from running out after him and tackling him in the car park. He was incandescent, self-immolating with fury until Darby grabbed his shoulder, extinguishing the fire, and time resumed its normal pace.

Brian gets up from his stool and walks to the cabinet behind the bar as Nik and Darby watch. He pulls out

75

the box of credit card receipts from the last full moon and finds the name of the jogger on a crumpled and re-flattened slip of paper. 'Server: Brian, Total: $100, Tip: $0 – worst service ever.'

FIVE

The neighborhoods west of the park feel like an entirely different city, a far departure from the warehouses, dispensaries and six-story walk-ups in the east. The affluent families in their stately rowhouses call it the cultural heart of the city, home to the museums, ballet and opera. The ravine of Thousand Acre Park bisecting the city maintains this separation. Locals love to complain about the headache of getting cross-town. Each has their preferred route, depending on the time of day. Public transportation projects to fix the issue are halted in their tracks with the city ordinates to protect the wildlife.

Brian has never felt compelled to go to the museum, ballet or opera. But after last week's realization about the whole marking thing, he's willing to make the journey for werewolf lessons. He has redoubled his efforts – listening to the TED Talks Tyler's sent him, reading the handful of mantras affixed to his bathroom mirror, going through his clothes to find the world-wearier shorts and T-shirts that will now serve as workout gear – and he's decided to take up Tyler's offer of a one-on-one coaching session. He sits on the vibrating bus with his shirt over his nose, clutching his duffle bag of workout clothes. He counts the time it takes for them to inch across the bridge in midday traffic. He peers over the edge into the depths of the park, a blanket of thick trees giving way to islands of open fields. Looking out toward the horizon, he focuses in on the bridges on either side, though miles away he can see them clear as day, a suturing urbanization over the city's wilderness. The trees and underbrush creep up the steep slopes of the ravine before being cut back with a clear definition of concrete and stonework on either side. Just then he hears the man behind him snort the phlegm from his sinuses into his throat. Back to reality, he is convinced he could run across town faster.

Brian finally gets off the bus and takes a deep breath. Even the air here tastes better. He Google Maps Tyler's address and walks through the tree-lined streets of opulent identical rowhomes. If it were possible to feel underdressed for the public square, it's here. He passes women on the street in athleisure that cost more than his rent. They push their prams, speed-walk with their gal pals and rare dogs, all of which growl at Brian as they pass.

He stops in front of the address Tyler gave him and double-checks. The three-story townhouse is stately, sophisticated, with careful attention taken to preserve the pre-war facade. The serpentine greenery and flower boxes wind along the stairway to the front door. Brian wishes his dad worked in high finance rather than insurance adjusting. He climbs up the platformed slate staircase and is about to ring the doorbell when Tyler throws opens the door. He's traded his usual business casual for workout gear: a loose, scoop-necked vest and split shorts over running tights. 'I heard you shuffling down the street.' He tosses Brian a wink and points to his super-hearing ears. 'Come on in. How have you been?'

Tyler gives him the tour of his home. It looks like it was professionally staged, a portrait of middle-class excess. The modern Danish furniture plays against the classic elements of the built-in bookshelves and vaulted ceilings. Brian invokes Tyler's father and mentally calculates the cost of everything he sees – modular cloud sectional: $5,000; 55" OLED TV: $1,000 minimum; skin-care products: $200 – but loses track with the gas range and countertop appliances in the kitchen. The fridge is the type that's connected to the internet of things, which Brian doesn't understand but assumes it's a cleverly disguised portent of the end of civilization. During the office portion of the tour, he feels like he should have taken his shoes off before entering. The stately built-in bookshelves are filled with matching hardback tomes without a single crease on their spines. The shelves are punctuated with French-paned windows and a reading nook overlooking the back garden. Tyler leads him to the formal living room (as opposed to the informal one, across the other end of the house), and tells him to take a seat.

'Not there, though,' he winces, as Brian plumps for a modest-looking wooden dining chair in the corner. 'It's an original Eames.'

'Here?' Brian says, pointing to a low-slung art deco-looking armchair.

'Oh, umm, that's a— Hey, you know what, why don't you just grab the couch. Now what can I get you to drink? Tea, coffee?'

Brian eyes the expensive-looking sectional; it's very bright and white upholstery. 'I'll just take a water, please.'

Tyler disappears into the kitchen and Brian hears a ding from the *Blade Runner* fridge, followed by a tap and the churn of an ice-maker. He pads back into the living room and hands Brian a glass of water. 'For this session, I thought I could show you my process for preparing for tonight,' he says, settling into a leather wingback. 'But before that, I wanted to do a little housekeeping at the top. What's your bandwidth looking like this week?'

'Uhh … robust?' Why Tyler was inquiring about his internet service provider was beyond him.

'Great, I had a couple of administrative items I was hoping you could take care of for The Pack, some foundational things to establish our web presence. Starting with a shared inbox, social media accounts, couple of cryptic posts to drive engagement. You're on Twitter, right?'

'Unfortunately.'

'Great. So, I'm thinking about the tone for our brand. It's like North Face meets Tesla. Rugged individualism and adventure-seeking, yet innovative and exclusive. Irreverent, but we support the troops. You know what I mean?'

Brian shudders at the unholy ventriloquy he will have to perform to speak as Tyler. 'How about I just start with an email address, and we go from there?'

'Sure, sure,' says Tyler. 'I'll do some more noodling on this, build out our brand story, and we can circle back.' Brian blinks at him as he continues to sink progressively deeper into the couch.

'Right!' Tyler suddenly exclaims, clapping his hands together and startling Brian into pulling himself out of the quicksand of the modern couch. 'Enough talk. Let's dive right in. You brought something to work out in, right?'

Brian nods to his duffle bag.

'Okay, guest bathroom is down the hall on the right. Sorry for the mess in there.'

Brian slings his duffle over one shoulder and shuffles through the hallway, trying to make himself smaller lest he nudge the individually lit paintings on his way. The guest bath is pristine, about the size of his kitchen. The marble countertops hold all manner of Aesop products, and he picks them up to decipher the minimalist black and tan bottles. *Hand balm. Hair oil. Bitch, is that lotion?* Brian reaches into his duffle and pulls out the half-empty kombucha bottle he was drinking on the bus. He tips the rest of it away, rinses it out and starts jerking off the handpump, his tongue sticking out of his mouth in quiet concentration. When the bottle is half full, he places it in his bag for later and slips out of his everyday clothes of sweatpants, T-shirt and trainers and into his workout wear of slightly older sweatpants, T-shirt and trainers. He checks his reflection in the colossal mirror, chucks a roll of toilet paper into his duffle bag and goes to find his host.

'Down here!' he hears Tyler yell, and Brian follows the voice down a short flight of stairs. Tyler's waiting at the bottom, a whole underground floor to the house spreading out behind him. Brian nods to a thick steel door at the end of the hall. 'Is that it?' he says. 'Where the magic, quite literally, happens?'

'Yeah, that's the dungeon. But that's not what we're doing. This way.'

Brian wonders if other guests have the basement tour too or if it is just for the werewolves. How else could he explain away the existence of a fortified cell? Perhaps when you're rich, people don't ask too many questions about how adjacent you are to potential human trafficking.

Tyler's gym is fully kitted out, replete with pull-up bars, dumbbells and floor-to-ceiling mirrors. Hooks along the walls hold weight belts and strings of metal chains. Brian drops his bag on the rubber floor and walks the length of the mirror, observing the dumbbells in their neat little rows. Much to his horror, they start at 60 kg and only go up. His eyes go wide and he doubles back, squinting at the numbers on all the kettlebells, but there's only one pink one in the single digits.

'We've been mainly talking in the past couple of weeks about strengthening the mind,' Tyler says, wandering over to a rack of outsized weights. 'But we also need to strengthen our connection to the body. How much have you *really* played with your capabilities?'

'What, the whole super speed thing? It's not really my thing.'

Tyler underarm tosses the green kettlebell over to Brian, which he instinctively snatches from the air one-handed. It feels light. He does an experimental bicep curl with it and turns it over; the faint white letters read 60 kg.

'Brian. *Make* it your thing.'

Over the next two hours, Tyler puts Brian through a variety of heavy-duty werewolf workouts. Brian didn't really know what CrossFit was, all he knew was what he'd gleaned from Twitter and hack stand-up comedy sets. If what Tyler put him through is indeed CrossFit, then the inventors need to be tried at The Hague. They jump, squat, press and lift in rapid succession, all the while Tyler yelling abusive encouragement to him over the sound system as it blasts post-grunge pop rock so loud that Brian can't think or dissent. 'Yes, Brian, push, push, push!' As if this weren't stressful enough, there's a stop clock on the wall counting down their completion times for each set. When it finally hits zero, Tyler nimbly hops down from a box, casually drops the cartoon barbell he's been lifting and grabs his water bottle. 'C'mon, Brian, five more!' he shouts, unscrewing the cap. Brian is beet red and struggling to breathe, but he's determined to finish his chin-ups, especially with an audience. He strains his way to the end of his set, his body hanging with multiple chains attached to heavy plates, and then he drops like ripe fruit and hits the floor with a sweaty slap.

'Good job, buddy,' Tyler says, turning off the music and peeling off his damp T-shirt. 'Don't you feel pumped?'

Brian's eyes wander. Tyler is *very* fit. Brian can pinpoint each ab; they're like fillets of chicken in shrink-wrap. If CrossFitting is what he has to do to get himself that kind of abdomen, he wonders if the costs outweigh the benefits.

'You … do this … every month?' he asks from the floor.

Tyler walks over to his side, unclips the chains and plates from Brian's weight belt and offers an outstretched hand. 'I do this every *day*, my man. It's addictive.' Brian grabs onto him as he's yanked into the air and onto to his feet. 'I'll take your word for it,' he wheezes.

Tyler leads him back upstairs and into the kitchen. 'Two special protein smoothies coming up,' Tyler says, popping the fridge door, retrieving a bushel of spinach and hand-shredding it into a blender. 'You know, I was thinking that maybe we can start with posting things like nutrition hacks and workout plans, keep the wolf references subtle, like a dog whistle. It'll make it that much more rewarding for those in the know, while also getting us a wider audience. For the wolfier stuff, throw it behind a "members only" area, give it an air of exclusivity, invite only. What do you think?'

'Posting where?' Brian says, gripping onto the marble countertop to steady himself as his leg muscles tremble.

'The Pack™ social media pages we were talking about.'

'We've got social media pages already?' Brian is tired, but he was sure he effectively put a pin in that discussion.

'Not yet we haven't, but when you sort out the email, you can sign up on Twitter, Facebook, Instagram, the Tok with the handle of The Pack? I'm looking into buying the domain name too. Just want to make sure we get these quickly. It's essential for a consistent cross-platform brand identity.'

Brian is about to ask why *he* has to sign up handles, when Tyler starts blitzing the smoothies. He decides to let it go. It's a small thing, he thinks. It'll take him ten minutes. He can't expect to get mentorship for free.

They take their smoothies into the backyard that Tyler has artfully turned into a contemporary woodland garden, offsetting the straight lines and hard edges of the townhouse's architecture. They follow the slate pathway as it curves through a mix of feathery perennials and broadleaf foliage ending in a sitting area with cushions and a water fountain. Tyler says that the next step is for them to center their minds through meditation. Brian breathes a sigh of relief, grateful that the next step is sitting in silence. 'Okay, so, what do I do?'

'Just take a seat here. Relax. Close your eyes. Notice your body. Notice your breath. And just clear your mind. It'll start to wander, but whenever you notice it does, recognize it and gently guide yourself back. I'll let you know when it's been an hour.'

'An hour? I'm going to sit here, doing nothing, for an hour and this is going to make me less homicidal tonight?'

Tyler hushes him. 'You're not "doing nothing", you're meditating. And yes, that is the goal. It'll fly by, I promise. Are you ready?'

Brian nods and closes his eyes. He can hear the trickling of the water fountain. He listens closer and he can hear

Tyler's breath. He tries to match it. Spending too much energy on listening, he can now hear the cars passing in front of the house. Someone is vacuuming in the house next door. *Bring it back*, he says to himself, taking inventory of his body. Everything is sore. This is going to suck tomorrow. *Wait, this is your mind wandering. Stop it, you idiot, get back to it … hang on, is this you 'gently' guiding yourself back? God, you suck at meditating.* Brian repeats this pattern. In the brief moments where his mind is truly silent, a sort of white, cold silence filling his skull, he bursts in on himself to celebrate: *look at you! You're really doing it!* and then the cycle starts all over again. At some point though, he really does let it all go, floating up into the higher reaches of transcendence, and he's surprised when he's brought back to earth as he hears Tyler's Apple Watch makes the digitized sound of a bao gong.

Brian opens his eyes. The sky has transitioned to gold and pink. He feels fresh, relaxed. 'It feels like my brain went through a dishwasher,' says Brian. 'That was actually pretty cool. I'm onboard with this part – it helps me stay with the human part of me. It's like calming the ego to my lupine id, if that makes sense. The workout stuff, though? I don't know. Isn't it just going to make me a more effective killer?'

Tyler grins. 'No, what we're working on here is the mind–body axis, Brian. One impacts the other. Master both and you'll have mastered yourself. You'll never not transition, and you should always be safe. It's why

I still use the dungeon, but most of the time I'm pretty much in control, the human in me fully present. I even use transition nights to listen to audiobooks. It's great to use the time for self-improvement tasks – well, the ones that don't require fingers. It's like getting an extra day of productivity each month – ooh, that's good. I should write that one down – but, anyway, you'll get there. We have plenty of time. You just keep working on it and I swear it'll all get easier. And whenever you want to do this again, if you have a rough day and want to re-center, just shoot me a text. That's what I'm here for.'

Brian nods, unsure if he'll actually take him up on it. He needs more evidence to make an informed decision. Tyler tells him he can shower in one of the guest bathrooms – apparently one of them has a rainforest shower – but Brian declines. He's just going to get dirty tonight anyways. He goes back to the bathroom, changes back into his clothes, hesitates, then throws two more rolls of toilet paper in his duffle.

'Good luck,' Tyler says at the front door, as Brian heads down the steps to the street.

'Yeah, you too. You got any plans?'

'Dungeon. Might put on a face mask. I'm midway through listening to *The Fountainhead*, so I should get that finished before dawn.'

Brian flicks him a thumbs up and heads off, the low evening sun lengthening his shadow. He's never been this prepared for a full moon before. He decides to take the extra time to walk to the park. He strolls through the streets, passing commuters returning from downtown. He notices he doesn't need his headphones to drown out the noise. He can focus on what he wants to hear. His body is sore, but his mind does feel less fidgety. Despite appearances, maybe there's something worth paying attention to underneath all of Tyler's bravado.

Coming to the park from the west side, he finds a trail down the ravine. He follows the path until he's deep enough into the tree line to cut away and delve deeper into the woods. He finds a spot next to a stream and strips, stowing his clothes in his bag. He may have mistimed it, he thinks, as he sits next to the stream butt naked. A better werewolf would be attuned to nature and luxuriate in its sights and sounds, and the moonlight on the babbling brook. But Brian pulls out his cell phone to doom-scroll Twitter. In the darkness of the park, the blue light illuminates his face. He's just in the middle of reading an article on how Kim Kardashian's shapewear is biphobic when, all of a sudden, it begins.

Brian lurches forward as he feels his bones rearrange underneath his skin. The pinpricks of fur pierce his body as they rise to the surface. He feels the skin pull as his ears migrate up the sides of his head. He falls to his hands and knees, and his jaw shoots forward. He struggles to keep it open as his teeth form fangs that split his gumline. He feels the sulfurous rage flood his entire body. 'Focus, focus,' he says to himself as his nails turn to claws and strike deep into the ground. He listens to the stream. He notices his mind is wandering but tells himself to come back to the stream. He sees the patchwork black fur coat shoot out of his skin and closes his yellow eyes. 'Let it pass through you,' he remembers Tyler say. He gives in to it, and he lets out a howl at the moon. The transition is complete.

Brian's transitions, at the best of times, feel like he's the only passenger on a runaway train. But tonight, it's different. Like a lucid dream where he can make suggestions to the train conductor. He bounds through the park at breakneck speed. He chases rabbits and foxes, galloping at them through the freshwater stream. When he gets close enough to the edge of the park to see passing headlights, he gently guides himself back. At one point, he raises his head, catching the scent of kids drinking beer in the park. He turns away, aiming himself deeper into the forest. Eventually, he finds a spot in a small glade of wildflowers and gently falls asleep. When Brian wakes up, blanketed in the morning sun, Tyler has a convert.

SIX

'What's the priority assessment before administering antitussive medication containing codeine to a patient?' Brian reads Nik's familiar bubble print off the cardstock from his seat at the bar. Nik has her back to him, counting the liquor bottles and entering checkmarks in a binder for the day shift. It's a quiet spring night in the empty restaurant. One of those days that serves as a preview for the summer weather where the trees false start with spring buds only to freeze in a sudden late frost, fall, and begin anew weeks later. Nik is halfway through another semester preparing for another set of mid-term exams. With Darby yet again distracted with Abe at the other end of the bar, Brian can help Nik prepare with fewer interruptions.

'Umm … respiratory rate?' she says.

'Nope. It's "lung sounds",' says Brian.

'Fuck,' Nik says under her breath.

'For what it's worth, I would've given it to you. I mean, how can you check the respiratory rate without hearing lung sounds.'

'Yeah, maybe if you're Superman …' says Nik. It's been three months since the transition that converted Brian to Tyler's vision. Since doubling down on the training program, he's gotten more of a handle on the werewolf abilities to the point that he's forgotten some of the human limitations. The precautionary bonus sessions at Tyler's place on full-moon days moved to a weekly occurrence. The agenda was different every time, depending on which part of the course Tyler was trying to develop. It could be personal training, or life-coaching, or lifting weights in Tyler's monster gym before re-centering with meditation in the garden. Tyler led targeted sessions to hone Brian's senses, helping him focus rather than dull his innate talents. They would climb to the top of his townhouse and Tyler would call out questions like a voyeuristic I Spy.

'1502 V Street, third floor. What are they discussing?'

Brian would dart his eyes to find the small gothic letters from blocks away. *1498, 1500, 1502. Okay, now, first, second, third floor.* He sees the couple sitting at the dinner table. They look disappointed. His ears twitch in each direction as if adjusting an antenna. He hears the bus outside, their television is on. They mumble. He focuses. 'It's their daughter. Grades. She failed a Chemistry test.'

'Yes! Okay, the woman on the 42 bus headed southbound on Grant Street. Article on the top right page. Light just turned green, go quick!'

Brian switches his attention to the bus. He hears the exhaust cough as he brings his ears close to his head. Then he sees her. '*How the millennials are destroying the …* Fuck!' The bus turns and putters down the street.

'It's the luxury watch market,' says Tyler, clapping a hand on his back. 'That was good though. You're getting there.'

Brian can now parse the migraine-inducing cacophony of disparate voices and clanging of plates into distinct conversations he can drop in and out of at will, readying drinks and dropping checks before his tables can ask. Nik and Darby are grateful for the extra help, though occasionally confused by his sudden-onset clairvoyance. Particularly the night when Darby was complaining about how long their customer's steak was taking in the kitchen, Brian took a deep breath in through his nose, inhaling the trace smell of irony meat and the nutty aroma of the browned butter wafting out into the dining area. 'It'll be two more minutes,' he said. Darby looked at him sideways and watched the clock until two minutes later they heard the ding of the bell in the kitchen window. They walked the length of the restaurant and picked up the plate, returning with a look of disbelief. 'Lucky guess?' Brian shrugged, determined not to show off like this again.

'Ugh, I'm so fucked,' says Nik, closing the binder with a slap.

Brian puts down the cards and dashes behind the bar to wrap an arm around her shoulder. 'You're gonna be fine, girl. That's why we're studying. One card at a time and one day at a time ...'

Nik stiffens. 'Wait, is that optimism I hear?' Brian smirks and squeezes her into a side-hug. She leans her head on his chest. 'Thanks, though. I'll take your word for it.'

She looks back up at him, but Brian's distracted, his attention caught by Abe.

'So, Darby hasn't worked off their community service yet?' Brian asks, nodding at the two of them whispering about Hollywood starlets in the golden age of cinema.

Nik breaks free from Brian's embrace and returns to the bottles. 'Ask me another.'

Brian picks up the cards and shuffles through them. His training sessions and pseudo-internship have made him more scarce and the after-hours drinks at the bar less enticing. After his third time vomiting on, and apologizing from, Tyler's floor, he determined not to drink before their meetups. While he has never been one for routine, the practice provides a structure to his days and a feeling of progress where he once felt he was standing still. On his morning runs in Thousand Acre Park, he sees the other joggers. He used to resent them and their performative wellness, but now they are his peers. He nods at them as he passes. When he is out of their eye-line, he sprints to see just how fast an out-of-shape werewolf can go without the handicap of a hangover.

When Brian does join the two of them at the dive bar, he won't stay until the last man standing like he used to. He'll have a couple drinks with them, bike home, and text Nik that he made it safely. What Brian didn't expect was that Abe would take the stool that Brian left vacant. He thought it should lie fallow or, better yet, be immortalized, like when they retire athletes' jerseys and hold a binge-drinkers commemoration ceremony as they hoist the seat into the rafters. Occasionally Abe will join their trio as they procession across the bridge for a drink. He looks out of place, just sitting there with sparkling water and adding nothing to the conversation, until eventually walking Darby home. There's no single offense that Brian can point to, which pisses him off even more. He's just always so … *there*, all the time. Brian tries different rationales for his resentment. Maybe he's controlling, or jealous, given the way Abe scoops Darby up from their post-shift cigarette without a word. Maybe he's selfish and out of touch? He tried this assessment on for size with Nik after the happy couple had left one night.

'Aren't you annoyed by the way he monopolizes the end of your bar all night? Couldn't you get more cash if he wasn't sitting there nursing a bottle of wine for six hours?'

Nik shrugged it off. 'He always tips well,' she said, placing Abe's empty wine glass in the dishwasher, 'plus it's one less asshole I need to worry about in addition to everyone else in this place.'

'Okay, fine, but you got to admit, that little Moleskine journal is pretentious as fuck. Is he cosplaying as a Brooklyn hipster circa 2010 or something? What is that all about?'

Nik sighed. 'I don't know, Brian. It's a journal. Who cares?'

'You know one time when he went to the bathroom, I read a bit of it,' Brian confessed.

'Brian …'

'I swear he left it there on purpose! I took a little peek,

and it was all in this weird ornate script, like German or something.'

'He's Dutch,' Nik corrected.

'Whatever. Anyways, down in the margin, in super tiny print, he wrote, "Hello, Brian".'

Brian waited expectantly for a reaction. She stared. 'Your point?'

'I'm just saying that's fucked up! It's entrapment.'

'If you're looking for sympathy after deliberately invading someone's privacy, you're not going to find it with me.' But that didn't stop Brian from trying.

He reads off a new flashcard: 'Which of the following is not treated with barbiturates? Seizures, insomnia—'

'Hypotension,' chirps Nik. 'You already asked that one. Did you mix up the piles again?'

'Oh, sorry. Speaking of barbiturates, you think old man Abe partied with Judy Garland back in the day? One of the original Friends of Dorothy?'

Nik sighs. 'Can you just drop it?'

Brian puts down the flashcards and puts his hands up in mock surrender. 'It's a joke! Honestly. What's the deal? We used to joke like this all the time.'

'*We* didn't, Brian. *You* did,' Nik says. 'Shh … here they come.'

'Are you guys ready? After the night I've had, I need a drink,' says Darby, slinging their tote over their shoulder and dragging Abe behind them. In classic Abe fashion, he hovers just outside the conversation to avoid having to participate.

'Almost – let me just lock this back in the office,' Nik says, departing with the stock list.

Darby leans on the back of a bar stool and pinches the hem of Brian's sleeve with their fingers. 'This is cute. New?'

'Yeah, uh ... Thanks.' Tyler recently had Brian recycle Marie Kondo's wisdom into a blog post on minimalism. Brian rolled his eyes as he plagiarized Marie's core tenets, but after firing off 2,500 words to Tyler on sock folding and sparking joy, he decided to give it a go. He stuffed his torn clothes and some of the laundry he didn't want to do into trash bags, pitching them from the window into the dumpster below. With his pocket a little fatter from fewer nights at the bar and more nights at home, he was able to buy some new clothes that highlighted the progress he had made with the were-workouts.

'Oh! Did you try out the planning app I sent you?' Brian had tried his hand at applying just a little of his training to Darby's hectic creative life, forcing them to sit down with their agenda after a particularly frantic shift so that they could work out when Darby could focus on the work that paid their bills, the work that made them happy, and when to make time for self-care.

Darby shifts their stance. 'No, not yet. I just don't know if it aligns with my process.'

'You've got to try it. It's been great for me to get organized.'

'It's just ... complicated.'

'It's not! There are these four quadrants of your life,' Brian says, reciting another blog post from memory. 'And then you just place the tasks in each quadrant. So for you, let's say, we've got work, art, friends and family. Then you prioritize them from one to ten, and—'

'Yeah, you told me all about it in exacting detail.'

'I ... I'm just trying to help,' Brian says, now clear that his advice to Darby was not taken in the spirit it had been intended.

'It's fine, really,' says Darby. 'I'm glad it's been working for you, though. You seem more ... *here*. If that's a thing.'

'Yeah. You know, I've been meditating a bit. Leading with my breath.'

Darby narrows their eyes with suspicion. 'Who are you and what have you done with my friend,' they hissed.

'Fine. I mean, it helps me and—'

'Brian, I'm kidding. Like I said, I'm glad it works for you. But listen, speaking of planning, are you free the night of my show? I need to give the theater names for my guest tickets.' Darby mentioned their show was moving to a bigger venue when they were jostling elbows at the kitchen hatch earlier that week, loading plates onto trays and sweating under the red heat lamps. 'It's no big deal. Well, it's kind of a big deal, given that it's at the Tate Theater,' Darby said casually. 'Some kind of mad cabaret business. It'd mean a lot to me if you came to the opening but you know, if you've got other things on, don't worry ...' Brian gave an evasive response; the third week of the month was always tricky with the full moon and his training schedule.

'Umm ...' Brian pulls up his calendar on his phone. Tyler has showed him how to set calendar reminders in his phone for the phases of the moon and helped him plan it out with his work schedule and set aside hours for The Pack™ logistics. Brian liked learning about the moon, how astrology and folklore brought a magic and a queerness to the werewolf stuff that was otherwise always so carnal and aggressive. Each month, Brian would return to the park for his transition and see how the landscape had changed. He could feel the ground thaw beneath his feet under March's Worm Moon. He looked up from the park to make out the rosy hue of April's Pink Moon. It helped him feel present, hopeful even, seeing how things change even if his daily life felt … boring. Tyler says being present takes practice. That it's all about approaching things with intention. Whatever that means, Brian thinks he's been doing it. At least his monthly transitions have been casualty-free. His last slip-up, he would later learn, was under the Wolf Moon, the irony of which made it easiest to remember. And Tyler had bought him a GoPro to wear so they could track what he did on full moons – 'And also for content,' Tyler had said, stretching the elastic around Brian's head. 'We're going to need this for socials. I'm thinking a time lapse for TikTok would gain some traction.' The next day Brian had been shocked during playback to see one moment in which a blue-black moth had landed on Brian's paw, and he had simply watched it until it had fluttered off back into the moonlight. Six months ago, he would have gulped it down like a seaweed cracker. His animal instincts were clearly under increasing advisement from their human counterpart.

Brian jumps to the week of the cabaret and sees 'BLOOD MOON' in all caps – thankfully, a couple of days before Darby's premiere.

'Busy week?' inquires Abe, wiping the lenses of his glasses as he peers into the display pastry case.

Abe always did this shit, jumping in when no one asked. 'No ...' says Brian. 'I'll be there.'

'I think it's an infographic,' says Tyler. He's shirtless in the kitchen, mixing up another batch of protein shakes. 'Something for the IG grid. Showing the contents of a go-bag for the full moon. Something funny like *'Tired of walking home naked at dawn?'* I think we can use it for some spon-con, you know?'

Brian is trying to gather his wits after a double-feature training session of weightlifting and jiu-jitsu. Shortly after Brian finally got the hang of the weighted pull-ups, Tyler suggested bringing martial arts into the framework. He thought the current training regimen was missing a certain militarism needed to unify The Pack™ philosophy of self-optimization. He was also sourcing new mantras every week, convinced that The Pack™ should have a stock of 365 minimum, enough for one every day from launch for the first year. A rotation of these are slapped on Brian's bathroom mirror for him to try out, written on cocktail napkins, old receipts and coloring sheets from the restaurant scribbled in crayon. They're all a variation on a theme, equating the vicissitudes of daily life being battles to be won or lost. Brian is hesitant to say anything. The rest of the training program has been so successful, poking holes in his framework would only slow his progress. What does it matter if some of the less palatable ideas sound like they're preparing for war? He posts them on his mirror, leaving just enough room for him to watch himself brush his teeth. Whenever Tyler is out of town for the expansion strategy, he texts to check in on how Brian is doing with the latest mantras. Unlike the physical training where there's visible progress, underlined by the increased hits on Brian's Grindr profile, Tyler needs continual assurance for the unseen work of his spiritual program.

'Wait – is this part of the listicle you wanted on the best four-way stretch fabrics for monthly transformations? Or is this separate?' Brian is having trouble keeping all these ideas straight, taking short, quick breaths while his ribs heal after Tyler broke a couple when he threw him to the ground during their very energetic sparring session.

'No, separate. But the go-bag could be a nice tie-in. How about we mock up both and see which one resonates more.'

Brian recoils at the royal 'we' that Tyler uses to get his way. It always signifies a new and ambiguous task for Brian to add to his list. 'Sure, I'll get on it.'

'Did you watch the talk I sent?' Tyler tosses the smoothie at him from across the kitchen. Brian snatches it from the air, wincing and grabbing his side.

'Which one?' he asks, through a sharp exhale. Tyler loves to send him videos at all hours of the day and night.

It's often a TED Talk from a corporate CEO, billionaire or former military commander. Brian realizes that these talks are less for his own benefit and more dry runs of Tyler's own TED Talk. Still, Tyler quizzes him whenever they meet up, so Brian saves up a queue of them to binge the night before. He watches them in the dark on his phone while lying in bed, chewing thoughtfully on pizza. When he gets what he thinks are the key takeaways, he moves on to the next one.

'The one on intentionality and career choices,' says Tyler. 'Thought it could help with the school stuff.' Tyler's mentorship has slowly expanded beyond the parameters of werewolf issues, bringing in his life-coaching to the rest of Brian's existence. They talk about careers, make steps to get him back into school, discuss mending his relationship with his parents. To Tyler's mind, these are all management challenges with clear next steps – something he demonstrated on his iPad over coffee at The Romanesco. He made various decision trees of each of Brian's problems, and Brian was shocked to see his challenges laid bare in such stark abstraction, as if a decision tree could mend a relationship with parents who fundamentally disapproved of him. Tyler doesn't like excuses; he's an expert at flattening complexity into a tick-box exercise. It was out of touch, but well intentioned. Where Brian saw a chasm between the boxes for 'Call your father' and 'Visit for Father's Day', Tyler connected them with a straight line.

'I get it, man. Dads are tough,' said Tyler. 'Trust me, I know. But he just needs to know that you respect him.

These are some easy things you can do to give him those assurances, so he doesn't have to question it.'

Brian felt that for some of these things, he did need an extra push. He could see that, in small ways, it *was* working. He had sent off for some university prospectuses, which had started arriving with a heavy *thwump* on his doormat. He had even recently reached out to his mom, by which he means that he remembered her birthday for the first time in years. Still, it was a start.

'Oh, yeah, I missed that. I'll get on it tonight ...' he says, sure that Tyler will forget.

'And are you practicing the scripts? The ones for managing conflict?'

'Yes, yes, I am ...' A particularly humiliating part of their training sessions is roleplaying confidence-building and assertiveness. Tyler sits at his dining-room table, eating imaginary food off an empty plate and acting like the most entitled customer imaginable. 'My food is cold!' 'This isn't skim milk!' 'Can I speak to the manager?' Brian's job is to diffuse the situation, all while standing his ground, with Tyler listening in to his heart rate. Brian should tell the imaginary customer to 'clarify their expectations', Tyler says; he needs to tell them, 'When you say X, what I hear is Y.' Brian doesn't want to point out that Tyler just doesn't understand that Brian can't get away with meeting entitlement with defiance, not while he's working for tips. Some people are just assholes, plain and simple. With the rotating hordes of tourists and conferences at The Romanesco, he knows that this need to exert control over others unifies the masses, having been on the receiving end of power trips from do-gooders and corporate execs alike. When they sit at that table and the performance of lord–subject begins, people take to their roles; they feel free to have opinions on your tattoos, your hair color, your fey voice, whether the wine is cold enough or how long they had to wait for their steak, and use their own criteria to see how much of their money you deserve. Brian is expected to be a mind-reader, a dutiful servant and a punching bag when people need it. He knows his role and he submits, letting customers' comments bounce off his force field of lassitude.

'Good, good,' Tyler says briskly. 'You know, you really need to keep working on that, Brian. You're still way too deferential. Even in roleplay, you still don't stand up for yourself enough. You can't just let all those emotions fester. Who knows when they'll bubble up to the surface?'

Despite Tyler's advocacy, Brian knows this emergent assertiveness is never to be used with his mentor. Tyler sees assertiveness through the lens of conflict, sublimating the entire emotional spectrum – loneliness, sadness, fear – into a language of anger and frustration, an us–them conflict between opposing forces that can be won or lost. You don't feel lonely, depressed or afraid; other people *make* you feel that way, and it's up to you to make them stop. Any pesky residual feelings of inadequacy and vulnerability are to be veiled by a smokescreen of stoicism. Rooted out, never made public, lest your enemies find them and exploit your weaknesses. Brian once casually questioned some of the core tenets of Tyler's overarching lupine philosophy – a sort of natural world versus Nietzsche mash-up.

'Isn't the whole thing about our innate supremacy and our will to power, like, a *little* bit ...' Brian trailed off and put a finger under his nose, indicating a small, clipped 1930s mustache.

He was surprised at Tyler's sudden flash of anger. 'Brian, you don't know shit. If you're not into this, then fuck off back to your little waitressing life or whatever.'

Brian squinted, trying to read Tyler. 'Are we roleplaying here?'

But Tyler just adjusted his face back to a smile and laughed.

Since then, Brian has kept his mouth shut and done as he's told, with the lessons awakening him to all the ways he could be belittled in his day-to-day life. Nik had to step in a couple of times at the restaurant and offer discounts to his disgruntled diners. It came to a head later that week after a confrontation with a mother of four. The woman was upset with the wait time during the dinner rush, probably because her children clawed at her, wailing for chicken tenders, grilled cheese, anything to satiate their endless want. She kept flagging Brian down.

'Please.'

'Any update?'

'Hello?'

In the past, Brian would have checked on the food and grudgingly brought some crayons in an attempt to bribe the kids. This time, he didn't do that. 'Ma'am, read the room. We're busy. They'll get here when they're ready.'

Brian didn't think anything of it until the next day when he saw the one-star Yelp review. He attempted to tiptoe into the restaurant to clock in, but Nik grabbed him and pulled him behind the wall that linked the bar and the kitchen. It was the only part of the restaurant where customers couldn't see or hear anything, like the backside of a Disney ride where you realize It's a Small World is an army of Skynet robots. It was for sliding half-eaten meals into the slop bucket, brief mental breakdowns when a new conference broke for lunch, clandestinely checking your text messages, and in this instance, stern talkings-to.

'God dammit, Brian! You know this is the only thing the owner cares about. I got an earful from him this morning. And now I gotta write you up,' she said, taking out a book reserved for only the most severe of waitstaff infractions, a murderer's row of no-call-no-shows and legendary acts of malfeasance passed down through the rich oral history of generations of Romanesco staff.

'I'm sorry. I was just frustrated, and it was super busy. I just snapped.' He felt irritated, childish at having his friend put him in time out.

'Honestly, I don't know what's going on with you,' she said, scribbling away. Behind her, Darby came jangling in with a stack of plates and silverware. They were just about to speak when they saw it, The Book, and quickly turned in the other direction without losing a second of momentum.

'Remember last week, when you told that two-top to "assess their need and get back to you"?'

'I told you, they were taking forever—'

'The woman you told her allergy "wasn't a thing".'

'Well, have *you* ever heard of a parsley allergy? Just *say* you don't like parsley and quit with the theatrics.'

'Then what happened with Mr. and Mrs. Duncan. They've been coming here for years.'

'If I ask you what you want to drink, please, for the love of God, just name a liquid ...'

Nik sighed. 'Who is this? This isn't you.'

'What do you mean? Of course this is me.'

'No, this is you after you started spending time with this Tyler guy.'

'What are you trying to say?'

Nik tore the carbon-print square out of the book and handed Brian a copy. 'Is everything all right?'

'Yeah, Nik, I'm fine. I feel the best I have in a long time.' Brian read Nik's familiar handwriting that he had only ever seen on flashcards and shared bar tabs; it detailed a fictional conversation where she had 'clearly explained the severity of his actions and the expectations of him moving forward'. For the infraction, Nik had checked the boxes for 'attitude' and 'insubordination'. 'Seriously, Nik?' he said, showing her the ticket.

'I'm just doing my job, okay. I know we're friends, but when I'm here I'm your boss. So please just don't give me any more headaches.'

'Sure thing, *boss*,' he said with a mock salute, turning

on his heel to get ready for his shift. He wished he had apologized, but another voice in his head told him to stand his ground, told him he was right, not to admit fault, and that Nik would get over it. Whether or not she did Brian didn't know. They never spoke of it again.

SEVEN

As the seasons change, the heat brings with it a lethargy where arguments are not worth the effort. The Romanesco is packed with customers in the summer. Tourists and locals dine al fresco and sip rosé on the patio. Brian and Darby now have double the tables they had in the winter, but at least they can be outside for some of it. Nik is trapped behind the bar and the air conditioning at The Romanesco is always on the fritz. She opens the large, paneled windows around the perimeter of the restaurant, desperate to feel the full effects of a cross-breeze that rarely comes. The three of them will each take turns standing in the walk-in refrigerator in the basement for a brief respite. On the odd occasion the three of them are in there at the same time, the first one in is the first one out lest the restaurant descend into anarchy.

At the close of yet another sweaty shift, the three of them count their cash at the bar while Abe scribbles at the other end. Although Brian keeps his head down, he can feel Abe there. He is always there, like the last party guest that cannot take a hint. He knows he is on edge with another full moon coming up, so he recites a silent mantra in his head.

'Whose is *this*?' Darby suddenly says, seeing a copy of the *Financial Times* on the bar and picking it up between finger and thumb like a dirty diaper.

'It's mine,' Brian snaps irritably.

'But … *Why*?'

'For news?'

Darby makes a monocle with their finger and thumb. 'Let me check the Nasdaq for you there, Brian,' they say in a nark voice. 'Please. Is this a cry for help?'

'No, Darby, it's not a cry for help. I'm thinking of going to business school. I've been talking about it with Tyler, and we thought it'd be good for my career prospects.'

Darby glances at Nik and then back to Brian. 'But didn't you call business school "capitalist indoctrination for the incompetent middle class"?'

Brian reaches across and snatches the newspaper from Darby's hand and stuffs it into his backpack. Nik decides now is a good time for an intervention.

'Okay, guys, let's finish up here,' she says, balling a bar towel and tossing it in the wash pile. 'I could murder a cold beer. Shall we?'

Darby hops off their stool and Abe closes his notebook, but Brian remains seated.

'Brian?' Nik asks.

'Can't tonight,' he says absentmindedly, counting the last of his tips. 'It's Tyler's birthday party.'

They stare at him.

'What? What kind of party?' Darby asks.

'A party party.'

'At his palace on the west side?'

'Yeah.'

'Who's going?'

'People.'

'What people?

'People.'

'Is it an invite-only thing or ...'

'I don't know.'

Darby rounds their eyes, horrified to be missing out.
'And?!'

'And I'll come to the bar next time,' says Brian, sliding his tips from the counter and pocketing them. He glances at Abe. 'You three have fun though.'

Brian rides his bike to Tyler's house, the summer breeze drying the sweat into salty white streaks on his T-shirt. *You should have changed your clothes*, he admonishes himself. He has put a lot of pressure on tonight – Tyler's and Brian's entire relationship has been one-on-one and this is the first time Brian is going to meet Tyler's friends. His inner sanctum. As he arrives at the house, he can feel the vibration of bass through his body. He chains up his bike and slips the expensive bottle of wine that he borrowed from work out of his backpack. When he walks up the steps, Tyler opens the door to greet him. It is clear he's been drinking. His hair is mussed, and his grin is wider than usual. 'Heard you coming,' he winks.

'Sorry I'm late. I just got off work. Got here as soon as I could.'

'No worries at all, my man. The party's just getting going. Come on in. Let me introduce you to everyone.' Tyler wraps an arm around Brian and guides him down the dimly lit hallway, before releasing him to high-five with a group of blazers. Brian waits patiently for the promised introduction and his own high five, but when neither seems forthcoming, he leaves Tyler to it and edges down the hallway. The familiar rooms that Brian has only ever seen empty somehow appear bigger filled with people. Brian peeks into the living room where a silhouette of a crowd jumps asynchronously to R & B. Across the hallway, groups of chattering thirty-somethings have gathered in the formal living room. A handful of girls in bandage dresses and high heels sip from champagne flutes and look down at a short guy in a suit as he explains to them that you can't just print more money to solve inflation. In the other corner, a handful of guys with gelled hair and waxed eyebrows shout sports at one another, crashing their beers together in agreement, the foam dripping down their hands onto the floor. Along the perimeter, pale guys in hoodies blend into the walls, their faces illuminated as they scroll through their phones. Brian feels out of place, self-conscious that he smells like hamburgers and sweat, unsure what his game plan is to evince effortless cool in this situation. He leans into the room just enough to scoop up a beer from an ice bucket and downs it quickly to settle his social anxiety. He wishes he'd brought some valium.

'Brian! Get back here!' Tyler waves him back down the hall. 'I want you to meet these guys.' Brian reaches down to grab another beer before doing as he's told, greeting the Blazers with a polite half-wave. Tyler ushers Brian through each of the rooms, introducing him to digital and creative types that make up the city's burgeoning flat-white economy, each with their full name and title – everyone except for Brian, who is just introduced as … *Brian*. But he doesn't mind; he's grateful to have Tyler as a life preserver as he acclimates to the chilly waters.

'And how do you know Tyler?' screams a white woman with an alarmingly high ponytail and a gold sequined dress that comes from, apparently, her own clothing line.

Brian glances at Tyler. 'Uh …'

'We're connecting on a project, looking at some IP ops,' Tyler says smoothly. 'Jackie, you're looking great by the way …'

'Oh, we're "Jacqueline" now,' she corrects, detailing her rebrand to Tyler. Brian backs quietly away from them as though at the end of an equine therapy session, careful not to startle Jacqueline or her ponytail. He downs his beer, pushing through the crush of people to get to the kitchen to grab another.

There are two almost identical men talking loudly about crypto to one another, barring the way to the fridge. They are both in performance-fleece vests over plaid button-ups, their Apple Watches on different wrists; one parts his hair to the right, the other the left – a kind of Leviathan of a tech bro, each of its four hooves clad in Sperry's boat shoes. Brian knows that if he wants more beer, he has to negotiate with them, slay them or answer their riddles three.

'Excuse me,' he says, trying to push past.

'Oh, hey there, buddy,' one of them stops him. 'Did we just see you with Tyler?'

'Uh, yeah. Possibly.'

'Great!' says the other. 'How do you know the birthday boy?'

Brian shuffles the contents of the fridge as he tries to remember Tyler's phrasing. 'We're connecting on a project. Looking at some ops. For IP. Ip ops. Ipops.' They look at Brian quizzically. He finds a beer and gratefully pours a gulp into his open mouth. 'Anyway, how about you – how do you know Tyler?'

Instead of an answer, he gets a sales pitch. 'You know when you're out with your friends, the spot you're at is dying down and you want to make a move to somewhere with bottle service?' says Leviathan's left mouth.

Brian sips his beer. 'Go on …'

'You want to find a close spot with good vibes. But you don't know where to go? Or when you find the spot, you don't want to be the last man standing responsible for the bar tab.'

Leviathan's right mouth jumps in. 'Well, we developed an app for that. It maps the nearest clubs, their prices, and syncs with Venmo for peer-to-peer payments. You should check it out next time you're out.'

Brian nods. Of all the intractable issues that big tech could resolve – food insecurity in the Sahel, rising sea levels or declining civic space fomented by authoritarian populism – it's good to know we have our best and brightest working on this one. 'And Tyler?'

'Tyler is a silent partner. He's always looking for the next big thing. I see a lot of people here who owe him a debt of gratitude.'

Brian scans the room through the lens of this new knowledge. He wonders how many of the revelers are Tyler's friends, debtors or both. And for that matter, which category does *he* fall into?

It's then that he sees Tyler break through the crowd to grab him. ''Scuse me, gents. I need to synergize with this one,' he says, as Tyler guides him away from the BOTTL pitch down the hallway toward the office. The sounds of the party get further away. 'There's someone I'd like you to meet,' he says as he closes the French door to his mahogany study. 'He's a very good friend of mine.'

A man who looks like a brown-haired version of Tyler spins around in the office chair to dramatically reveal himself, like an arch villain in his lair. A drunk arch villain, that's clear from the tumbler of Scotch tilted precariously in his hand, and the sunglasses sitting askew on the bridge of his nose.

'Brian, this is Mark. Mark, Brian.'

'Uh, hi …?' Brian tries, more of a question than a greeting.

Mark mockingly salutes him in return.

'He's an old friend,' Tyler says, 'like a brother. But more importantly, he's one of us.'

Brian shudders to think of what they could possibly have in common before it dawns on him. His eyes go wide. There's another person. Tyler's been mentoring another werewolf, this whole time.

Mark looks at Brian and casually howls.

'I didn't know there was someone else,' says Brian. 'Uh ... how long have you two been doing the Monster Mash?'

'Well, you could say he's my protégé. He was the first one I've worked with on this framework – and to great success, I might add.' Mark lifts his cup in a toast. 'I didn't want to introduce you two too soon. Had to make sure you both got individualized attention from me. But with all the great progress you've been making, I'm excited for you two to finally meet. The pack is really coming together! Anyways, I'll leave you two here to get to know one another.'

Tyler turns and closes the door behind him. Brian is left to process the fact that their duo is now a trio. 'There isn't going to be another werewolf walking through that door, is there?' he asks.

Mark shrugs before helping himself to more Scotch from Tyler's decanter, slopping some over the sides. 'You know Tyler. Plays everything soooo close to the chest. Business, friends, girls. All of it. When we would do group projects in school, I felt like he wanted me to sign a non-disclosure agreement. Just in case he stumbled on some great innovation.' Mark spins in his chair back to Brian and gestures at the decanter; Brian nods and Mark glugs four fingers into another crystal tumbler and slides it recklessly across the desk. Brian covers the distance quickly to catch it as it drops off the other end. He takes a seat in one of the leather chairs in front of the desk, worrying vaguely about the trail of condensation the tumbler left on the desk lacquer. The office is mood-lit, the rows of books and oriental rugs soundproofing everything but for the bass of the party outside.

'So, you didn't know about me either?' Brian eventually asks, after several minutes of watching Mark twirl himself around on the chair.

Mark stops spinning and peers at him from over the top of his sunglasses. 'Nope, no, I knew. Said you had some rough edges he had to work on. Not ready yet. But look, you made it. Here we are.' He spins around again, leaning back a little too far, and slaps his hand on a slat of the bookshelf to steady himself, creating a domino effect of sliding hardbacks. He curses under his breath and hastily stands them back up.

Rough edges? That stung a little, but it probably wasn't untrue. Brian remembers how he used to skip dinner on the full moon to save money and time, knowing he'd invariably end up eating something (or someone) in the park anyways, before Tyler laid bare how terrible an idea that was. After years of him going it alone, Tyler *did* find him in a sorry state, and after seeing the results of the past few months, Brian's sarcasm has very much warmed to actual appreciation.

'Soooo,' Brian says, as Mark starts wheeling himself across the floor. 'How long have you known Tyler?'

'Oh man … uh … forever? Wait no, like, since college. How many years is that?' He briefly starts counting on his fingers before he loses track. 'Anyways, we were roommates the first year of college. Paired together by some university software and we've been best buds ever since. He's like a fuckin' brother … been with me through all of it … the awoo stuff …' he says with a warbling howl, 'and all the rest of it … girls, work. He's always looking to find the areas where I'm' – he brackets his fingers for air quotes – '"suboptimal".' Even with Mark slurring the word 'suboptimal', Brian detects a tinge of resentment.

'But what can you do? Y'know? I owe him a lot. He talked to his dad to get me this job. Tyler moved on ages ago, but I've been there since … climbing my way up the food ladder … corporate chain … *food chain* of the acquisitions department. He knows how that place works 'cause he was born into it. Always makes time to help me figure that place out, even with all of his other projects.'

'What, The Pack?'

'The Pack T-M? Yeah, and the rest. I can't keep track of 'em all. I know there's the coaching stuff, corporate retreats and the like. HR makes us do that dumb shit every couple of months when someone fucks up. I think most of his money is tied up in real estate, managing all the family's properties around town. If you have the money, it's a great way to make passive income.'

Brian cannot imagine income ever being 'passive'. His has always been active, edging toward outright aggressive when he needs to work a double shift to make rent at the end of the month. Apparently when you have money, it just begets more money – you get paid in the service of being rich.

Brian has been holding back the question he really wants to ask, though Mark is too drunk to feel the heft of this silence. 'So, when did you, you know, become one of us?'

Mark gets out of the chair and, with the concentration of a curler, tries to roll it back to the desk. It veers off and hits the glazed doors with a thud. 'Umm ... about a year after college? Me and Tyler were on one of our fishing trips. We were drinking in the boat all day. Don't remember much of the attack. When I woke up, Tyler had bandaged me up good. Told me everything – that he was one too, that that was the only reason he could fend it off. Without him I would have been wolf meat. He's always looked out for me. When we got back to the city, he even found me a place with a basement for the full moons – he loaned me the money for reinforced doors ...'

Mark wanders from behind the desk to come and sit on the front of it, about an arm's length from Brian. He casually leans back a little, his legs spread apart. 'But sometimes, I like to just run free,' he says, his voice lowering conspiratorially. 'I hear that's what you do too. Huh ... I wonder what else we have in common?'

Wait, is Mark ... hitting on him? Brian shifts uncomfortably in his seat, trying to find an eye-line that isn't taken up by Mark's crotch. It wouldn't be the first time a drunk straight guy hit on him. One more month at home with his parents and he would've been chased out of town with pitchforks and torches by the moms on the PTA. He's no stranger to the approach. Some just want the attention; others, more. When Brian's self-esteem is particularly low, he succumbs to the pictureless Grindr messages from straight married men. It makes him feel sexy, to be desired by someone that, according to their own self-classification, is never and could never be attracted to him. That even though his weight makes him an undesirable in the eyes of the 'no fats, no femmes' crowd, somehow here he can break through. Plus, it's utilitarian – there are never any strings, no repeat customers, no repercussions, just once or twice a fleeting moment of recognition and terror in the face of some guy in a grocery aisle, out shopping with his wife and kids. And, like it or not, it's hot. It's a category on Pornhub for a reason. Rather than see how this will play out, Brian shuts it down. He looks away from Mark's crotch and drains the rest of his whiskey. 'I need another drink. I'll see you back out there.'

Brian follows the sound of the party down the long hallway, bumping gently along the sides of the walls as the drinks hit him all at once. He should have eaten at work. He cuts through the revelers until his path is blocked by a guy spraying champagne on a group of people dancing, unable to read that the girls screams aren't in excitement as their blow-outs are soaked with brut rosé bubbles. Brian ducks into the guest bathroom to gain his bearings, but he is confronted by a trio of sweaty suits hunching over a mirror of cocaine.

'I thought you locked the door!' says the one sitting on the toilet.

'You were the last one in!' says another.

The third offers him a rolled-up bill. 'Well, since you're here. You mind locking that?'

When in Rome. He locks the door and snorts a sting of chalky powder. He waits patiently as the tech industry Cerberus engages in rapid-fire conversation on B2B cloud solutions, the toll he must pay to get a couple more lines to course correct his drunkenness. With his chest now pumping with a euphoric courage, he slinks out of the room unnoticed and ducks into the kitchen. The party's beginning to thin out a little, and the Leviathan is no longer standing sentry, so he has a straight shot to the fridge. He grinds his teeth as he surveys the beer options and is just about to choose between a brightly colored tin of pale ale and a bottle of continental lager, when he is suddenly tackled into a hug from behind with such force that it activates his fight or flight response. He spins around, either ready to pop someone in the jaw or tuck and roll away, when he sees that his attacker is a petite blonde girl. She's in a crop top and a high-waisted pant and her long ombré hair, parted in the middle, reaches her midriff. She smiles at him, looking for a glimmer of recognition through big blue eyes. Her cheeks are pink and she smells like white wine and peonies. Tyler approaches behind her.

'Brian, right? Tyler told me you were coming!' she says. 'I'm Sarah, by the way. I'm sure Tyler's told you all about me.'

'Sarah …?' Brian asks, trying to place the name.

Tyler peers at him from behind her and pantomime-nods. 'My girlfriend Sarah?'

'Sarah! Yes, of course,' Brian says, feigning recognition. 'He does not. Shut. Up. About you. Great to finally meet you.'

She grabs his hand. 'Listen. I need a cigarette. You smoke, right? I'm dying for one. I quit – well, I only smoke when I drink now. Come out with me to the patio – I want to know everything about this mystery man Tyler has been spending all his time with. He's always so secretive about his projects …' she says with faux disapproval, towing him through the kitchen and out into the garden.

The garden is filled with an overflow of revelers who chatter amidst the greenery in a cloud of skunky smoke. He hands her a cigarette; she holds it in her lips and casts her big blue gaze at him until he realizes she needs a lighter too. She leans in as he lights it for her, then the Wikipedia entry of her life begins, from birth right up to the present moment. '… and I know what you're thinking – where's the ring, right?' she says, having just mentioned that she and Tyler have been dating for ten years. Brian nearly chokes on his beer – did she just say the quiet part out loud? She must be drunk. Or have zero self-awareness. Or both. 'Well, you know how it is,' she continues, blowing a column of smoke into the night air. 'We're both really focused on our careers right now. And we have a good thing going, we don't need to rush anything.' It can't have been easy to be with Tyler all those years. Brian wonders if Tyler would be more open to the idea of marriage if she just framed it as a 'collab'.

Sarah is vice president at a public relations firm downtown. She made her way through the ranks working on crisis communications, diving in and out of corporate maelstroms, leveraging her pathological optimism to diffuse tensions and reframe challenges as opportunity. She keeps her client list close to her chest – it's part of the gig. She has her own place a couple of blocks away from Tyler, a cute little one-bedroom overlooking Thousand Acre Park. They have talked about moving in together, but Tyler doesn't want to until they're married – he's old-fashioned that way. 'So,' she says, now on her second cigarette. 'What about you?'

The cocaine takes the wheel as Brian and Sarah talk for maybe an hour, one of them occasionally sliding open the patio door to collect more drinks from the fridge and Brian lighting up cigarette after cigarette for the two of them. Brian gives her the broad strokes of where he's from, his family, friends, working at The Romanesco. He's talking a mile a minute, but she keeps up with his breakneck pace; active listening is an essential skill for her. She asks him about growing up in the suburbs, where he lives in the city, and gives him the names of a couple of restaurants in his neighborhood he must try, though he's fairly sure he can't afford them. She doesn't inquire further about school; she must assume he's a college drop-out in the same way that Bill Gates is. Though she's briefly puzzled by the fact he's a waiter, trying to find the link between him and Tyler. Brian says it was a chance encounter at The Romanesco and alludes to a couple of projects that he's invested in, a few big, disruptive ideas that Tyler's helping him with, which seems to satisfy her fairly minimal curiosity. Sarah's a little basic, true, but he finds that he likes her company, how easy it is, how she laughs at everything he says.

'You're so funny,' she says for the hundredth time that night, slapping his arm as he tells her about selling a textbook last week to pay his electricity bill.

The guests drop off one by one. As they leave, Brian gets to see Tyler's inner circle – the folks who stay around till the end of a birthday must be the ones he is closest to. When there's only a half-dozen people left in the living room, he and Sarah come in from the garden to occupy the couch, sitting down next to Tyler. He instinctively puts his hand on Sarah's inner thigh and keeps talking to the champagne assailant, disheveled and sticky, sitting on a cushion on the floor, waiting for his Uber. Mark's barely awake in the Eames chair. Brian's just wondering how to make his exit when another thirty-something guy in a polo and khakis comes in from the kitchen with a fresh beer in hand and his curly-haired brunette girlfriend under his other arm and suddenly addresses the room, cutting across the smaller conversations. 'Hey, guys. What about the trip?'

Mark seems to spontaneously wake up at this. 'Yeah,' he mutters, sitting up again. 'What's the plan?'

Every year, the group goes away to a campsite nestled between the lakeshore and an alpine forest that climbs up the mountains. It's about a two-hour drive outside the city, but a stone's throw from their ivy-snared alma mater. On their holiday breaks they would pack up their dorm rooms to binge-drink in the forest. Though this has become much tamer in recent years, they keep the ritual alive, trading truth or dare and hallucinogens for hiking and cast-iron cornbread.

'Remember when we took all those shrooms and went skinny-dipping?'

'Then Jason freaked out, convinced that there was a sea monster licking at our feet?'

'Hey! I'm just saying, there has to be more than one Loch Ness monster.'

While the shiny happy people and Tyler start talking about sleeping-bag gauges for mountain territory, Brian feels the shine of the cocaine wear off, leaving him drunk, fussy and with an insatiable craving for more cocaine. It's time to leave. He stands up and leans over to Sarah.

'Hey, really enjoyed meeting you,' he says in a low voice, so as not to interrupt the spec breakdown of a Hyke & Byke Snowmass bag. 'I'm going to head off.'

'Wait, you should come too,' she says as a polite reflex, but as the suggestion dawns brighter on her, she turns and addresses the room. 'Guys, shouldn't Brian come too? On the trip?'

Brian would rather be eaten alive by the underwater monster that nipped at their wading heels all those years ago than go camping, given his hatred of nature and his predilection for keeping his personal, professional and mystical worlds separate, but he doesn't make an excuse – he knows Tyler will do it for him. He waits for Tyler to interject, giving him an easy get-out. To his horror, however, Tyler agrees. 'You should come, Brian. It'll be great to get out of the city.'

The whole room looks at Brian expectantly. 'That's …
wow, that's super exciting,' Brian lies. 'I'll have to see about
getting time off of work, though. They can be pretty hard
on us. You know, late capitalism, gig economy …' He
mimes a noose round his throat and makes a strangled
noise. Silence. 'Anyway, I'll be off … thanks for everything.
I'll definitely come if I can.'

'I'll see you out,' says Tyler, levering himself up from
the couch while the conversation starts up again around
them. When they get to the front door, Tyler comes in.
Brian can see the trace of coke on the tip of Tyler's nose
and instinctively rubs his own. 'Just between me and you,'
he says, 'I think it'd be good for you to come. Commune
with some nature that isn't a city park. Mark will be there.
It can be a bit of a team-building exercise.'

'Yeah. I really will try. Work though … it is hard.' Taking
time off work is a considerable dip into his pocket. 'I really
will see what I can do.'

'Great,' grins Tyler. 'The Pack's first trip.' He offers Brian
a fist bump, then closes the door.

EIGHT

'You coming to the bar?' Darby says casually, picking up their bag and slinging it onto their shoulder.

Brian looks up from a receipt he's reading. One of his customers has scrawled *asshole* on the bottom. 'You guys go ahead without me,' he says, distractedly trying to think which customer it might have been. 'I'm going to Tyler's tonight.'

'But you're still going to come to my show, right? I've got you all on the guest list for the premiere.'

'Who's on the list?' Maybe it was that customer that wanted a salad instead of fries. Whatever, he ate the fries anyway ...

'From here, you, Nik, Abe ...'

Brian looks up sharply. 'Abe,' he repeats. Brian resents how much Abe seems to have upended the dynamics of the group. Always perched on a bar stool, either at the restaurant or the bar after work, a passive observer like a needy Gilded Age ghost. Brian was getting worse at hiding his irritation, too, Darby increasingly aware of his low-key hostility to their new partner.

'Is there a problem?'

Brian sighs. 'No.'

'Good. Because I want all my favorite people there together. You promise you'll come?'

'Yes, yes. Wouldn't miss it.'

Darby pauses at the door before they head outside to wait for Nik. 'Cool, 'cause if you flake, our friendship is terminated. Okay, love you, bye!'

Another dynamic that's changed recently in Brian's life is the one he has with Tyler now that Mark has been welcomed into the pack. Or rather now that Brian has integrated himself into *their* pack. Gone are the chummy one-on-ones – in the weeks since Tyler's birthday, their training sessions have been less two-man wellness retreat and more three-way Stanford prison experiment. Biking over to Tyler's for their sessions, Brian would wait out front of the door for a couple of deep breaths before ringing, bracing himself for the onslaught of raw masculinity.

Although Brian had only recently gotten accustomed to the physical training, Tyler switched up the routine to be more of a boot camp, bringing in all the trappings of high-intensity circuits and combat to create what felt like an elite juvenile detention facility in the basement of his multi-million-dollar townhouse. Brian would ready himself as the two of them chained weights around his waist that would cut into his sides as they jumped, pushed and pulled their bodies across the room. Tyler and Mark would strip their shirts off and grunt and scream, throwing 100 kg weights at one another, fist-bumping and slapping one another's asses in congratulatory praise, while Brian would lie on the floor, his threadbare T-shirt wet with sweat and blood and clinging to his body like a wet blanket, just waiting for the day they would invariably perform the windmill high five from *Top Gun* without a tinge of irony. It didn't take long for a hierarchy to take root. The two of them would shout about toughening up, going stronger and harder at it. Unfortunately, this was always directed at Brian, given how long it took him to finish. They were generally machismo oriented, a vague 'GET IT!' 'BE A MAN!' or its analog 'DON'T BE A PUSSY!' He would stay silent and do his best to drown out the two Adonises shouting on either side of him. But the personal ones, the ones designed to humiliate him, those would snap Brian to attention. 'JUST QUIT, QUIT LIKE YOU QUIT EVERYTHING' and 'YOU'RE JUST GOING TO LIE DOWN AND TAKE IT LIKE A BITCH.' It pissed him off just enough to pull out what little energy he had left – which, he only later realized, reinforced the insults. But even if Brian did have the opportunity to shout back at them, he wouldn't take it. He wasn't sure degrading someone for their perceived physical weakness could ever be motivating – making cutting comments under his breath was more his style. Late at night, warming up leftovers in his microwave, he'd thrust his chest out and roleplay what he might shout back at Tyler and Mark.

'Your father doesn't respect you!'

'No amount of muscle mass will slow the steady march of time.'

'You will be forgotten and everyone you know will one day turn to dust.'

The jiu-jitsu, which Tyler had initially introduced as a metaphor for redirecting emotions and using someone's own momentum against them had slowly been reframed as an act of domination. Tyler would referee Mark and Brian's sparring matches. As the two of them 'rolled' on the floor, Brian tried to look for a glimmer of recognition in Mark's eyes that this whole thing was absurd. But Mark never thought if he didn't have to; there was always this exquisite blankness behind his eyes, one that reminded Brian of the flow state he so desperately sought through hours of meditation. Mark did what he was told, and, ever the loyal servant, was determined to put on a show. Brian remembers the first time his tapping out during a submission hold went ignored. Mark had him on the floor, his legs snaked around Brian's right arm. Brian was trapped, he felt his bones give way and begin to splinter under his skin like fresh wood. He tapped and tapped, but Tyler just watched him, his eyes narrowed, and he nodded at Mark, who snapped his arm with a deafening crack.

'What the fuck?!' Brian yelled at Mark while scrambling to his feet, realigning his forearm and thumb from their 90-degree angle.

'There is no tapping out, Brian. Not out there,' said Tyler, gesturing out the basement window. 'You'll be fine. That'll heal in no time.'

It's true, it had healed by the next morning, but Brian's body remembered. The possibility of playful violence followed him outside the sparring sessions, ostensibly to ensure that they were always at the ready. It could be a punch on the arm, a push to shift your balance, or a kettlebell shuttled across the room at your head. Brian was on edge, always waiting, and prayed that he could catch whatever was incoming without being ridiculed for flinching. He eventually learned that, to gain respect, he had to be feral in those sessions, like a trapped animal. After one training session when Mark frisbeed a barbell plate at him while he wasn't looking, Brian galloped across the room and pounced on top of him, tackling him to the floor and pummeling him until his fists bluntly erased the semblance of Tyler from his face. He pulled himself to his feet and grabbed a drink of water, basking in the rare exaltation of Tyler's praise. Brian practiced his dissonance in that moment, convincing himself that this violence wasn't who he was, that this was just him learning the skills to protect himself. But it was difficult to make this leap after watching Mark lumber onto his knees to collect his teeth from the gym mat and jiggle them back into his gums.

The transition from the basement-level Colosseum to the civility of protein shakes and meditation was abrupt. They never addressed whatever they did in the gym. Down there, they were animals. Up here, they were taming those instincts. The ole id-ego division separated by a 2-foot layer of floorboards and insulation. The interstitial conversations between these sessions were awkward, with Brian feeling like a foreigner in a strange land. As the three of them sat around in the kitchen, drinking energy drinks and cooling off, Tyler and Mark would talk in a language that Brian understood but could not speak, throwing around terms like 'capital gains', 'blue sky thinking' and 'innovation' like a venture capital Mad Libs. Plus, there were only so many conversations about sports and blockchain that he could handle. This was all within the backdrop of their 'bromance', which Brian observed with anthropological fascination. Their infatuation with one another existed in the liminal space somewhere between a fist bump and a Cape Cod civil union. They play-fought and grabbed at each other, years of conditioning telling them they could only touch one another in the guise of combat. They would pretend to hump one another in jest when the other bent down for a kettlebell. Brian prickled at this; he would find it more homophobic that they thought two men having sex was something so ludicrous that it was inherently comical if it weren't such a clear example of both their immaturity and, at a level deeply inaccessible to them, their longing for intimacy. To balance their mutual man-crush, their other favorite topic of conversation was the lurid detail of Mark's sexual conquests. Mark is single, good-looking in a lobotomized action-figure kind of way, and has the kind of job that pays him enough to wear tailor-made suits to work (at least that's what Brian thinks, having peeked for a tag on a suit hanging in the guest bathroom, only to see Mark's name embroidered on the inside pocket), so naturally his Tinder is a graveyard of women he's ghosted.

'And then she was like, "You don't remember what you said to me last night?" and I was like, "Bitch, I don't even remember your *name*".'

Tyler whooped and offered Mark a seismic high five. 'Lady *kil*-ler. You're getting what's yours, bro!'

Brian is sure he gets laid more often than Mark, but doesn't think his app-based exploits with, say, JUSTAHOLE420 would earn him the same reception. After a couple of failed attempts at challenging the casual misogyny – 'Guys, I don't think we're calling women *bitches* anymore' – Brian has given up and retreated inward. He's even more evasive about the camping trip whenever Tyler brings it up – if it's going to be anything like these training sessions, he would prefer to pass. He can continue to humiliate himself in the safety of Tyler's home without having to bring nature into it.

Mark's career is a topic of much conversation. Tyler loves to discourse on the smallest of management challenges, and he really enjoys something he calls *windows of opportunity*, which Tyler is always imploring Mark to climb through, no matter how narrow the opening. If he didn't know better, Brian might assume that Mark's a cat burglar without a collarbone rather than a well-paid executive. Mark seems to take all Tyler's advice without debate. But with all this attention on Mark's job, it becomes more and more apparent that Tyler never talks about his own career. Brian starts to wonder how this guy could have all this time for a passion project. He's always assumed there's an actual job there in the background, and the vague way that Tyler occasionally mentions 'work' has always seemed to confirm that assumption. But in all the time that Tyler has mentored Brian, he's only once rescheduled one of their sessions. On the occasions he's traveled out of town, it has always been for The Pack™ and, as far as Brian knows, he has always returned without any new recruits.

While Mark's input to The Pack™ is preparing to be the eventual poster boy, Brian resents how he's carrying the lion's share of its administration. On several occasions he's countered one of Tyler's 'we should …' statements about some half-baked idea that Brian would later have to translate into 'a thing' by suggesting Mark take it on instead.

'Maybe Mark could compile the mailing list? He's likely more adept at Microsoft than I am.'

'Pshh, Brian. Come on. Mark's got a job. He's too busy,' Tyler deflected.

While it would be too obvious for Brian to point out that he did also, in fact, have a job, he resigned himself to 'the work', hoping this upfront investment would lead to an eventual pay-out and bring an end to his days in the service industry. At least that's what he told himself as he shot off another email to a graphic designer in San Diego on the umpteenth iteration of The Pack™ logo. 'Could we get the wolf to look less like a wolf?' Why couldn't Tyler just do this himself, he thought, as he used his own credit card to buy a fleet of North Macedonian bots to follow The Pack's Instagram. He scrolls through the followers and wonders if any of them are even real people. The only messages they've received are spam. When will this even go live? Brian asks as he continues to fuss with the beta of The Pack™ website. He's drafted blog posts, Facetuned photos and sourced enough New Age aphorisms to start a Palo Alto cult, but Tyler keeps pushing back the launch, waiting until they reach 'critical mass', whenever that is. Clearly it's larger than what they have now, after Tyler upbraided him for selecting '0–11 employees' on The Pack's LinkedIn page.

When it's finally time to meditate, Brian is thankful for the silence. He has noticed the slow encroachment of his signature nihilism. It has taken considerably more effort to keep his sarcasm at bay, especially when Tyler and Mark are such easy targets, like the time Mark thought if we all just opened our doors, we could solve global warming with eight billion air conditioners. It's wild how they think that whatever shit comes out their mouths has intrinsic value, as if their focus on being *men* inoculates them against any kind of introspection, unable to see how they must sound to others. He sometimes wishes he could tell Darby about it – they would have a field day tearing these guys to shreds. But this makes Brian question his own levels of introspection – lying in bed at night, staring up at the ceiling, he wonders whether the scorn he sometimes feels for Mark and Tyler is just another defense mechanism, a rejection of them before they can reject him. Of course, rather than meeting these feelings head on, or worse, revealing his insecurity, he does what he's always done with difficult feelings: he buries them, opting instead to look for subtle ways to demonstrate to them how few fucks he gives. He'll show up late and leave sessions early; refuse to do that one *last* burpee; mute their group chat and leave their texts on read – or worse, read them so they can see the blue ticks, but *still* not respond. All the while he has ramped up his own training at home, doing a thousand one-armed push-ups while watching season three of *Love Island*, or creaking his bachelor pad mini-fridge onto his back to hold a plank for hours on end, sweat drip-dropping in a pool on the floor of his studio, pretending to himself he's just taking his program seriously, but somewhere, deep at the core of him, determined to prove to these guys that he is not as weak as they must think he is.

It's golden hour when he jumps off the bus in Pleasant Heights, an established neighborhood where wide, tree-lined sidewalks with single-family homes and housing projects coexist in relative harmony. The sun's low on the horizon, the city bathed in a warm glow. He's never been to Nik's apartment complex before – and since he spends most of his time now with Tyler and Mark, it's an invitation that has been increasingly remote – but tonight's the premiere of Darby's show and so they're all pretending that everything's fine for at least the next twelve hours. Brian walks through footpaths of identical cinderblock buildings in the courtyard, following Google Maps up to the third floor. He stops at the door, adjusts the lapels on the ill-fitting brown suit he borrowed from his dad, and then knocks.

Nik opens the door. 'Hey, stranger,' she says, not without warmth. She looks amazing, a far departure from her usual T-shirt and clogs behind the bar at The Romanesco. He has never seen her with her hair down – a broad sweep of chestnut, cascading down the back of her jewel-toned wrap dress. 'Wow,' he says.

'Oh, this old thing?' she says with a twirl. 'Come on in, I'll just be a minute. There's liquor out on the kitchen counter – you can make the drinks for once.'

Nik's lived here for years now. Knowing the city so well, she pays next to nothing in rent and is determined never to move. Brian's always been curious what her place might be like, and he now walks through it as if at a museum. The mix of furniture represents her gorgeous eclectic style to a tee; every piece of wall space has something to look at, a mix of rock posters and canvases, abstract acrylic artwork, vintage photos in mismatched frames, a stained-glass and rose-gold parrot hanging in the window which casts blue and red hues across the floor, an antique pistachio-colored lamp with a gold fringed lampshade in the corner; the mix of colors and eras shouldn't work at all, but somehow they come together, the sum of their parts a stunning display of originality.

Brian finds his way to the kitchen and the liquor bottles, and free pours bourbon and sweet vermouth into a shaker. He grabs ice from the freezer, lingering over the family photos on the olive-green refrigerator. There are more recent photos interspersed with older ones whose curled corners are blanched by sunlight – a shot of her family at Disney World, Nik in a Mickey Mouse hat flanked by her brother and sister. Another of that same brother, now decades older, holding a newborn. A wedding photo of her parents, her mother in a cream lace dress and sheer sleeves, her father in the same color barong. A handwritten letter addressed to 'Monika' on Dr Bacaycay's stationery that he can't make out but for bits of Taglish Nik taught him and the heart at the signature.

Brian takes the Manhattans and finds his way to Nik's bathroom, where she is finishing up her make-up. 'Here,' he says, putting her drink next to the basin and then taking a seat on the edge of the clawfoot tub. 'Your place is great, by the way.'

'Thanks,' she says, and he's unsure whether it's in response to the drink or the compliment.

'Sooo, how's Darby doing? About tonight, I mean.'

'They're a little nervous, I think. There are a couple of reviewers for some art magazines coming. Someone from the *New York Times* too, but that might be just a rumor.'

'Huh. That's great. I can't imagine Darby getting nervous, though. They seem so … fearless.'

'Darby? They've been nervous about this one for weeks now. You'd have seen it had you been around a little more,' she says lightly, more as an observation than a rebuke.

Brian goes quiet. He sits and watches her as she does her make-up, leaning her face close to the mirror, touching a mascara wand to her eyelashes. He remembers this same ritual with his mom. His parents had date night every Saturday. His dad would be doing yard work until the last possible minute before showering and slathering himself with drugstore cologne. Hanging out with Mom was much more fun. He would sit in the same spot and just watch her get ready as they talked. Brian would talk a lot, as most kids do. And his mom would listen. When she did speak, she never spoke to him like a child, never used the patronizing lilt that the other mothers on their block would. She would even let him curse, providing he promised not to do it in school. Back in those days, things were easy, but as Brian grew up, things got complicated and their conversations grew quiet, as he hid more and more of himself from her.

It feels the same here with Nik, things being hidden. They talk, but it stays superficial. They stick to easy topics – school, work, TV – but there is an elephant in the room. Brian is careful not to talk about Tyler. He suspects she still disapproves, that she sees Tyler as the locus of the changes that have happened to Brian over the last few months, the shifts in his outlook and behavior. He'd love to tell her how much better he feels about himself – that Tyler might be a colossal douchebag and a shitty tipper, but he has still really helped Brian get his life together – but Brian's not sure that Nik would see it that way. He would love to tell her that things with Tyler haven't all been hunky-dory either, and to ask for her advice on how to navigate the dynamic he's found himself in, but surely she would seize any opportunity to take a sledgehammer to any cracks in their foundation.

'There,' Nik says, finishing her make-up. She glances at her phone, then swears softly. 'Shit. We're running late. Okay, let's take an Uber.'

'Very fancy,' Brian says, while Nik concentrates on her phone.

'Done. Five minutes away. Let's go wait outside.'

Most of the established theater in the city is west of the park, showing regional tours of Broadway musicals and plays, and catering mostly to tourists. But downtown is where the independent theater scene lives. The Tate Theater, nestled among the office buildings, cinemas and restaurants, is an institution for those in the know – the tastemakers, the gallerists, producers and patrons. They exclusively put on shows that they believe to be at the vanguard of performance art. The fact that they placed their bets on Darby's cabaret is quite an achievement – after some glowing online admiration from the city's hipster glitterati, Darby's gone from various small, grungy art spaces to an actual theater with a dress code.

Brian goes to stand at the end of a long queue, slowly making its way through the doors, but Nik grabs his arm and marches them to the velvet rope at the very front, where she briefly confers with a burly security guard that Nik catches Brian ogling. He checks a clipboard, then smiles and waves them through. 'Guest list,' Nik whispers to Brian. They enter the courtyard-style theater and find their seats in the center about a dozen rows from the stage, as more than 200 people follow them, jostling into their seats. Brian scans the crowd to see some of the regulars from the restaurant, the time and attention Darby spends with their tables having resulted in a loyal following. In the front row, stage-left, Brian sees Abe, decked out in all black. He points him out to Nik. 'You've got to admit, the man is dedicated to a color palette. Either that, or the only suit he has is for funerals.'

'You know, Brian, you've got to stop with this. It upsets Darby, these constant little digs. I know you don't get Abe – and to be honest, I can hardly get a word out of him beyond his customary order of Côtes du Rhône – but this isn't about what you and I want, this is about Darby. Abe makes them *happy*. He makes them feel safe. He gives them confidence to be themself. What Darby needs from you is not your critical evaluation of their partner, but just a friend who has their back. Okay?'

Brian reels a little; her measured response hints at it being premeditated. He's about to defend himself, to say once again that he's only *joking*, but … maybe Nik's right. At some level he knows he's been a prick, that he's turned away from Nik and Darby in recent months, but that's because, despite Tyler and Mark's flaws, they understand him in a way that Nik and Darby never could. Perhaps his needling of Abe isn't just due to a basic level of jealousy at someone taking Darby's attention away from him – maybe it serves as a way of getting Nik and Darby to push him away, so that it hurts less when inevitably he has to cut and leave, move towns again because of another early-morning snaccident with a jogger, or when real intimacy means that they'll start wanting to know things about him that he can't tell them. 'Listen, Nik …' he begins, unsure of what he's about to say, but in that moment the lights fade, and the audience falls silent.

The orchestra in the pit begins playing and the curtains open. But no one is there. The music continues to swell and then finally, when the horns come in, Darby unravels from a pair of silks, tumbling in a barrel roll from the ceiling before catching themself in an upside-down split. The audience gasps, and Darby lets them, turning slowly like a mobile, letting the anticipation build before belting out an original aria, still upside down. And that's just the opening: over the next hour there's singing (at times in German), and storytelling juxtaposed with feats of athleticism that showcase their charisma, uniqueness, nerve and talent. Somehow, they all work together. Brian never would have thought of knife-throwing as a symbol for grieving a loved one, but the pairing of Darby's controlled monologue on the theme of loss with the thud of each dagger into the board makes Brian feel each blade in his chest. He knew Darby was talented but had no idea what was stirring beneath the surface of their dayglo irreverence. He sees shades of Darby that he has never seen. They are romantic, hopeful, optimistic. They see life as a gift and are acutely aware that one day it will end, that our driving force is to survive, and the only certainty is that we won't. As he sees all of this in Darby, he wonders why he's never heard or seen any of this in them before. He thinks this must've just been Darby being their usual evasive self – no time for origin stories, limitless horizons, etcetera, etcetera. Then it hits him – he's never truly asked them about any of this before.

The lights go up and the crowd erupts in applause. Brian can feel himself choke up. He wants to cry, but he doesn't know why, and he surely doesn't want to explain it to Nik. They stand up and applaud. He turns to see Nik wiping away her tears. She looks at him and smiles, and that opens the floodgates. As Brian's tears flow, she pulls him into a hug. 'I'm just so proud,' she says. 'They are amazing. And now everyone else gets to see what I see.'

Nik and Brian head to the side entrance of the stage to wait for Darby amid the throng of well-wishers. Nik chats with a group of passing regulars from The Romanesco's bar. Brian recognizes them but has never bothered to really *talk* to any of them. He's surprised that they've come out to support Darby, but then … Darby makes an effort with them. They remember their birthdays – though Brian suspects this is to keep tabs on any Scorpios and Geminis in their midst. They know how they take their martini, their kids names, and when and where they're going on vacation. Brian wrote this all off as a tactic for tips, but they seem to have built a real community for themself.

Brian spots a makeshift bar, a trestle table loaded with beer for the backstage crew. 'Hey, Nik, I'm going to get a drink,' he says, miming chugging a beer.

'Wait, let me come with you.' She wraps up a conversation with a smiling older couple he's seen haunt Nik's bar on the weekends. They see him and their smiles drop, as Brian recognizes them as Mr. and Mrs. Duncan, each holding a glass of Pinot Grigio. It seems like Brian's comments taught them how to order beverages, though he's sure the bartender who served them got a ten-minute preamble of perfunctory small talk. He looks thoughtfully at his shoes as Nik takes his arm.

'Okay, listen. What I said to you before the show. There's something else.'

Brian's body stiffens. The elephant in her bathroom has followed them to the Tate Theater.

'Don't be mad. But I really wanted to talk to you about the new kick you've been on. I know you've been working through things. You seem much more in control. You're drinking less. You look great. And I love that for you, really.'

Brian focuses on the faux bar. 'Uh-huh.' It's so close, yet so far. He instinctively reaches out his fingers, wishing he could stretch his arm through the crowd to the bucket of beers like a drunk Mr. Fantastic, grabbing one or two of them, maybe even the bucket judging by where this is going.

'I'm just wary of your friend Tyler and these ideas he's been putting into your head. Being confident and assertive is one thing. But ... don't you think you may have, perhaps, gone too far the other way?'

'Meaning?'

'Honestly? You can be aggressive. Mean-spirited, even bullying. I sometimes don't recognize you anymore.'

'Is this still about the Abe thing before the show? Because I was going to say that—'

143

'It's not just Abe. It's everything. It's the customers. It's Darby. It's even me. You're flippant. I just don't want you to lose who you are with this evolution you're going through. What happened to that funny, sensitive, know-it-all guy? He's not here anymore. I miss you. I know Darby misses you too. You've just got to be critical of anyone offering you quick solutions. Especially when they're coming from this rich, ambiguously employed guy who has succeeded with every possible advantage afforded to him.'

'Listen, I know Tyler has his faults. But he gets me. He's trying to help. He knows what I'm going through and—'

'And so would we if you would just let us in.' She's exasperated. She grabs his shoulders and looks into his eyes. 'I know it's not easy. But I've told you about my stuff with my family. How I'm working on myself. You've helped me out with balancing school with the restaurant. I let you in. Darby trusts us to introduce us to Abe. They've just bared their soul in front of hundreds of strangers. They let you in. We're here, Brian. We can handle whatever it is. No matter what. And I'm sure we can understand better than this guy.'

Brian feels dangerously exposed. Nik's still holding on to his shoulders, looking into his eyes as if she can read his entire fucking soul. How can he possibly let them in? The moment they knew that he casually transitioned into a fairytale-horror monster once a month they'd be gone. No boxes of dishware or beach towels as a consolation prize. But he's just so tired of keeping it all in. He just wants to tell her, to unburden, whatever the consequences, to be done with it, and maybe there's just the slightest, smallest, unbearably hopeful chance that they would—

'Are you two going to *kiss*? Now that would be one way to upstage me.' Darby's draped in a silk robe, flushed with triumph and vodka. 'Okay, enough about you two … what did we think of *me*?'

Nik drops her hands from Brian's shoulders, and the two of them rapidly adjust the atmosphere. Nik wraps Darby up in a deep hug and Brian starts gushing. 'It was amazing. Incredible. Honestly. I can't even put it into words.'

'Try?'

'To put it into words? Uhm, it *was* amazing … and incredible. Um, mystifying—'

'Babe. I'm kidding. It just means a lot that you came.'

'Are you too busy being famous to come out for cocktails?' Nik asks.

'I'm *never* too busy for cocktails,' Darby replies. 'I just need to go get changed, then there's a whole gang of us heading over to …' Darby drifts off as a stagehand comes over, carrying a bouquet of a dozen purple blooms. He hands them to Darby. 'For me?' Darby says coquettishly to the stagehand. 'You *shouldn't* have.' The stagehand blushes and scampers back into the darkness of the wings, while Darby laughs and turns over the card. 'Aww, they're from Abe. Aren't they gorge?'

All of a sudden, Brian's nose wrinkles and he gags, his stomach cramping. He hasn't drunk enough for it to be an early-onset hangover. It could be the Manhattans on an empty stomach, but Brian's a three-tour veteran of that kind of behavior. It's just something about the flowers, the stench of them overpowering. A migraine starts at the base of his skull and splits his head in two. He closes his eyes and tries to cover up his reaction, but it is too late. Darby's seen it; their face is going pale.

'You've got to be fucking kidding me.' Darby looks at Nik in disbelief, then back at Brian. 'You can't keep your snide little comments about Abe to yourself, not even tonight?'

'Darby … wait, about Abe—' Brian begins, but his stomach cramps again and he gags theatrically.

Nik's looking at him in horror. 'It's not funny, Brian—'

'Leave it, Nik. I am sick of this shit. I get it, you don't like him. That's abundantly clear. You're just jealous. That has got to be it. That I've got someone, that I've got this,' they gesture wildly at the theater, 'and you're chasing a straight guy who just wants to mold you into a Barbie version of himself. Well, good luck with that. I'm fucking done.'

Darby storms off, the flowers hugged protectively to their chest. The air thins, and suddenly Brian can breathe again. 'Nik,' he gasps, 'it's not what you think.'

'What do I think, Brian?' she says, coldly.

'That …' He pauses. What can he say? That something about the flowers combined with his wolf-based super smell threw his brain into a cement mixer? He can't believe he was on the cusp of telling Nik everything. There's no way she could understand. He shakes his head. 'Nothing.'

146

'Yeah, that's what I thought. Well, I'm going to see if Darby's okay. Have a good night, Brian.' She turns on her heel and walks away through the crowd.

Brian shoulders his way to the bar, lifts a beer and stows another in his oversized suit pocket, then leaves the backstage area, past the stage and into the now-empty theater. He hurries up the aisle and out into the forecourt, wondering briefly whether he should just get a taxi home. An Uber would probably bankrupt him. I'm so tired of all this, he thinks to himself. Of hiding, of misunderstanding, of hurting people he cares about, of never having money. He drains the beer and tosses the bottle into a bin, then starts another for the very long walk home. As the night slowly lightens toward morning, and the skyscrapers slowly transition to the familiar warehouses and storefronts of his neighborhood, he takes out his phone. Ignoring the missed messages in The Pack group chat, he fires off a text. 'Hey, about that camping trip: I'm in.'

NINE

Getting four days away from the restaurant was no easy feat, but Brian had to get out, even if it was to the great outdoors. He had called up Nik one Wednesday morning, a cloth held over his mouth.

'Flu.'

'Flu?'

'Yeah, it's bad.'

'You sound … you sound as if you're talking through a cushion.'

'Sinuses. They're pretty bunged up.'

'Uh-huh.'

Since Darby's premiere, no one had talked about the Abe thing. Brian turned up to work on time, behaved himself with the customers and was polite to Nik and Darby. It seemed to pain Nik, the loss of casual intimacy, but even weeks later, Darby was still angry enough seemingly not to care. This was confirmation enough for Brian that their little troika was now beyond repair, that he had made the right decision to keep them at arm's length, and the full-moon stuff under wraps. Each night, he left as soon as his shift was over and went straight home to exercise or

148

work on The Pack's sprawling social media output. Tyler hadn't said a word about his absence from the thread – he had simply texted him dates for the trip and some corny Bitmoji enthusiasm and then emailed him revisions to ThePack.com beta. Brian's job was to proofread the entire thing, from Tyler's opening mission statement to the twelve-step program to better lupine control, to the recipes, the tips for glossier fur and the associated ad copy for The Pack's branded supplements, which were really just prenatal vitamins in werewolf drag.

'Okay,' Nik had said on the phone. 'Take the weekend. See how you feel next week.'

He had just been about to hang up when she had said his name. 'Flu. Feed a cold, starve a fever. Eat well, get plenty of fluids in you. Call me if you need.'

Brian has never camped before. He does not come from a camping family. Vacations were for obligatory visits to extended family to see their piece of suburban paradise; for sleeping in a twin bedroom with your feet hanging off the edge as you focus on the glow-in-the-dark stars on the ceiling, pretending not to hear your cousin masturbate. Brian is woefully unprepared; he has no hiking boots, camping bag, or, notably, a semblance of enthusiasm for camping. But he sleeps naked in the park once a month, so how hard can it be? He packs an old pair of jeans he's cut into shorts, some T-shirts, his toothbrush, and makes a last-minute trip to the bodega down the street to stock up on some protein bars. This will be *fine*.

Tyler pulls up to Brian's apartment building in his BMW SUV. Brian stands up from the curb he's been sitting on, brushes down his jeans and raises a hand in greeting. Sarah is in the passenger seat; she looks up from futzing with the radio to wave excitedly back. He shoots her a smile, throws his duffle bag in the hatchback, and jumps in the backseat with Mark. 'Hey buddy, you ready?' asks Tyler from the rear-view mirror.

'As ready as I'm going to be,' he responds. 'Be gentle. It's my first time.'

Sarah cackles with laughter and they hit the road.

Brian feels every minute of the two-hour drive pass with brilliant clarity. They play a mix of yacht rock and Neil Diamond the whole time, all three of them singing along to 'Sweet Caroline' while Brian tries to go into a Zen trance. Whenever there is a lull in the conversation – topics ranging from the office (drama) to *The Office* (comedy), reciting Steve Carell quotes that have been done to death – rather than bask in the brief, precious moment of silence, one of them has to mention how glad they are to be doing this.

'This trip is *so* awesome, guys,' Mark says, because no one has said anything for thirty seconds.

'Totally,' confirms Sarah, taking the baton and detailing just how awesome.

Brian grits his teeth and prays for death, already regretting his decision to come. He focuses on staring out the window, watching the verdant negative space between the suburban homes get larger and wider until they're fully immersed in the pastoral countryside. Mark continues to manspread in the back. It irritates Brian, so he is determined to stand his ground. Their legs touch for the rest of the ride and neither moves away.

Finally, they pull off the main road and cut down a dirt track flanked by an alpine forest on either side. A river empties into a lake where a clearing meets the shore. 'Here we are,' announces Tyler, pulling the car up next to another SUV. The campsite covers the necessities: there's a picnic table with initials and hearts etched crudely into the gray wood, a cinderblock firepit in the clearing covered in ash and stubby logs, and, thankfully, Brian sees a toilet shack through the clearing that, unfortunately, he can also smell. Four of Tyler's college friends are already in the clearing, busying themselves with unloading equipment from their car. Boy–girl, boy–girl. Brian recognizes them from the birthday party but does not remember their names. 'Hey,' one of the boy ones says to him, throwing up a cheery wave. 'Glad you could make it.' The couples introduce themselves to him again, and as soon as they mention their names, Brian immediately forgets them, like drinking from the River Lethe. They are all wearing the same quarter-zips, hiking boots and convertible pants that zip into shorts, so it's impossible to tell them apart. He'll have to listen in for context clues rather than ask for clarification. He realizes he's been staring at them too long while they wait for him to say something. There's only one way out.

'I'm *so* glad we're doing this.'

'Right?!' says one of the girls, while the guy claps Brian's hand and pulls him into a half-hug.

'B, can you help me over here?' calls Mark, standing by the open hatch of Tyler's SUV. No one moves. Brian looks around, trying to identify which of them is B. Mark is staring at him. 'Oh, me?' When the fuck did he become B? Still, he plays literal happy camper and instead of telling Mark to unhand his initial and call him by his proper name, he goes over to help unload their wares. Apparently camping requires a lot of equipment – an outdoor camping oven, a portable water heater with a shower head, inflatable sofa beds, and a two-room tent with enough square footage that it could require a credit check.

'Okay, into teams,' Tyler shouts. 'Menfolk to me, let's put up the tents. Girls to Sarah, you start prepping dinner.' The men all hoist heavy bundles of tents onto their shoulders and walk off down into the clearing, while the women start talking excitedly while they rummage through coolers. Brian belatedly realizes that he's classed in the menfolk category and so grabs a tent bag too.

These people camp so often they've long since lost the written instructions. Brian goes off of vibes. It's just poles and nylon. His ancestors have been camping since they discovered fire. How hard can it be? Pretty hard, it turns out – the competitive 3D-puzzle group project is beyond his grasp. As the boys grunt and command one another to pull, hold and hammer, Brian looks enviously at the girls drinking and laughing around the picnic table. Is that a jug of G & T? With a fucking *rosemary garnish*? Did they bring rosemary *just* to be used as a garnish? What *is* camping? After the second tent is erected, during which one of the quarter-zips showed a flash of impatience with Brian's inability to identify the difference between a cross rod and a base rod, Brian gradually, so as not to be obvious, backs away from the men. No one seems to notice – in fact, they seem to be getting on faster without him – so he takes another step back toward the three girls. 'Is that gin and tonic?' he asks when he's edged himself near to the picnic table. 'Sure is,' says one of the college friends. 'You want?' Brian takes this invitation as tacit permission that his construction support is no longer needed. 'You've no idea,' he says, taking the offered drink.

Brian attempts to ingratiate himself with the girls by playing the Gay Best Friend role. The GBF card only comes out under duress, but in this case, it's the path of least resistance, a way to quickly earn the girls' favor that obfuscates his social anxiety. They drink and chat about their jobs, their boyfriends and, again, how glad they are to be doing this. He eventually gets their names. When the girls mention them, he repeats them over and over in his head for maximum retention. '*Emily, Emily, Emily.*' '*Jen, Jen, Jen.*' '*Max, Max, Max.*' He's still not sure about Jen's partner though, the quarter-zip boy who snapped at him. It's definitely Jake or John.

As the boys finish Brian's tent, the girls ask him his opinions on different Hollywood A-listers and the pop stars of the moment. Brian, being a judgmental bitch himself, is happy to provide his thoughts on their career trajectories and which ones are talentless hacks.

'All I'm saying is that there's a system – a ginger hierarchy, if you will. First, you send your screenplay to Jessica Chastain; if she says no, it goes to Amy Adams; if Amy passes, Emma Stone; then it's on to, say it with me, Bryce Dallas Howard.'

'But what if Bryce is a no?' asks Jen. The table is quiet in thoughtful contemplation.

'Isla Fisher,' Brian and Emily say in unison. He brings his fingers to his eyes and points back at her. 'See, Emily gets it.'

He pulls from his database of Darby's one-liners, keeping them laughing as he proposes a boycott of Cameron Diaz's wine to lure her out of retirement and back into romantic comedies, slowly working his way into their good graces. Sarah particularly seems to have imprinted on him. She brings him into side-hugs whenever one of his jokes lands. 'Isn't he funny? I told you he's funny!'

At some point around the second jug, the human identified as Max comes over. 'Ladies, are you ever going to start dinner?'

Brian wonders if this now includes him, if his not-so-clandestine switcheroo has resulted in double work. He does not really know how to cook much of anything in his own kitchen, so he's not sure if he'll be much help here either.

Emily giggles. 'But babe, we're having fun getting to know our new friend, B. Trust us, we won't let you starve.'

Still, as Max saunters off to help the boys light the barbecue, the G & T committee jump to attention. The girls pull out pre-packaged burgers, chicken skewers and brioche buns from the cooler and Brian's put to work chopping vegetables. Their pedagogical approach is a lot more palatable than the sweaty guys yelling at him. 'B, you're going to lose a finger. Look, curl your fingertips inward, like this,' Jen says to him, removing his ham-hands out of harm's way as he massacres a red onion. 'See, now you try ... That's it.'

'How do you work in a restaurant and not know how to use a knife?' asks Sarah.

'Gross negligence in the onboarding process.'

'Woof, I know all about that.'

'Really, Miss High-Powered PR Executive? I find that hard to believe.'

'Aww, you're sweet,' Sarah says, minding her knifework of the portobellos. 'But I wasn't always the maven you see before you. I figured since I studied communications and marketing, that's what I would be doing, till I discovered it was a boys' club of mad "geniuses" that take all the credit and dish out blame. After another year of being passed over for opportunities, seeing guys who were younger than me, guys that I'd recruited and trained taking those positions, I couldn't take it anymore. Got a career counselor and, long story short, crisis comms felt like a great fit. CEOs don't care what you've got between your legs as long as you solve their problems.' Sarah punctuates this with a forceful chop of a carrot.

'Wait, so, like … what crises have you managed?'

Sarah looks to confirm Emily and Jen are down the hill at the grill helping Max with the burgers and she gestures for him to lean in over the table. 'Have you heard about the chemical spill out on the west coast? The one that flooded the marina, killed all those turtles?'

'No?'

'Exactly.'

'Jesus Christ.'

Sarah leans back and resumes her chopping. 'What can I say? I'm good.'

Max finishes up the burgers, skewers and grilled vegetables as they crowd around the picnic to assemble their dinner on paper plates. Looking down at his multicolored plate, Brian thinks this is likely the most well-rounded meal he's had since moving to the city. He spends most of the night talking with Emily and Max at his end of the table, feeling a particular kinship with Emily as a co-conspirator for the Bring Cameron Diaz Back campaign. Turns out, Max has actually tried Cameron's wine, and says it's 'fine', which offers the kind of endorsement they hope spurs a national movement. On occasion, he'll see Tyler looking at him from the corner of his eye, overseeing his conversations, lifting a toast to him for how he's integrated himself. As the sun sets, Brian heads down to the stream to rinse his hands. The only thing he can hear for miles is the chirp of crickets, deer bending and snapping branches, and the trickling water. When the sun goes down, he looks up at the stars, which are always blocked out by a cloud of exhaust and light in the city, even for werewolf vision. Brian can't help but feel how easy it is with these guys. How they're completely devoid of the low-grade anxiety that underpins his every waking moment. The city seems so far away. They sit around the campfire in folding chairs until late in the night, drinking beer. Jack/James brought a guitar, which is unfortunate, but Brian passes around a bottle of bourbon he borrowed from the stock room to make his unplugged cover of Oasis's 'Don't Look Back in Anger' somewhat tolerable. After one too many s'mores, Brian bids adieu and struggles to unzip his tent with his sticky marshmallow fingers. Once inside, he crawls into his borrowed sleeping bag and thinks to himself, if this is camping, it's not that bad, as the sound of crickets, the smell of the campfire and the buzz from the booze wrap him in a sensory blanket that lulls him to sleep.

On day two, Brian realizes he may have spoken too soon.

'Brian?'

He peels open his eyes. The interior of the tent is lit up by soft daylight. 'Mmm?' he says, his mouth dry.

'You ready?' It's Tyler's voice.

'Ready for what?'

There's a noise of someone conferring in a low voice.

'Ready for the hike, B!' That's Sarah. Said with way too much energy.

He glances at his phone, wondering what kind of monsters go hiking at 6 a.m., and then he unzips his tent.

The whole gang's there, fresh-faced, practically dewy, and dressed like an ad for Berghaus.

'I'm going to need a minute,' he grumbles, wiping the sleep from his eyes and into his hair.

After scarfing down the remaining campfire beans and toast that someone must have got up at an ungodly hour to make, Brian follows as they file out of the campsite, Tyler at the front with a wooden staff like Gandalf, Brian bringing up the rear. He tries to be optimistic. It'll help him sweat out the hangover that, apparently, he is the only one coping with. And hiking is just walking after all. He walks all the time.

About an hour later, having gone through about a mile of pine trees before fixing onto a trail whose gradient started to become near vertical, Brian realizes with dull horror that hiking isn't walking. He clocked their dorky, polished hiking boots as they set out, and even thought smugly to himself that people with money were idiots, but now he was beginning to think that his Chuck Taylors weren't activity appropriate.

'How are you doing there, B?' John/Jake asks with a smirk as they summit what feels like a small peak, but which Mark jauntily refers to as only a 'hill'.

'Oh, yeah, fine,' Brian replies. 'Great, actually.'

Brian is not great. He can feel every root and rock under the soles of his feet. Sarah slows her pace to check in on him from time to time, but Brian's attention is focused on breathing, hydrating and keeping the frustration and pain from his face. After they traverse a small mountain stream, and the icy water soaks right through to his socks, every step he takes makes a soft squirting sound.

'Too many beans, Brian? Your shoes make it sound like you're farting!' Jen chortles, waiting for him while he catches up.

'Ha ha ha,' Brian says with a touch of mania, and opens his mouth into a violent silent scream as soon as she turns away again.

About two hours later and what feels to Brian like 1,000 meters of expert-level rock climbing, Tyler throws his bag and staff to the ground and takes a deep inhale. 'We're here,' he announces, turning to gesture at a view from a point at which the cliff face drops away. Everyone slings their bag in a pile and joins Tyler, and they solemnly look out together over a mountain vista of the entire forest.

Brian limps after them. 'This it?'

'Yeah. Beautiful, isn't it, buddy?' says Tyler, clapping a hand on Brian's shoulder.

Brian takes in the view like a desktop background. 'Uh-huh.'

He leaves them admiring what Max describes as 'transcendence' and sits heavily on the ground by the bags. He cradles his feet and winces as he slips off his Chuck Taylors, then he wrings out his socks. *You're a werewolf, God dammit*, he thinks angrily to himself, *you should enjoy this or at least be better at it*. Mountain ranges are literally his spiritual home. Maybe if he crawls on all fours, he'll be more adept – at the very least it would shift some of the burden away from his maimed feet. But all he wants to do is delay the inevitable journey back down. His blisters sting, it's way too hot, and when he's not fighting for his life, he's bored. The forest, the trees, it's just ... *the same taste over and over again*, he hears Darby suggest in his mind. He thinks maybe he's just a city wolf. Like an American Werewolf in London.

They finally make it back to the campsite three hours later. Brian wants to down a shot and then spend the afternoon asleep in his tent, but as soon as they're back in the clearing Sarah claps her hands together and exclaims, 'Lunch!' and then everyone cheerfully scatters like demonic von Trapp children to get to work. Brian is exhausted and camping is starting to feel like housework with the difficulty turned way up. 'C'mon, boys,' Max shouts, rallying the penis-owners to the barbecue. Brian is again left to figure out whether he goes with the girls or the boys when Tyler chimes in.

'You coming, Brian?'

'Oh, no,' Sarah answers proprietorially. 'Brian's with us.'

Brian winces. He's got zero interest in heating foodstuffs over an open flame after nearly succumbing to heat exhaustion, but although he's grateful for the opportunity to peel and chop from a seated position, he wonders what Tyler will think if he again chooses housewifery over manual labor. And it annoys him that Sarah so freely sorted him into her own cosmic gender football team by claiming him as one of the girls. There are other things that are beginning to annoy Brian about Sarah, too. Her unearned closeness. He feels like he brought it on himself with his warm-up act yesterday, but he doesn't like how aggressively she's friending him like a human Facebook poke. He decides that he'll leave the girls to the lunch prep and the boys to their fire-bonding and instead he volunteers to stack firewood for the evening campfire. He disappears into the undergrowth, searching the ground for kindling and drier logs. He walks further into the forest, the laughing and conversations in the clearing left behind, until finally it's near silent, only the birds in the branches above him for company. He starts a small stack of wood at the base of a birch tree whose bark peels and curls like antique wallpaper. He likes the task – it's another 3D puzzle project, but less competitive, and more Jenga than Ikea, which Brian finds strangely relaxing. It allows him to seek revenge on nature by creating order out of her chaos. Then he hears the branches snap and the sweet scent of peonies and he comes gasping to the surface of his flow state.

'Brian?'

'Sarah? What are you—'

'Oh, I'm just getting away from the bustle, you know. Thought I'd come and see if you needed help. I see you – wanting a little alone time, huh? That's another thing you and I have in common.'

Brian doesn't answer. Instead he tries to puzzle out a) how two people together constitutes 'alone time' and b) what else Sarah imagines they might have in common. She comes over and links her arm through his, guiding him to a large fallen trunk and sitting down.

'Okay, so don't tell, but I actually came out here for some screen time,' she says, pulling out her iPhone from the pocket of her vest. Her background is a picture of her and Tyler at what appears to be a gala. 'You can't tell Tyler. We do this whole "digital detox" thing while we're out here. He's so much better at it than I am. I guess that's how it is when you work for yourself – you get to make your own hours. But an hour is a year in the work I do.'

'Your secret is safe with me,' Brian says, which is true – though not because he's great at keeping secrets, but because he doesn't care.

They sit in silence while Sarah triages her inbox, then she sighs performatively. 'Look at us,' she says, showing him her iPhone background. 'I love this picture. This was at Jen and Jason's wedding, must've been five years ago.'

Jason, Jason, Jason, he reminds himself. 'Oh really? Looks fancy. Thought they'd have more of a "reclaimed barn" aesthetic. But again, I only know them from this ...'

'Yeah, everyone's getting married. You're likely a year or two out from it happening with all your friends too. I feel like every summer I'm flying from one to another. We've got nine this year. You want to see what I've picked out?'

Brian attempts to decline, but she's already in her camera roll, flipping through all the dresses she's bought for upcoming weddings. Her manicure is intact. He wonders if she keeps a schedule for it. Staying at the ready if Tyler ever pops the question so she can share an immediate photo of the ring on Instagram. Maybe she got one expectantly before this trip? And perhaps the trip before that?

162

Paying half-attention to the Ganni fashion show, he continues to puzzle out what it's like to be a Sarah. First, how could she be invited to this many weddings? Brian can count his friends on one hand. And surely this is cost-prohibitive. She's also got a big-deal job where her absence can topple corporate empires. Who has this many vacation days? But also, he wonders what he said that brought about this impromptu haute-couture conversation. Why was it him and why now? It's plain from looking at Brian that he has no fashion sense. His clothes are a mishmash of thrift-shop finds and the errant flannel left by one of his sexual conquests. All of which he has worn into the ground and had decorated by flyaway condiments. Yet still, she persists.

'These look nice,' he tells her, hoping that it's the quickest way to make the fashion show stop. He sees from her face that it was not the response she was looking for. 'I mean, iconic,' he says, cringing as he corrects himself.

'Aww, thanks!' she giggles, grabbing his arm and putting her head on his shoulder as he looks longingly at his diminutive pile of wood.

After lunch, and after everyone has cooed appreciatively as John (*wait, that's not right* …) and Mark play a competitive game of Wiffle ball in the clearing, Tyler claps his hands together and announces – to Brian's dismay – that they should get ready for the evening hike.

'More of a short walk this time, B,' Mark says, tossing him a wink. Being asked to put his damp trainers back on and spend another couple of hours trudging along a trail feels like an exquisite torture designed to break him, but he cannot show weakness. Especially in front of Wiffle Ball King Mark. He has to toughen up. Camping sucks and it's boring, but again, he reminds himself, he's a *literal werewolf*. And so he forces his swollen feet into his shoes and they file out the campsite for the second time in a day, hiking along ridge paths and shale slopes, only to arrive at a slightly different elevated view of the same forest.

'Beautiful,' Emily coos, while taking multiple pictures on her iPhone. 'B, will you take one of me and Max together?'

Brian limps over to them, holds out his hand for the phone and then takes three shots in quick succession, barely looking at the screen. ''Kay, you look great,' he says in a monotone, tossing the phone to Max before turning away to fall face first into the pile of bags.

On day three, Brian realizes he is a gay frog in Sarah's pot of slowly boiling fag hag water. Whenever he has a moment to himself, he has to contend with her constant questions. She asks about Tyler's projects, of which Brian admittedly knows nothing. She wants to know what they're working on, how it's different than his other investments and why he spends so much time traveling. But perhaps most of all, and always approached from the obliquest of angles, she wants to be reassured about her relationship with Tyler.

'You guys have never discussed whether he'd go back to his dad's firm?' she asks him over breakfast.

'Nope,' Brian responds, spooning porridge into his mouth.

'I know his dad casts a big shadow – the "rat race" and all that. But it's good money, flexible hours. I'm sure he could create his own job description. I just know it's tough out there trying to make it on your own, especially in this economy. Maybe with more stability in the present he could have the headspace to think long term, don't you think?'

Brian just wants her to go away and be left alone to nurse his physical and psychic wounds in silence, to not be hoodwinked into letting slip that the love of her life turns into a furry homicidal monster once a month. There are other people here. If she wants to pump people for information about her boyfriend, Mark knows him better and their friendship goes back for years. But judging from Tyler, Max and the other one's conversations with their partners, they don't seem all that interested in their interior lives. Maybe Brian is the first person in Tyler's orbit that's shown genuine interest in her drive and ambition. He's her way in, a Rosetta Stone to decode her partner, a tool to translate Tyler's seemingly colossal solipsism into a language that shows her that he really and truly cares for her. That everything he does, everything he's building, is for their eventual life together. But Brian can't crack the code either. Part of him feels sorry for her, for not being able to give her the answers she seeks; the other part wants to shake her awake, to break her free from the Matrix. He'd cover the red pill in peanut butter, put it in her mouth, clasp one hand over her lips and rub her throat with the other to ensure she swallowed it. He has to get her to realize what *she* is bringing to the table in this relationship, that at any time she can cut her losses and run. It wouldn't be easy to make this decision, though, particularly given the upfront investment she's made in their relationship – and if it's anything like Brian's internship, Tyler's undoubtedly given her just enough vague assurances that she'll eventually reach her goal. Despite his best efforts though, throughout the day – and another pointless death march to another alleged beauty spot – Brian increasingly retreats into monosyllabic responses to Sarah's questions.

By dinner time, Sarah starts to notice Brian's withdrawal, so she redoubles her attempts at friendship. While the group sits around the long picnic table eating chili, discarded hiking boots in a row by the tents, cold beers fished out of the stream where Max put them before they set out on the morning trail, Sarah turns the conversation to *Sex and the City*.

'So, which one are you?'

Jen ponders for a moment before smirking and grabbing James/Jake. 'I'm a Samantha,' she says, littering her man's neck with kisses.

'You know, in retrospect, Charlotte actually had the most adventurous sex life. But no one ever talks about it because she's portrayed as this buttoned-up WASP,' says Emily, ever the astute observer.

Sarah turns to Brian. 'And what about you, Brian?'

'Haven't seen it.' He will *never* admit to these people that he's Carrie sun, Samantha rising.

'You're kidding!' says Sarah.

'He's lying,' Emily says flatly, which no one hears.

'Okay, well, are you typically the guy or the girl in relationships?' Sarah asks, tossing her hair, evincing a no-big-deal-I-talk-about-this-with-my-gay-friends-all-the-time intimacy.

Brian looks around the table to see if anyone else is hearing what he is hearing. Apparently not, as they all stare at him expectantly. 'Well, we're both "the guy" in a relationship. That's the point.'

Sarah laughs. 'No, you know what I mean …'

'No, I don't think I do.'

'Come on, Brian! In every relationship there's a flower and there's a gardener,' she grins, intoning it as if she's reciting a children's fairytale. 'The flower needs to be adored, cared for, tended to. While the gardener provides …' She cocks an eyebrow and looks at Tyler. '… *support and attention*.' Brian squints at her and then looks around the table, praying that he will catch a single eyeroll. But he is alone. He wants to ask Sarah why she thinks these roles are gendered. He wants to ask her why she thinks it's okay to ask him this. He wants to ask her who the fuck she thinks she is. But instead he redirects, aiming for diplomacy. 'Okay, well, which one are you?'

She laughs. 'I'm the flower, of course. And I need a *lot* of watering.'

Jen giggles and Mark offers Tyler a high five across the table.

'So,' she says, turning back to Brian, still grinning. 'Which one are you?'

Brian wouldn't describe himself in landscaping metaphor to someone he deeply loves, let alone someone he half knows. He takes a pull of his beer and tries to steer the conversation elsewhere. 'Emily, you said you work in the entertainment industry – have you seen—'

'Briiiiiannn, don't be boring,' Sarah implores. She's pink-cheeked, and Brian realizes she's already drunk.

'Sarah, leave the man alone,' Tyler chides.

'What? He's like my BFF already. I'm just *interested*. I might know someone I could set him up with. Okay, let me reframe it. Brian, are you a top or a bottom?'

Brian can feel his heart race. He lifts a shaky hand to pinch the bridge of his nose to calm his temper. But after days of hiking, sweating and itching, he has had enough. Tyler's breathing exercises go out the window. He can feel the words work their way up his throat before he can stop them. 'Okay, Sarah, which are you?'

She frowns. 'I don't get … what do you mean?'

'Okay, let *me* reframe it,' he says briskly. 'You prefer it in your pussy or your ass?'

There's an audible gasp from around the table. Jim/Joe's hand has literally frozen in midair with his beer en route to his mouth. No one says anything.

'Well, Tyler?' Mark asks, laughing, blissfully unaware of the tension in the group.

'Shut up, Mark,' Tyler mutters, shifting in his seat.

Sarah looks scandalized. 'I can't believe you just asked me that!' She looks around everyone for confirmation that Brian's just stepped out of line. How the picnic tables have turned. She's in a crisis of her own communications, and there's no way she's managing herself out of this one.

Brian pounces. 'Exactly. But yet you ask me shit like am I a top or a bottom?'

'What? No, I didn't mean it like … it's just different.'

'How?' he asks. 'I just don't understand why you feel entitled to this information. As far as I know, we aren't fucking.' Sarah's cheeks go from pink to red.

'Brian—' Max says with a conciliatory touch to his shoulder, but Brian shakes him off.

'No. Chopping vegetables and looking at your fucking dresses is not the fast-track to friendship you think it is. You don't get to ask this, and surely not with an audience. Am I a fucking caricature to you?'

Tears start welling up in Sarah's eyes. 'I'm sorry, I just … I was just playing around. I thought you'd be cool about it.'

Around the table, everyone sips their beers in silence, doing their best not to make eye contact. He notices Emily has taken Sarah's hand under the table. He realizes too late that his self-righteousness is not going to earn him any points with this crowd, especially when faced with her I'm-listening-and-I'm-learning tears. He wipes a hand over his face and takes a steadying breath. 'No, it's fine. I'm sorry. Really. I'm just tired. It's been a long day. I'm … I think I'm going to turn in. Whoo, I'm beat. Max, the chili's great by the way. Your mom's secret recipe, with the adobo.' He makes a half-hearted chef's kiss, then stands up from the table, drains his beer and heads back to his tent. No one tries to stop him. As he zips up the entrance behind him and crawls into his borrowed sleeping bag, he wonders what Tyler thought of all this. He noticed that he didn't seem to defend Sarah, but he didn't defend Brian either. Some 'gardener' he is. From beyond the nylon partition, Brian hears the conversation rustle back to life and he takes great care not to listen.

The next morning, Brian wakes up to the sound of his tent unzipping. 'Wuhng ... ung?' he slurs from his pillow.

Tyler's face appears at the opening. 'Come on. Time to get up,' he whispers. The campsite behind him is silent and the light's still gray. It must be super early.

Brian pulls on his clothes and carefully places his shoes back on over three pairs of sun-dried socks. Exiting the tent, he sees Mark is there too. 'Hey, buddy. I planned a special hike today. Just the three of us. Grab some water. Let's go.'

Brian stifles a yawn as they leave the camp and follow a path that cuts up through the tree line before turning into a particularly unforgiving trail. It feels as if they are breaking new ground. They walk in near silence for hours; the only sound the animal calls in the forest. The sun finally comes up over the horizon and burns away the morning dew. Brian trails behind Tyler and Mark, struggling to breathe. He wonders if this is a punishment. Retribution for humiliating Sarah last night. Maybe they're bringing him up here to push him off a cliff. It would probably be fun for a second, Brian thinks while huffing and puffing.

His Chuck Taylors are held together now only by hope. His blisters have blisters. At least if they kill him, it will save him the journey back down.

When they reach the top of the overlook, the sun is high in the sky. Brian looks out to see yet another view that's entirely indistinguishable from the other hikes and wonders whether this was really necessary. 'Here's the spot,' says Tyler as they drop their backpacks and Brian collapses onto the ground. Tyler takes off his shirt and sprays himself down with his water bottle. He's clearly up to something. Brian catches Mark's eye to see if he knows what they're there for, but Mark shakes his head quickly and pulls a couple of gulps from his camel bag.

'This is it, boys! This is us at our most authentic. Pushing ourselves to the limit. Communing with nature. Dominating the elements. Look out there, boys – everything here, everything the light touches, is ours.'

Brian pulls himself up to sitting. '*A king's time as ruler rises and falls like the sun,*' he intones.

Mark squints at him. 'Huh?'

'Nothing,' Brian mutters. 'Anyway, Tyler, what were you saying?'

Tyler laughs. 'What I was *saying*, Brian, is that we should feel alive!' He lets out a howl that echoes through the valley. 'C'mon. Stand up, the pair of you. I want to remind you of the power we have here.' He begins to limber up his shoulders as Brian and Mark get uncertainly to their feet. 'Okay, tops off!' Tyler orders. Mark doesn't need a second invitation, he's already stripped out of his hiking shirt, his sleek muscles bunching and knotting under the skin, but Brian hesitates.

'Errr, do we need to be topless?'

Tyler rolls his eyes. 'Brian, you're a werewolf! You. Never. Have. To. Be. Ashamed.' Tyler was clearly never the kid at the pool party hiding his body under a T-shirt on the pretense of sunburn, but Brian takes his sweaty New Order T-shirt off regardless. Tyler lifts his arms and places them on Mark and Brian's shoulders, standing on either side of them as they admire the view. Until, suddenly, Tyler's grip tenses, Brian feels his feet lift from under him, and then he's smashed into the ground with such force it knocks the wind out of him. He looks to his right and sees Mark in a similar heap.

'You didn't think just because we're on vacation we're going to skip training, did you?' Tyler says, looking down at the two of them. 'I told you, you've got to be ready for anything. C'mon, let's practice, spar a little bit. Have some fun.'

Though Brian's not thrilled with the idea, at least it's something to do to break up the monotony of hiking and peering meaningfully at nature. Tyler begins with a demonstration of some of the more powerful combat techniques they haven't been able to do within the confines of his townhouse. But no one is going to mind a little collateral damage up here in the mountains. They start with a contest to see who can judo throw one another the furthest. After Tyler demonstrates on Mark, sending him crashing through a substantial oak tree in the process, it's Brian's turn to experience it before he can perform it. He grits his teeth as he reluctantly offers himself to Tyler. 'Okay, but be careful. I had childhood asthma and I'm n—' and he's in the air, sailing across the clearing, past where the oak tree once stood that caught Mark's impact, and then he's hurtling down to make a sizeable crater in the underbrush. 'Fuck,' he breathes, staring at the sky. That was … fun?

It soon becomes a contest to see how far they can send one another, laughing together as they send one another crashing into the landscape like fleshy boulders from a catapult, but as the sun creeps up overhead, Tyler calls time on the game. 'Okay, guys, that's enough. We're here to learn. Now, see if you can work those moves into a fight. Let's roll.'

Brian and Mark square up to one another in the center of the clearing. As they prepare themselves for a high-noon duel, Brian is dimly aware that they're competing for Tyler's approval, which means Mark is going to come for him with everything he's got. When Tyler starts the fight with a loud hand clap, Mark launches himself at Brian, but Brian stays calm – he moves to one side and uses Mark's momentum and body weight to judo throw him into the thicket of trees. 'LET'S GO!' cheers Tyler, the highest praise one can achieve. Brian takes a moment to bask in this rare adulation, and that's all it takes; Mark sprints back across the clearing and slams him onto his back full force into the gravel, sending it up in a cloud of dust. Brian can't see, but he feels the familiar snaking of Mark's legs around his arm and up his sweaty torso. *Not again*. Brian growls and focuses all the energy he has into every sinew in his trapped arm, lifting Mark overhead and then pounding his face into the dirt with a terrifying crack. Brian rolls onto all fours, picks up Mark like a sack of flour and throws him ten feet onto his back, then bounds after him and pounces onto his shoulders. He's about to strike as the dust finally settles, he sees Mark's nose sitting askew on his bloodied face, and he catches himself before giving the Ken doll any more opposable parts. He rolls off and they lie next to one another, panting hard.

'Oh, here,' Brian says, noticing one of Mark's teeth by his hand. 'You'll be needing this. Might wanna rinse it off first.'

Mark snaps his nose back into place. 'Thanks,' he says, pocketing his missing incisor.

Tyler jogs over and lets out a whoop. 'Guys! That was just great. Just so good to let off some steam,' he laughs, lying down on the ground next to them, all three staring up at the sky. 'I feel like all the work we've been doing; we've got something great here. The three of us. Strong. Solid.' He props himself up on his arms. 'That's why I brought you up here this morning, actually – to remind you of that. Now, I think it's time we have a real talk about next steps for our expansion strategy. As you know, I've been tracking. Looking for these patterns. Trying to find wolves to bring into our pack. But it has been difficult, I must admit. Finding new wolves takes time. *Most* of them are really good at covering their tracks, and not all of them have been as receptive as you two. And others, typically the loners, don't last too long on their own.' He glances meaningfully at Brian. It's as if Tyler sees himself as Brian's savior from an inevitable and untimely demise, which might not be entirely untrue – Brian can't remember the last time he encountered salad on his own dinner plate before he met Tyler – but it'd be nice if he stopped finding every opportunity to remind Brian of his werewolf failings.

'We need to get more aggressive with our tactics if we're going to grow. We can't just stay in this start-up phase for months on end. Then it struck me. Our whole philosophy is that we're a *pack*. It's not just me here. Your success is also linked to the work we're doing. For our expansion phase, I want each of you to recruit two new people.' Brian sits up too, ready to interject, but Tyler holds up a finger to silence him. 'I know what you're going to say. That's why these new recruits would be your responsibility. I've given you all of my mentorship and you have both grown into such strong, capable men. You have everything you need. This would then give me the opportunity to take an advisory and oversight role.'

There's silence while Mark and Brian take in what Tyler's proposing. How can they find recruits if Tyler can barely find them? He has all the resources of wealth, business-class flights, and time at his disposal – Brian has about $200 in savings, full-time wage labor and a bike.

'Tyler,' he begins. 'It's just … it's unworkable. I'm happy to keep doing some of the back-end admin stuff, the website thing and social media, but I wouldn't even know where to start in recruitment. I don't even know what kind of werewolves we're looking for.'

Tyler bats away his concerns. 'It's easy. I can share some of the candidate criteria when we're back in the city. In the long term, we want *every* werewolf. But in the short term? We're looking for high-value recruits who'll bring something new to The Pack™. Skills, expertise, networks. The kinds of candidates that would really get it. You know? The fact that being part of a pack isn't just about financial investment, but *emotional* investment.'

Brian trades glances with Mark. 'Emotional investment?'

'Yeah, responsibility to one another. You can't just opt in and out of a pack. You've actually got to be there. You've got to show up. It's not enough to, like, send a check once a month or pay for tuition or whatever, you've got to come to the fucking Little League ballgames every week, you know?' Tyler has gone quite red.

'Wait. There are werewolves in Little League?'

'Brian! You're such a— It's a fucking metaphor.'

Mark chimes in. 'Listen, man, if this is about your dad or whatever, I don't think that—'

'It has nothing to do with that!' Tyler snaps. 'This is purely a business decision. Two new recruits by the next full moon. That's my final word on the matter. And if you can't find them, you'll make them.' He stands up and stomps over to his T-shirt, pulling it on over his head and then hoisting up his bag.

'Make them?' asks Brian, still sitting.

'Well, yes. Bite them, maim them, just don't kill them. Surely you can control yourself by now. Once they're fully established in the pack, then each of them can recruit new werewolves of a similar pedigree. And then *they* find two people. It's the easiest way to build a network and sustain the pack.'

Brian finally gets his wits about him and pulls himself to his feet. 'Tyler, listen, this sounds crazy. Being a werewolf has upended everything I wanted to do in my life. I wouldn't wish this on anyone. I can't in good conscience pass this on to anyone else.'

'We're offering power that any man would kill for,' counters Tyler. 'I'm sure there will be an adjustment period. But the pack needs to grow.'

'Grow into what, exactly?' asks Brian. 'I thought we were doing this more as a community help thing. To try and manage this blood curse you so glibly think is a gift. Why don't we just take a step back and think this through. This whole idea is sounding awfully like a pyramid scheme.'

Tyler laughs at him. 'Pyramid scheme? Please. It's just nature. All packs need an alpha and that's me. Why? Do either of you think you have the business acumen or the temperament to lead?'

'I can't … This is fucking *ridiculous*. I get that an organization needs to make money; the website, the fees – hell, even Oxfam has merchandise – but you're replicating the same hierarchies from the modern world in the mystical, the ones that take any good or precious idea and then strip it of anything worthwhile.' Brian wrestles his own T-shirt on and grabs his bag. He's furious; he feels like he's been betrayed – or just lied to all along. 'But I guess it makes sense, huh? Your life, your family, your wealth was all created in a world that was built for your success and benefit. So what do you want to do? The same shit. I guess when all you have is a hammer, everything is a nail.'

'Shut up.'

'Also, what the hell are we even recruiting them into? Hard to start a cult with a beta website full of typos, an unfinished manifesto on Google Docs, a full-time waiter and …' He gestures toward Mark, who's still sitting down, watching the argument as if it's a tennis match. '… and terminally horny Malibu Ken over here.'

Tyler drops his bag with a snarl, covers the distance between them in a single leap and then unhinges his jaw to roar fully into Brian's face. He feels it reverberate through his whole body, snout to tail and, just for a moment, he sees Tyler's irises flash red. Brian braces himself to be attacked by a 250 lb wereboy, but Tyler closes his eyes and starts Ujjayi breathing. He then opens his eyes again, which are back to their deep blue color, and slaps his customary manic grin on his face. 'This is my final word on the issue,' he says quietly, wiping away some of his spittle from Brian's cheek. 'I'm not discussing it further. Two new recruits by the next full moon. If you can't find them, make them.'

'Jason, can you ask Brian to pass me the ketchup please?' Sarah says frostily, even though Brian is sitting practically next to her.

'Uh, Brian, can you pass Sarah the ketchup?' says Jake/Jeff to Brian.

They're eating hotdogs at the picnic bench, all of the collegiate bonhomie evaporating in Brian's presence. When Tyler, Brian and Mark walked back to camp in silence that afternoon, Brian was left alone to sit outside his tent. Sarah seemed to have decided that Brian's hastily thrown apology last night was evidence that he was in the wrong, and so further indicated that she should feel like a victim, and her friends have all come down heavily on her team. *Et tu, Emily?* he thinks as she quickly breaks eye contact with him at the campfire. The only other person that Brian thought of as something approaching a friend just bellowed in his face and encouraged maiming innocent people. Camping really did suck. Still, at least he wasn't asked to join in Wiffle ball or food prep. He's been thankful for the space as he's desperately cycling through his options for how to extricate himself from this situation. What can he do? Does he move again? Surely not back to his parents. He briefly imagines living in a research outpost in Antarctica with a few bearded geologists, stripping down at night to sandwich himself between them in a big fleece sleeping bag, transitioning once a month to slide down snowbanks and bound across ice sheets, stomach bloated with rich, blubbery penguin meat. What a dream ...

But that dream will have to wait. He now sees that Nik was right: he got in too deep. He should have recognized the warning signs. But it's too late for that now. He finishes his hotdog and then excuses himself to go and spend the evening downing the bottle of bourbon he prudently stole from supplies and hid in the foot of his sleeping bag.

'Knock knock,' comes a soft voice outside his tent, several hours later. Brian groggily looks at his phone. It's well after midnight and his bottle's very close to being empty. For most of the night, the others sat around a giant bonfire, burning the last of the logs, finishing up any and all alcohol they could and performatively having fun, as if to make clear to Brian that there was *no* way he could be having as much fun as they were, alone there in his borrowed tent. It had fallen quiet a while ago though, people heading to bed before the long drive home tomorrow, and Brian assumed he was the only one still awake.

'That you, Tyler?'

The zip opens and Mark tumbles head first into the tent. He's drunk.

'Oh. It's you. Thanks for having my back up there, by the way. Really impressive how you helped me stand up to Tyler.'

'You called me Malibu Ken!'

'Yeah, sorry about that.'

Mark shrugs. 'I've been called worse. And I've heard much worse from Tyler. I've known him for a long time. It's best to just do what he asks and not get in his way.'

180

'I think this might be a bridge too far, don't you think? He's diving headlong into Marvel villain territory. What's going on here? What's the real issue? Something about his dad?'

'Oh, no, no, no. I'm not going there.'

'C'mon, it's just us. If it's nothing, then why'd you say it?'

Mark peers around the tent as if searching for bugging equipment and then leans into Brian. He smells like beer, body odor and dirt, which Brian unfortunately finds … sexy. '*No.*'

'Come on. Give me a hint. Just one word.'

Mark's drunk face screws up in deep thought. 'One word. One word. Okay, what about: *trust*. No, wait. Is *trust fund* one word or two?'

Brian smiles; the financing vehicle for The Pack's business-class travel and Tyler's caviar lifestyle is finally made public. He holds out the rest of the bottle of bourbon to Mark as a reward, hoping that, even though he's *so, so dumb*, he'll still respond to classical conditioning.

'Thought so. Daddy Warbucks trying to lure Tyler back into the nest? Tightening the financial thumbscrews?'

'I told you, you get one word.' Mark locks his lips with an invisible key and swigs from the bottle.

'Well, Mark. It's been great wrestling with you, but if this thing is dead on arrival, which I suspect it is, I'm out. I just can't do it. I will not do it. You shouldn't do it either. You've got to talk some sense into him.'

Mark just nods and sips the bourbon. 'I'm not sure I get the problem,' he slurs.

'Wait, you don't see the hyper-toxic-masculine problem in murderous-pyramid-scheme that makes up The Pack Tee Em?'

'I just don't see how it's any different from what I was taught growing up,' says Mark, leaning even closer to Brian. 'I was always told to be strong, aggressive and stop at nothing to get what I want.' There's a lot of slightly unfocused heavy eye contact coming from Mark.

'And what … do you want?' Brian hates himself for asking it.

Mark grabs Brian's crotch. He is hard, drunk and doesn't care anymore. It's only a matter of time before this whole pack implodes anyway. He leans in and kisses Mark, grabbing the back of his head, bunching Mark's hair in his fist. 'This is a terrible idea,' he says. Mark grins, his lips pink from being kissed so hard. 'Fuck it.' They lunge at each other, tearing open each other's jeans, ripping the T-shirts from each other's bodies, biting and clawing like the animals they are. In the dark of the tent and the haze of cheap alcohol, Mark looks even more like Tyler than usual. Through spit, will power and a prayer, Brian fucks him. He thrusts into him and covers Mark's mouth tightly with his hand to keep the other campers from hearing. The way he arches his back and pushes back onto him, Brian can tell it ain't Mark's first rodeo. After he comes, he rolls off Mark and laughs to himself. He doesn't know how or why yet, but he knows he's right. That *was* a terrible idea.

TEN

He enters his apartment and drops his bags, the thud sending up dust into the stale air. After nearly a week away being tested by Mother Nature, Brian is delighted to see a microwave, a mattress and a shower.

When he woke up in his tent that morning, Mark was gone. The atmosphere was thick as the campers packed up and piled into their cars. Max, Emily, Jen and Jaden/Jaxx hugged the others, lingering over Sarah as if she had been recently bereaved, before giving a canon of stiff waves to Brian. The ride back was silent. No American soft rock. Mark and Brian's legs didn't touch. After they pulled up to Brian's apartment and he climbed out, he briefly wondered whether he had turned into a ghost – or Abe – as not a single one of them said a word to him. He shut the door and the car smoothly pulled away and disappeared into the afternoon traffic.

He heads to the bathroom, turns on the shower as hot as it will go and begins to see if he can separate his camping clothes from his skin. As he pulls up his top, he stops. He can see the scratches across his chest from Mark last night. Absurdly, now that he's managed to alienate both Nik and Darby *and* his werewolf mentor, Mark is the closest thing Brian has to an intimate. He recoils at the thought and hangs his head over the pedestal sink. How did he get so alone? He looks back up to the mirror, blotted out with affirmations and mantras, written in blue and black pens, markers and crayons. He reaches up and pulls one off. 'I'm a warrior, not a worrier.' This one is patently false, he thinks, crumpling it up and tossing it in the bin. 'I am not a drop in the ocean. I am the ocean in a drop.' Despite daily repetition, its meaning still isn't any clearer. He peels the tattered pieces of paper off one by one until he can finally see himself. Then he looks at the last one in the corner, jotted on a corner scrap of a flashcard. 'It's not what we have in our life, but who we have in our life that matters – J. M. Laurence'. He doesn't remember writing it – there are too many to keep track of – and he surely has no idea who J. M. Laurence is, but he could recognize that cardstock anywhere. In that instant, he turns off the water and grabs his T-shirt.

'You look like shit. That must have been some flu,' Nik says, when she finally opens her apartment door. He hesitates, unsure whether after everything that's happened that he's welcome to show up on her doorstep unannounced. She rolls her eyes. 'Come in, take a seat.'

He follows her into the living room, and she shuffles across the floor in her sandals and carefully pushes the textbooks and flashcards out of the way to make room on her couch. 'Don't move too much. The cards are in a very specific order,' she says from the bathroom, returning with a first aid kit. She perches on the coffee table in front of Brian. He doesn't look her in the eye.

'So?' she prompts, uncapping a tube of ointment.

'Sooo. I didn't have the flu.'

'Doesn't take a semi-trained nurse to figure that one out.'

'Nik, I'm ... I'm sorry. I took time off to go camping with Tyler. I shouldn't have done it. If you want to fire me, then I get it.'

'I want to strangle you, but ...' She sighs. 'No, Brian, I don't want to fire you. I *just* about still want to help you. Here, take the corpse of Chuck Taylor off and give me your feet.'

While Nik dabs cream onto the various cuts, bites, stings and blisters on his feet, Brian gingerly picks up one of the flashcards.

'Hey. A triage nurse has four clients arrive in the ER within fifteen minutes. Which do you send back to be seen first?' Brian lists the clients with hints to their maladies.

Nik stops. She looks up at him for a long while, then breaks into a half-smile. 'The teenager who burned their hands on the stove,' she says. 'That's the wrong pile, by the way – grab the other one.'

While she gently finishes tending to his injuries, he shuffles through the cards.

'A sixteen-year-old female who ingested fifteen tablets of maximum-strength acetaminophen forty-five minutes ago is rushed to the emergency room. Which order should the nurse do first?'

'Gastric lavage.'

'A nurse reviews the labs of a patient receiving furosemide. Which result indicates an adverse effect is occurring?'

'Decreased magnesium. And stop scratching your poison ivy. How many times have we talked about this at work? I've no idea how you come into contact with it so often,' she says, applying hydrocortisone to his ankles.

Brian continues to shuffle through her deck. Symptoms and treatments, causes and comorbidities. Nik knows the answer to every one, which puts pressure on him to finally work up the courage to broach the real reason he's there. 'I thought about what you said at Darby's show. About Tyler …' She does her best to appear neutral, but after field-dressing the wounded animal that arrived at her doorstep unannounced, she certainly knows that this camping trip can't have gone well.

'You were right. Tyler didn't want what was best for me. He wanted what was best for him. He wanted to turn me into another version of himself. Someone he could influence. I just … I thought I had to do it. I'd been struggling to get my life together for so long. And for a while there, it worked. It gave me a sense of control that I was missing. I thought I had to learn to be hard. To toughen up. Be more assertive. And it felt great to feel powerful, like I had a say in what I could be.' He puts down the deck of cards that he's been hiding behind. 'I just didn't realize it would come at the expense of the people I care about most. You've always been there for me, Nik, and I chose not to see it. I'm truly sorry.'

186

Nik puts down the blister pack she's holding. She nods, as if weighing out her response. 'It means a lot to hear that. It does. These lessons take a long time to learn, and they take practice. Trust me. But understand that being strong doesn't just mean being aggressive and dominating everything in your path. Being vulnerable and asking for help when you need it – now *that* takes a lot of strength. So does admitting you were wrong.' She says this last line with a raised eyebrow, insinuating that hers is just the first stop on Brian's apology tour.

'About Darby, that was just a misunderstanding. I swear I felt ill. But don't worry – I'm going to make this right.'

'Good. They're not going to like me telling you this, but they do miss you. I know they were really hurt that night. But I think there's an opening there.'

Brian goes in for a hug. But Nik pushes him back. 'No, you need to get out of my apartment and wash those clothes.' She hands him antihistamines and guides him out her door. 'Remember: don't scratch, and short lukewarm baths. Take two of these and call me in the morning.'

After multiple loads of laundry, a two-hour shower and a full-body application of calamine lotion, Brian locks up the apartment, shrugs on his coat and bikes over to The Romanesco early for his first shift back. The restaurant is alive in rich technicolor as cosplayers huddle around tables and pose for pictures with one another; the Comic Con must have started, the best week of the year – they're good tippers, effusively kind and never dull. Brian cuts through Goku and Optimus Prime, whose cardboard costume is blocking most of the entryway, when he sees Darby at the end of the bar. They've dyed their hair blue since Brian last saw them, the server apron around their waist the only thing that distinguishes them from the obscure anime characters congregating at the end of the bar. Brian briefly makes eye contact with them before Darby looks away. Brian pushes his way through the characters, the restaurant humming and clanging with the changing of the guard from day to night shift. 'Hey, can we talk outside?' he says, when he reaches Darby.

Darby examines Brian from head to toe. 'No thank you,' they say coolly, before strutting to their first table.

Throughout the night, Brian tries everything he can to get time with Darby. He runs drinks and plates to their tables, hoping to earn some gratitude. He runs to the point-of-sales when Darby is ringing things in, pointing out the spandex-gothic eye candy that walks in. This, unfortunately, has the opposite of the desired effect. 'I'm in a relationship, Brian. But you know that.' But Brian continues, determined to wear them down.

'Darby?'

'What, Brian?'

'If you're not busy, my table over there wants a picture with you.' Brian points at the two-top by the window where Goku and a head-to-toe purple Frieza from *Dragon Ball Z* are halfway through their burgers and sipping on IPAs, Frieza's prehensile tail wrapped gingerly around the leg of their chair to prevent any obstacles for the waitstaff. 'They said they like your modern take on "Sayaka Miki", whoever that is ...'

'Fuck, did it happen again?' they say, peering down at their diaphanous cyan tunic. 'Last year it was *Final Fantasy VII*. This year it's ... what is she from?'

'Something called *Magi Madoka*? I don't know.'

'Okay, but is she a—''

'Yes, they assured me that she is a slay. And to answer your follow-up, her preferred weapon is a sword. A cutlass is a sword, right?'

Darby smiles for an instant, but Brian catches it.

'Fine. Tell them I'll be over in a minute,' they say.

After a mad dash of a night slinging drinks and diner food to an array of colorful copyrighted characters, they finally close the restaurant and count through the wads of cash they've left in their wake. When Darby gets up from the bar and goes outside for a smoke on their after-hours bench, Nik nods to Brian. 'I think this is your chance. Good luck.'

Brian walks out the French doors of the restaurant and Darby shifts in their seat away from him. Crossing their legs, they pull a cigarette from their tote bag. They don't offer Brian one. Brian feels like he's now the one putting on the show. He paces a bit in front of them. He's rehearsed this in his head a bunch of times. Rather than double down on the flowers, which would only result in further questions, he concedes.

'Listen, Darby. You were right. I was jealous.'

Darby's aloofness immediately warms by a couple of degrees to intrigued. They take a drag on their cigarette, then they gesture with it for Brian to continue.

'I wish I had your innate confidence, a calling – hell, even a relationship. I've been aimless, looking for answers in the wrong places. In trying to take control of my own life, I've turned into a domineering asshole, and it's hurt those around me. I am sorry for not showing up for you. And I am sorry for how dismissive I've been of Abe. My reaction at the show was completely uncalled for. I know he makes you happy, and that's everything I want for you. Really.'

Darby is not immune to flattery but will not let him off that easily. 'You have been an asshole,' they say. 'But it's not just that. You've been completely MIA these last couple of months. I know you've had this whole self-help journey with Ms. Tyler. But I needed you too. This whole show. Everything with Abe. It was finally happening for me, and I was terrified that I could lose it. That I could fuck up and it would all be gone in an instant. And you … you weren't there.'

Brian is surprised. 'I'm sorry. I had no idea. You always seemed so confident and self-assured. We've never really talked about it.'

'I didn't know if I *could* talk to you about it. I figured you would just tell me to toughen up and get over it. Seems to be your whole vibe recently. And even if I did open up to you about it, it's not like that's ever been reciprocated. You teach people how to treat you, Brian.'

'I'm truly sorry. I just hope that I'm not too late. If you'll have me, I promise, I'll be there.'

'And?' Darby wheels their hand, as if they're expecting more.

'And ...' Brian was stumped. Wasn't this the forgive-and-forget part? 'And ... I'm truly sorry and I hope it's not too late and if you'll ha—'

Darby cuts him off with an eyeroll. 'Okay, Brian. I know you're new to apologies, so let me help you out. Now, what are you going to do? How is this going to change?' Damn emotionally intelligent Darby. Brian pieces the ideas together.

'I'm ... going ... to be ... open? And honest. I'm going to get to know Abe. And I'll do what I say I'm going to do.'

Darby puts out their cigarette and examines him again. 'You promise?'

'Promise,' Brian says, holding out his hand for a pinky-swear.

'Oh, we're good. But you can keep your hands to yourself. Is that rash contagious? You look like shit, and you smell like a nursing home. What is that? Eau de oatmeal?'

Brian laughs and sits next to them on the bench. 'I really *am* sorry for being a dick about Abe, you know. How are things with him?'

Darby swoons. 'It's going great. He's such a romantic. Sure, he owns the flower shop, but every time he sends me a bouquet, I die. Whenever he's in town, he'll meet up with me after my shows and walk me home. Such a gentleman. Oh, and he got me this!' Darby opens their tote bag to show Brian a shiny revolver amid the gum, make-up and receipts. 'Jesus Christ!' Brian closes their bag, looking around the empty parking lot in case the feds are watching. 'You just keep that thing rolling around in a tote bag? Shouldn't it be in a safe or something?'

'What good is it going to do in a safe? Honestly, Brian, think. The safety is on, and it's not loaded. I'm not dumb. Abe is just protective. My little papa bear. He was concerned about a pretty little thing like me walking home alone at night with all my cash from the restaurant.'

'Couldn't he have just gotten you mace or a taser or something?'

'Puh-lease. If I get attacked on the street, I'm not giving them pink eye. I'm going to shoot that motherfucker down.' The gravity of their sentiment is undercut by the 'pew-pew-pew' from their finger guns.

ELEVEN

In the weeks since the camping trip, Brian has been able to regain a sense of balance in his life. He hasn't seen Tyler and Mark since they dropped him off at his apartment. He figures he has said his piece. He's left The Pack™ WhatsApp group, he's quietly and unilaterally retired himself from admin work, and he's scrubbed his GoPro footage and 'before' photos from the beta version of the website. He's done with them.

Now that he's freed up from navigating pack dynamics, he has been able to spend more quality time with Nik and Darby. Their after-hours trips to the bar are back on and he's getting better at moderating his drinking, which means he's better at forgiving himself for the one-off nights when he does stay out too late partying. Brian has kept the pieces of Tyler's program that worked for him, and that has seen him through another casualty-free transition. While the mantras went out the window on day one, he has continued with his morning runs in the park and his ritual of meditation in the evenings. He actually enjoys it – both disciplines help him turn his brain off and maintain control of his other senses, though he is annoyed that the common advice of fresh air and exercise actually does work and isn't, as he'd always assumed, a conspiracy by Big Nature inc.

Tyler still tries to contact him, though. He calls and texts, and when Brian doesn't answer he shows up on Brian's lurking-only Twitter account. Brian soft blocks him on every app on his phone, but every few days or so, he'll send a flurry of texts and the restaurant customers will frown at Brian due to the incessant vibrating in his server apron. After that first full moon since the trip – which Brian spent mostly perched on a rock by a stream in the park, almost peacefully meditating his way through the transition, like a shaggy version of Rodin's *Thinker* – Tyler leaves a voicemail message at The Romanesco.

'Hey, message for Brian. It's Tyler. Don't know if your phone's broken or something, but … touch base, please: we need to debrief on our awkward moment. I know things got heated but … let's catch up. I really think we can find a way to move forward.' Beep.

'Ooh, who is that? Boyfriend trouble?' asks Darby. They, Nik and Brian are closing the restaurant for the evening, wiping down tables, sharing a bottle of tequila as Nik goes through the various booking queries and customer complaints on The Romanesco's voicemail.

'No. it's Tyler,' Brian says. Nik and Darby exchange a glance.

'Didn't that sort of end on the camp thing you did?' Darby asks. Brian's only ever told them both the bare minimum about Tyler, and certainly nothing about The Pack™. But Brian's turned over a new leaf. While leaving key werewolf details out of it, he decides to bring Nik and Darby in. He tells them Tyler is – *was* – his life coach. He took Brian on pro bono to build his training program, and in return, Brian helped him with some of his business admin for a couple of lines on his non-existent résumé. But after creative differences, he wanted out. 'But it's like this guy has never heard no in his life.'

'Well,' asks Nik, 'have you actually told him no?'

'Uhh …' Brian has not. He has just been evading his every advance. 'I told his friend Mark. The other guy in his program. I'm sure they talk …'

'Brian, Brian, Brian. People can't read your mind. Remember? If you want a clean break, then just tell him that. He'll move on,' she says.

'And if he doesn't, he's a sociopath,' adds Darby.

If only they knew how potentially true that statement was. Still, Brian feels gutsy after their drinks. 'You know what? You're right.'

'Yeah!' cheers Darby.

'I'm going to call him now.'

'Yeah!'

Brian throws down another shot and retrieves his phone from his apron. His thumb hovers over Tyler's old number. He remembers just how strong Tyler was when he tossed him through the trees up on the mountain. 'You know what? I'm going to *text* him.'

'Yaaay,' Darby says, not quite so emphatically.

'Tyler, if it wasn't clear from everything I said on the camping trip and my absence over the last month, I'm done. I'm out. It's over.' Brian says it aloud as he types. 'Sent.'

Nik rubs his back. 'Good for you. I'm sure that couldn't have been—'

Brian's phone lights up and vibrates on the bar. They all see it. Tyler is calling. It sends a chill down his spine. They watch silently until it stops. Then he gets a voicemail notification.

'Oh God! He's left *another* voicemail?' says Darby. 'I thought the first one might have been an accident. What kind of monster leaves voicemails?'

'I do!' Nik says defiantly.

'Ah yes, the generational divide. I always forget. Brian, you got to block his ass. Here, you want me to do it?'

Brian quickly snatches his cracked phone out of Darby's hand. 'No!' Darby rounds their eyes in surprise. 'No, I mean, *I* should do it.' He struggles for a moment, scrutinizing the menus. 'Wait, how do you do it?'

'Aww, you really *are* opening up. You just admitted you've never had a jealous ex-lover before. Give me that.' Darby grabs the phone back, taps the screen three times and hands it back to him. 'There. Done.' Brian breathes in deeply, searching for that feeling of a weight being lifted off of him. It never arrives.

The next morning, there's still no sense of relief. He hopes that it will hit him during the day. He goes on his run to jumpstart the process, but it doesn't work. He tries to distract himself with Pornhub, but that doesn't work either. He spends the afternoon lying in bed diving in and out of TikTok rabbit holes. He pores over a stream of Disney Adults in their forties and fifties bawling their eyes out as they get to meet Mickey and Minnie before settling into a livestream of a woman scratching off hundreds of lottery tickets. He watches this with rapt attention until she references her love for the 'scratcher community' which shakes Brian free from the hypnosis, realizing it's time to go down into the lock-up, pick up his bike and head to work. It's a late summer afternoon, the first cool day that feels like the first day of school. The leaves are still green, but the sky is a burst of autumn golds and reds as the sun begins to set. People passing in the streets have pulled out their lightweight coats and cardigans over T-shirts and tank tops. As he rides across town, he feels his lungs opening up, but as he reaches the bridge heading to The Romanesco, he's hit powerfully by the familiar smack of vetiver and pine. The scent is so strong to Brian's wolf nose that he can almost see its trail, shimmering in the air. It's Tyler. He follows the scent, smells it getting stronger and stronger as he races down the tree-lined block until he can see the restaurant, the epicenter of Tyler's oud. Brian pulls on the brakes in the parking lot, jumps off his bike and locks it up, then runs into The Romanesco.

The restaurant is crowded. Tyler sits at the table closest to the entrance, facing the door. He's not taking any chances he'll miss Brian. He has pushed the dirty dishes from the previous diners into the center of the table. He inclines his head to Brian to signal him to come over, his eyes wide but his smile gone. 'Brian, can we talk?' he says, as Brian approaches. It doesn't sound like a question. 'I think we need to clear the air.'

Brian glances toward the bar. Nik and Darby are in the middle of talking with Abe, but they must have caught Brian's entrance as they're both looking over. 'What the fuck?' mouths Darby. They lean back into their conversation with Abe, who turns around to look at him too. Great. Is there anyone else in the restaurant that needs to know about this?

'Tyler, listen. I've said everything I need to say. Now is not a good time. My shift starts in a few minutes.'

'This won't take long. Please, just take a seat.' Brian hesitates, but then pulls out his chair, throwing a quick eyeroll to Nik and Darby to signify that everything is fine. Their support is not needed.

'Let's just get right to it. I'm sorry. I'm sorry you felt the way you did about our expansion plans. I imagine you said what you did because it caught you off guard. You haven't been yourself ever since I brought Mark into the mix, and I should have known you would get defensive with new recruits. That's on me. It's just this philosophy and the pack we're building here, it requires a certain baseline of masculine energy and aggression. Of course you were going to struggle with it. But I never said it was going to be easy. You just have to work harder at it, toughen up, and you have to be way less emotional if you want to succeed.'

Brian wonders if it'd prove his 'baseline masculinity' if he cracked one of the dirty plates on the lip of the table and stabbed it into Tyler's jugular, but instead he takes advantage of the opening Tyler has given him. 'You're right. This whole endeavor isn't made for me. I'm done trying to make it work. It's best if you just move on.'

'Move on?' Tyler echoes.

'Yeah, you know.' Brian mimes walking with his fingers. 'Move on.'

Tyler bangs his hand down on the table. The customers nearest to them look, but Brian shoots them a smile to deflect their attention. 'That's not what I said. I said that it *could* work but you're not trying. You're obstinate and you have been the whole time. You think you know better. But you don't. You were a wreck before you met me. Remember? And out of the kindness of my heart, I gave you, an absolute nobody, an opportunity to get in on the ground floor of what we're building here. Then we have one disagreement on the growth strategy and just like that you want out. I'm giving you one more chance, because this train is leaving the station. Mark is already working on recruitment. And if you don't get back on, you're going to be left ...' he struggles to extend his metaphor, '... on the platform.'

'What do you mean, Mark is working on the recruitment?'

'If you actually showed up to training, you'd know this already. But over the last few weeks we have identified profiles – people in the city with power and influence that can fill gaps in the organization. People in business, politics, tech and society. The plan is in motion and Mark's going to move on it. Tonight's full moon. Just like we agreed.'

Brian leans back into his chair. New recruits under the Harvest Moon. You had to hand it to him, it was *very* good branding. 'Listen, Tyler, we didn't agree to *shit*,' he hisses. 'Have you lost your goddamn mind? You're really going to werewolf-ify innocent people for a fucking multi-level marketing scheme?'

'It's not a scheme, Brian, it's a movement.'

'It's a power grab! Literally the only thing that gives me comfort right now is just how much of a mouth-breather Mark is and just how hard you've been failing at this whole thing for the last six months. Turns out it's hard to build something from the ground up when you can't leverage your pedigree or Daddy's money to get things done, huh? All the travel and hours of training sessions, and what do you even have to show for it? Have you been able to find another beside me?'

Tyler is about to speak, but Brian cuts him off. 'And don't say Mark. He's been in your thrall since college. Come to think of it … isn't it suspicious how he became a werewolf? He told me about the fishing trip. How it was just the two of you. How could Tyler, the most powerful werewolf that ever was, possibly have missed another wolf in their midst? How could he not have fought it off to protect his closest friend. Tell me, Tyler, does Mark know it was you?'

For the briefest moment, Tyler's irises gleam red. He folds his hand across his lap, closes his eyes and starts Ujjayi breathing again.

'I *knew* it,' says Brian. 'No wonder this plan seemed like the only path forward for you. I thought *I* was having a hard time with the werewolf thing, but in all honesty, I was probably better prepared for it than you. I knew since I was a kid that I was going to always be outside my comfort zone, that if I wanted to achieve something then I'd have to do it myself. No one was going to open any doors for me. But you? I'm sure it's got to be rough. For the first time, living in a world that wasn't designed explicitly for you.'

Tyler's breathing has quickened, becoming more erratic, but then he starts a low yoga hum, a single monotone to center himself.

'God,' Brian mutters.

Tyler continues to hum until the rise and fall of his chest slows to its usual restful cadence. When he is ready to speak, his manic grin returns, though it has more of the appearance of baring his teeth.

'You have no idea what you're talking about. Mark is a natural. He's thriving. And it's rather audacious for you to be speaking to me like this considering how we met. Do I really have to remind you about the people you've killed? Tsk, tsk.'

'That hasn't happened since … whatever, there's no way you could possibly pin it on me.'

'Oh Brian, I followed the trail straight to you. Right to this sad little diner.' He points to the table in the back where they had their first coffee together. 'I bet others could too. I doubt they'll be as accommodating as I've been.'

'There's no proof.'

'No?' At this Tyler *really* smiles. 'Your DNA's all over that jogger. And do you know where else it's all over? My tent, my sleeping bag, both of which I *so* kindly loaned you. You don't think I wouldn't use *Daddy's money* to have a forensic specialist swab it down? And I wouldn't use *Daddy's contacts* to have your samples handed to the right people?'

Now Brian is the one who is silent. The dinner rush continues to come in and crowd around the host stand. The two of them have been rather cavalier throwing around the word werewolf. They just have to hope that anyone who might have overheard them assumes they're a couple of unlikely *Twilight* fans.

'You've said some things here that are going to be hard to forget,' Tyler continues, for the first time sensing the advantage. 'But I can forgive, if you bring in new blood. Tonight's the night. It's not too late. But you will have to understand who's actually in charge here. No more of your emotional little outbursts.' Tyler grabs his messenger bag and stands up from his seat. 'Oh, and by the way, Mark told me how disgusted he was with you hitting on him the entire camping trip. It was all rather pathetic. Have some self-respect.'

TWELVE

Brian tosses and turns. His muscles are sore, his head is pounding. Even with his eyes closed, he can feel how bright it is as he bakes in the sunlight. Today is the day he becomes a bona fide adult, he tells himself. He will finally buy curtains.

After Tyler had left, Brian had scooped up the dishes from the table and taken them over to the kitchen hatch.

'Everything okay?' Nik asked as he walked by.

'Uh-huh,' he grunted non-committally.

Everything was not okay. He was happy to work his shift; moving from table to table afforded him the opportunity to frantically pace to his heart's content as he cycled through the thankless decision he had to make. Brian couldn't survive in prison – they don't have Netflix, the food sucks and there's truly nothing to do. At least with the full moon transitions, they would probably give him his own cell. Plus, it could help him really get into shape, add some muscle mass. The other option is he could change someone tonight – and who knows, maybe his bite wouldn't actually change people, since he was never bitten himself. Maybe it would be a kind of werewolf-lite thing, the only side effects being that they'd no longer be a cat person, they'd have a predilection for raw meat, or they'd start scratching behind their ears with their foot. But no, biting someone was too risky, and frankly, way too much responsibility. Brian can hardly manage his own life; taking on someone else's would be such a chore.

His shift had gone quickly as he was distracted by his internal monologue. When Darby had pulled Abe from his stool and suggested a trip to the bar, Brian had been all too eager to join. 'Yes, please, dear God.'

'I knew I could count on you. C'mon, Nik. Just slap an IOU in your register and let's get out of here.'

'Ugh, I keep coming up short. I need to review these receipts.' Nik had laid out about fifty credit-card slips face up in five-by-five rows on the bar, desperate to find the misplaced decimal that had eaten her earnings. 'You guys head out without me. I'll meet you there.'

Darby talked at Brian as they walked across the bridge, and for once he was thankful for Abe's silence. He tuned in and out as he recited the same haunted carousel of anxieties in his mind, briefly holding and weighing each decision.

'Briiiannnn, are you retreating into negative self-talk and unproductive interiority again? Come back, join us in the land of the living.'

'Sorry, weird night,' he said, walking through the divebar door Abe had opened for them, the cool fall wind whistling through the doorway.

'I can imagine. I want to know all about it. So, two questions, second one first: what the fuck was that all about with Tyler? And do you want a shot?'

'Yes to the shot. Oh, and a beer. Actually, two beers.'

'That's the spirit!' Darby skipped down to the far end of the bar to order their drinks as Brian and Abe sank into their stools.

'So, what *was* that all about?' This was the longest sentence Brian had heard from the man so far.

'Ugh, not to rehash this multiple times, 'cause I'll have to recount all of this for Darby, but it's just this guy, Tyler. He wants me to join his weird social network scam of a start-up. I told him I was done helping him with it, for free might I add. But you know rich kids and their passion projects. He's probably just mad he has to pay someone to work on their web presence and marketing now. He wouldn't take no for an answer. So, get this, he comes to confront me at work.'

'And how does that make you feel?' Abe asked like an armchair psychologist. With his black blazer with elbow patches he certainly looked the part.

'Just, anxious, I guess. Trapped. I'm trying to find a way out, but I don't have any good options.'

'Hmm …' Abe folded and unfolded a cocktail napkin. 'Sounds frustrating.'

'Yeah, I guess it is frustrating.'

'You said you don't have options. But what would you do right now if you *knew* that, whichever option you chose, you would be successful?' Brian pondered this while Darby doubled back their way with the drinks and dropped them in front of them, their eyes widening as they saw Brian and Abe actually talking. 'Be right back,' they said and headed to the bathroom.

Brian grabbed a shot and drained it, followed by a sip of his beer. 'I'd stop him, them, *it*. Whatever, I'd end it, the whole enterprise, burn it to the ground.'

'Hmm …' Abe studied the lime in his soda water. 'I think you have your answer.'

As the night passed, Brian continued to drink like the old days. Each beer with a complementary shot for optimal inebriation. Abe was right, it *was* frustrating. Why was Brian the one to be commanded, pulled and prodded in each direction? Why were these always Tyler's decisions to make when Brian was the only one who'd been putting in the work? Who the fuck did they think they were, putting him in this position? Those wealthy fucks using him as a pawn in their sick expansion strategy, not caring whose lives they ruined to get their way. They wanted him to feel in control, but only on their terms, for their gains, to their financial benefit and influence. After another shot, he sipped his beer in silence. And Mark, that fucking closet case, how *dare* he paint him as this obsessive pathetic chaser – he'd initiated it. Brian ordered another beer and promised himself that it would be his last shot – or second-to-last, for sure. And blackmailing a waiter for mauling a jogger, how would that even work? Oh, hey, Nik's here! He looked at her with one eye open and toasted her beer before stoking the fires in his mind.

He replayed all the times that Tyler and Mark had yelled at him, belittled him, broke his bones, his sense of safety, his confidence and his spirit. It was like pouring gasoline on the flames. His eyes flashed red, his mind burning up with one singular desire …

Brian rolls over in bed, trying to escape the tyranny of the sunlight. Maybe he needs blinds rather than curtains. Feels more … *bachelor*. He's just falling back asleep when he catches a whiff of what smells like the slop bucket at The Romanesco. Raw meat, iron, something slightly sour. When he opens his eyes, Mark's bloodshot eyes stare back at him. Or rather, *eye*. Where the other should be, there's just an empty, gaping socket. Brian shoots upright and scrabbles backwards. He clasps his hand over his mouth – he's not at home, he's in a meadow in Thousand Acre Park. Lying next to Mark's dead body.

Brian looks around the meadow, making sure there's no dog walker around, a jaunty Labrador chasing a tennis ball into a murder scene, but he and Mark are alone. The grass around him is trampled, matted, half wet with tacky blood. His hands shake as he takes stock of his own naked body – he's covered in dried blood, but all his fingers and toes are accounted for. The claw and bite marks on his sides, back and arms are hot to the touch as they slowly suture themselves back together, but at least his organs are all still safely stowed inside of him. The same cannot be said for Mark. The signs of their battle are all over his corpse. All the slashes and punctures must have opened back up after he died, his werewolf healing expiring at the same time he did. He's split at the seams like a cheap trash bag, a string of something that looks like dark blue anal beads hanging from a little hole in his side. His face is weirdly purple, a treacly black bile running out of his mouth and down his chest. That's not normal. And Brian can't find any obvious kill mark on him either, the usual *Mortal Kombat* fatality of ripping out a victim's jugular. Mark's is still intact. It looks more like he was poisoned or something, like he choked on his own vomit and drowned right there on dry land.

Brian's hangover and the scent of Mark's corpse cooking low and slow in the morning sun makes him gag. He vomits in his mouth and swallows it. He has got to get out of here. He pulls himself to his feet and runs for the tree line, a bloody, naked man zipping across an otherwise idyllic autumn field. He follows the familiar trail through the forest, down to where his go-bag is stashed in an old hollow stump. He grabs it and then scrambles down the dirt bank to the stream. The cool water stings his half-open wounds and Mark's blood and crusty saliva sluices off him, turning the stream pink like the little enamel spittoon at the dentist. He hastily pulls on his clothes, which stick to his wet body, then plods through the woods, up the familiar hiking trail to the street. It's still early and a congregation of commuters start jostling one another on the street as a bus pulls up to the curb. Brian breaks out into a speed walk, and crams himself onboard with the rest of them, making his way toward the back. He is quite the sight for the rest of the suit-clad commuter class. His jeans are covered in pond scum and dirt up to his shins and he smells like a drunk farm animal. A deep purple bruise on his cheekbone is bisected by a trickle of blood from his hairline. Several people tut as he pushes past them, and when he's finally sitting down, an old lady with cloudy hair openly glares at him.

'What can I say, I'm in LOVE! I really think he's *the one!*' She turns away, lips tight.

Brian tries to retrace his steps after he left the bar. He pulls out his cell phone to check his texts. There are three missed messages from Nik, making sure that he made it home all right. He just about remembers leaving the bar, but then what? Given where he woke up, he knows he ended up in the park, but where the hell did Mark come from? He closes his eyes and focuses. Okay, so, he's out the bar, down the street, back past The Romanesco – so far, usual route to the park. But wait, then there are streetlights, rowhomes, a tree-lined block. This isn't right. A closed Prada store? What was he doing on the west side? He's running, panting, filled with a searing hot rage; he's beginning to transition as he runs, his bones shifting under his skin ... then he sees it in all its posh urbanite glory. Tyler's house.

'Fuck, fuck, fuck,' he says aloud. The passengers nearest him stand up and inch closer to the front of the bus. He closes his eyes again and gropes through the dense fog of his memories. All he gets are flashes. Jumping the fence into Tyler's garden. Throwing himself at the double-glazed glass doors ... bouncing off? Rich people *really* got the best of things. Climbing up the drainpipe but then … a howl, in the distance. Leaving the garden, running toward it. He's in the park, a faint trace of recognizable scent in the air … beer, body odor and dirt. Follows it, sees a young couple cutting through the park, then movement behind them. A shape in the shadows, stalking them. Another werewolf. He tackles it just as it's about to pounce, sending them both crashing through tree trunks, away from the couple. There is a battle. Gnashing fangs and claws. He swallows mouthful after mouthful of chestnut fur saturated with thick blood. The iron and wool poultice coats his mouth as he struggles to swallow it. The pain, it stings. He is hurt, but he can't stop, there's no retreat. Then he has the feeling of being watched. Another figure in the dark. A man? The battle ends abruptly. Then there's nothing.

Brian opens his eyes and nearly misses his stop. He grabs the pull cord and the bus lurches to a halt. He dashes out the side exit, dodges through the busy street and heads back to his apartment. Entering his bathroom, he turns on the shower to its hottest setting and strips himself of his damp clothes. As the bathroom fogs up, he slows his breath, taking in the steam and humidity in deep, cleansing inhales. *Everything is fine.* After finally gathering his composure, he asks the age-old question: after committing homicide, do you do your entire skin-care routine? The answer, of course, being yes. He dabs on the vitamin E-infused face mask to reduce the potential scarring. As it dries, he dips out of the bathroom to toss some spoons in the freezer for application under his puffy eyes. He clips his nails and digs the blood and dirt out from under them, using his tweezers to pull out the splinters in his hands and then to pluck a few errant eyebrow hairs. As he's about to jump in the shower, he realizes he cut a few of his nails too short as his index finger begins to bleed. Adding the lemon garnishes to the drinks tonight is going to suck. And that's when he remembers: he has to work tonight. He begins to spiral again. Tyler will surely find him there. But he also needs to look as if everything is normal, as if he hasn't been dueling to the death with a rogue hell-beast. He jumps into the shower and sits in the tub, trying to remember any other details. Did anything happen when he went to Tyler's? Did he even kill Mark? Who else was in the park that night? But his memories are punctuated with these blank swathes of time, like intertitles in a silent movie. This would be so much easier to deal with if he weren't hungover.

He is in the shower so long, absentmindedly soaping his body over and over again, that when he finally gets out, the body wash bottle is empty and it's nearly time for his shift. He has no idea where his bike is, so he takes the bus, settling into a seat and opening a window, staring out at the changing cityscape. The glass and steel buildings have multiplied even in the last short year, wresting the rowhouses and old brick storefronts from their owners and turning them into sleek, shiny, hipster gathering centers. It begins to make Brian dizzy, so he closes his eyes and tries not to bring up the Pop Tart he ate while getting dressed. When he finally hops off the bus, his relief at being stationary and out in the fresh air very quickly curdles when he sees who's waiting for him outside the restaurant – Tyler, smoking a cigarette.

Brian is caught briefly between the desire to chase the bus down and throw himself bodily back onto it and the need to play dumb, act innocent. He walks toward the entrance, almost breaking out into a nonchalant whistle. 'Hey, Tyler, nice surpr—'

Tyler strides toward him and grabs his arm, stopping him in his tracks. 'Shut up,' he orders. His face is red. His business-casual smarminess is gone. 'What did you do last night?'

'Same as I do every night. Just went to the park. Did the Monster Mash, you know, ate a raccoon or two,' Brian says with a shrug.

'Then what?' Tyler asks and takes a drag of his cigarette. His hand shakes as he brings it to his lips. His manufactured calmness is starting to break.

'Umm, then I went home and watched *Love Island*. I'm halfway through season six, so no spoilers, but I'm really rooting for Paige and Fin—'

'No, Brian. Then you slaughtered my best friend.'

Brian's resolve folds. 'Oh, so *that*. I don't know what happened, Tyler, I swear. I guess things got out of control again. I just woke up and Mark was *there*. I didn't mean to ...' He drops his voice to a stage whisper. '... to *kill* him.'

'Oh, yes you did. You were so pathetically angry at him after he rejected you that you marked him, then you killed him.'

'I did not mark Mark!'

'You did too mark Mark.'

'Hold on, Funky Bunch, *if* I was going to mark Mark, it'd be for his willingness to hurt innocent people, but I'm telling you, I don't remember anything.' He tries to pull away, but Tyler's grip tightens. He pulls him closer as a couple of customers coming into the restaurant look at them quizzically.

'Let me fill in the blanks. You were rooting around my house. Digging and digging, like a desperate little animal. I've got to commend you, you really did some damage. Nothing that can't be fixed – I told you, no one is getting in or out of that cell – but trying to get to me like that? Tsk, tsk. Hardly a fair fight. Where's the honor in that?'

Brian swallows hard and stares straight ahead; he thumbs his hands where he took out the splinters.

'But you couldn't get in, could you? So you gave up and went for him. You killed him. And worst of all, you tried to kill me!' Tyler grabs Brian by the collar of his shirt and pulls him close. He is frozen. He can feel Tyler's hot breath and spit in his ear. 'Do you have any idea what you've done? You've set this movement back years.'

'Let him go!' shouts Nik. She's standing in the doorway to The Romanesco, flanked by Darby and Abe on either side. The customers have all stopped eating, their heads turned to look out the glass front. Tyler decides against making a scene. He lets Brian go and jokingly puts his hands up in the air. 'We were just catching up!' he says,

213

his signature grin disarming the onlookers but bouncing off Nik, Darby and Abe.

'I'm fine, really. Go inside,' Brian says, but they stand their ground. 'We're done here.'

As he takes some steps toward the entrance, Tyler grabs his wrist and pulls him back to face him. His smile is gone. 'I just need you to know, what you've done here, yes, it's a setback. But there are other ways that I can make you more … compliant.' He peers meaningfully over Brian's shoulder to his friends at the entrance. He waits to see the gravity of his statement register on Brian's face before he lights up the smile again. 'Now we're done.' He waves at Nik and Darby. 'See you all later! Have a good night!'

Brian stands still, sure not to move until Tyler has disappeared at the end of the block. Nik and Darby hustle over to him, Nik wrapping an arm around his shoulders, and they guide him into the restaurant.

'Seems like a messy break-up,' says Darby.

'You don't know the half of it,' mutters Brian. 'Thanks for having my back out there.'

'Always,' says Nik.

'You too, Abe,' he says, wondering if that is the first time he has willingly addressed the man directly.

Abe nods. 'Of course,' he says gruffly, then walks back inside.

'I told you he's protective. My li'l papa bear,' says Darby.

THIRTEEN

There are twenty-nine and a half days between each full moon, a fact Brian is acutely aware of after his last confrontation with Tyler. If this were just his problem – if Tyler hadn't pulled his friends into this with a really meaningful side-eye – then Brian would face the possibility of being mauled to death with the same casual nihilism he approaches any and all adversity. Like when he didn't know how to set up his electricity bill, so he only ate takeout and charged his phone and laptop at work for a month. He'll continue to avoid the issue until the anxiety reaches fever pitch, then promptly half-ass a solution that he whips up last minute. If his solution is successful, then it's evidence that he spent his time wisely by ignoring the problem for as long as he did. If unsuccessful, then there was clearly nothing he could have done to prevent it in the first place. He has wasted the last ten days of potential prep time going through the motions to distract himself. He wakes up, he goes to work, he takes the orders, he goes home, he starts season seven of *Love Island*, picks the sluttiest ones and roots for them with his whole chest. Step 1: Complete.

But with Nik and Darby involved, this is a lot more complicated. After his last shift, when he and Darby were sharing their ritual cigarette, Brian scowling up at the half-moon, Darby gently butted his shoulder with their own. 'Hey, are you okay?' they asked, guessing he was brooding about Tyler.

This small, casual show of support from Darby plunges Brian immediately into Step 2: Overwhelming anxiety. *They know something's up*, his hyperactive internal monologue begins. *I can't tell them the truth. Can you imagine? 'Hey, Darbs'* – Brian never refers to Darby as 'Darbs' – *'I'm a mythical beast and that guy you think I've been secretly dating? He's one too, and he's out for revenge after I accidentally shredded his friend, and by revenge, I mean ... well, you. And by shredded, I mean ...' They'd freak the fuck out. And then leave me. And I don't know how to do this on my own—*

'Brian?' Darby's looking at him with mild concern.

'Oh. Sorry, just got a lot on my mind.'

'Sure you do,' says Darby.

That night Brian can't sleep. He fidgets around on his mattress for hours, wrestling with his conscience. He owes Nik and Darby a fighting chance, but at 3 a.m., staring into the dark, he feels powerless. The past grows and the future recedes. He lays in bed, watching the reflections of passing headlights cascade across the ceiling, trying to think his way out of this. Why couldn't they have just gone inside when he asked? *Because they care about you, you idiot*, his inner monologue chips in. And they do –

they really do care about him, and that means he needs to care about them too. He kicks off his duvet, stomps to the bathroom and pulls the light cord. Looking at himself in the mirror, the lonely scrap of Nik's flashcard looks back. 'It's not what we have in our life, but who we have in our life that counts.' He can't have his friendship group go from two to zero. He takes a deep breath, nods and makes his decision. He is going to tell them tomorrow.

The following morning, after eight hours of preemptively trying to come to terms with the imminent loss of the two people that he cares about most in the world, he plucks up the courage to rip the Band-Aid off. They'll come over, he'll sit them down, and then he'll just do it. Even if they want nothing to do with him after he tells them, that's fine. As long as they're safe. He composes and retypes the same text message over and over until he finally sends something short to their group text.

BRIAN: GUYS. I NEED TO TALK TO YOU. CAN YOU COME OVER?

He watches Nik and Darby's ellipses start and stop. This is taking forever. Darby messages first, teasing that it must be serious if he's finally inviting them over to his inner sanctum. Nik follows up more soberly. SURE, she says, clearly having guessed something is up. WE'LL BE OVER IN AN HOUR OR SO.

Fueled by his low-grade panic, Brian throws himself into cleaning. He folds his laundry, collects up armfuls of takeout boxes and washes the dishes. When those are done, he looks for new monotonous chores he can use as a distraction. He scrubs his baseboards with an old

T-shirt and rehearses his speech. *Nik, Darby. I need to tell you something. I'm a werewolf and we're all in peril.* Peril? Try again, Gandalf. *We're all in mortal danger.* Better, but perhaps a bit cosmic-doom-y? While alphabetizing the condiments in his fridge, he tries to remember how he came out to his parents. Maybe he could use that as a template … although there is no werewolf equivalent of finding gay porn on the family computer.

His phone suddenly vibrates on the counter and he thumbs open the text message.

NIK: HEY, WE'RE DOWNSTAIRS.

He takes a deep breath and heads to the door, pausing in the doorway to look back at his apartment. It looks show home ready. Amazing what a little anxiety can do. He stands in this moment, savoring this time before his friends know and everything changes. 'No time like the present,' he mutters to himself, finally compelling himself to move.

He plods down the fluorescent-lit hallway to the entrance. Nik and Darby wave at him through the glass door, and his heart begins to race. 'Everything all right?' Nik asks, pushing a bag of warm bagels into his arms. She looks concerned.

'Yeah, everything's fine. Come on in.'

He ushers them into the stairwell, then leads them up to his apartment. The two of them putz around the room, making the very short walk across the living space and back, stopping to admire the mattress. 'Well … this is more or less exactly what I was expecting,' says Darby.

'It's efficient,' says Brian.

'Yes ... spartan,' says Darby, searching for a compliment. 'Very butch.'

Nik seems to be vaguely looking around for somewhere – anywhere – to sit.

'Just this, I'm afraid,' he says, embarrassed, gesturing to the mattress. 'But take a seat, it's fairly clean.' He opens up the paper bag that he's still clutching to his chest. 'Bagel?'

'No, I'm good,' says Nik, while Darby reaches in and takes three.

'How about a drink?' Brian asks, stalling for time.

'Coffee?' asks Nik.

'Uhhh, I'm out of filters.'

'Green tea?' tries Darby.

'Uhhh, I'm out of that right now.'

'What have you got?'

'Vodka. Or water?'

'You know, Brian, I think we're both pretty hydrated over here. Why don't you tell us what's up? What did you want to talk about?'

Here we go. Brian takes a deep breath and steadies himself. 'Okay, so ... I've known you guys for a while. And I know you've had your concerns, wanting to make sure everything is all right with me. I know I haven't been too open. I could've been better at that, and I'm sorry ...' Brian notices he's pacing and stops. His hands are shaking and he clasps them together awkwardly. Looking up, he sees Nik and Darby watching him. Their eyes are wide. *Just get on with it.*

'Well, so, you know how some nights I have to do my disappearing act. And how I get really moody sometimes. And there are certain smells and sounds that I can't deal with. Well, there's a reason for all that. This was what Tyler was really helping me with. But I realized too late that he was ultimately only helping me to help himself.' They are rapt with attention. He wishes he could disappear.

'See, the thing is ... I'm ... I'm a werewolf.'

He closes his eyes. He cannot bear to see his life explode under the nuclear bomb of his announcement. The silence feels like a lifetime.

'Duh,' says Darby. Nik slaps their arm.

Brian snaps to attention. *Duh*?

'Babe, you haven't exactly been hiding it,' says Nik. 'A lot of the signs were there. For one, you know I make the schedule each week. And then there was that one time you requested all the days off that had the little full moon on them. I don't know why they feel the need to include that in the scheduling book. I mean, holidays, sure, but ...'

'*I* thought you had a menstrual cycle,' says Darby, pulling out their phone. 'Nik said I was crazy. But you're always so bitchy at that time of the month. I downloaded an app for it and everything. Took a couple of cycles until I realized what I was actually tracking. It really puts your flimsy excuses for missing my shows into context. Speaking of which, it looks like we're in your fertility window, moon sister.'

Nik laughs and slaps them on the arm again. 'And how many times have I had to tell you how to deal with poison ivy?! At first, I thought you were just cruising for dick in the woods, but ...' She looks up at Brian and sees tears welling in his eyes. She clears her throat; her tone is softer. 'Honestly, we were just waiting until you felt comfortable.'

Brian tries to speak, but he doesn't for a moment trust he can do it without crying. He walls it in, Ujjayi breathing through it, desperately trying to control the moment. The two get up, one after another, and come over to him. They gently put their arms around him, letting him lean into them, holding him up between them.

The dam bursts wide open.

'You're not freaked out? I mean, I understand if this is all too much ...' he sobs.

'Of course not,' says Nik, rubbing his back. 'You can't get rid of us that easily.'

Brian ugly-cries like a widow at a Mediterranean funeral. He cries for feeling accepted, for a feeling of safety, for the feeling of having family, community – albeit a small one, but it's made up of people he can be his full self around. He cries for this feeling of weightlessness, relieved of the burden of always having to translate or hide what he's feeling. He cries because for the first time in years, in this shitty studio apartment, it actually ... finally ... feels like home.

Only when his breathing slows and his tears are no longer torrential does Darby break away. They pull out a bottle of cheap champagne from their tote bag. 'I told Nik my suspicions on our way over. So I brought bubbles,' they say, jingling the bottle. 'It's not every day your friend comes out of the were-closet. Seems appropriate to have a toast.' Brian snort-laughs, both emptied and blissed out with relief. He wipes away his tears and heads to the kitchen to root around in the cabinets of old dishware to find three Icelandic yogurt jars.

Behind him, Darby is telling Nik that they told her so. Then they shout to him, 'I knew it! I did. I have a sixth sense for these things. Plus, I figured after whatever went down with you and Ms. Tyler that it was just a matter of time until you gave us the whole story.'

Brian stops in his tracks. He spent so much time thinking about the 'coming out' part that he hasn't rehearsed the 'imminent threat on your life' piece.

'So, about that …'

'Is garlic like *a thing*?'

'Garlic? No, Darby, that's vampires.'

'But you're basically the same thing, right … ?'

While Nik starts lecturing Darby about magical essentialism, Brian quietly marvels at his friends. They're sitting in their after-hours bar, which – in the days since Brian told them that Tyler is planning to maybe, you know, potentially kill them all – they have basically turned into a war room, the three of them coming every night to strategize in hushed tones and to sketch out plans on cocktail napkins.

They took the possibility of their demise much more calmly than he imagined they would. When he told them, they stood silently at the foot of his mattress, threw back their champagne like a shot, and Nik, ever practical, said, 'Right, we need to plan our defense.' She took the lead on all this prep work, bringing the same care and attention she had previously reserved for pharmacology to defeating a werewolf with a vendetta. Slowly, through their evenings of wargames and clandestine spycraft, they're finally putting the finishing touches to a plan.

'Okay,' Brian says, interrupting Nik's lecture. 'Let's run through this one last time. We know that we don't need to go to him – he'll come to us. So we barricade ourselves in The Romanesco. I'll take the lead with support from you guys from behind the bar. If things go sideways, then you save yourselves and lock yourselves in the walk-in refrigerator until morning.

'That going to hold against an angry werewolf?'

'Should do. The metal is way too thick for him to get through – I couldn't even get through double-glazed French doors the other night.'

'Okay, but that's not an eventuality, because we're going to kill him first, right?'

'Oh man, I super-duper want to,' says Brian. 'But that's definitely the hardest part.'

'What about silver?' Nik asks. 'Is *that* one a thing?'

'Whoa, excuse me, *I* can't ask about garlic but *you* can ask about silver?'

'Shut up, Darby.'

Brian pauses to think. There are many gaps in his werewolf syllabus. 'I don't know, actually. It's never come up.'

Nik is exasperated. He can tell she's thinking, *how has this kid lasted so long?* 'What do you mean, it's never come up?'

'Tell me, Nik, when do you think I touch silver in my day-to-day life?'

'Good point.' Nik thinks for a moment. Darby pulls out their phone and reads the Wikipedia entry on the many varied uses of silver. Brian's family is not in whatever echelon of the suburban middle class that keeps a matching set of 'good china', so silverware has never been an issue. He also assures them he hasn't built any household appliances, satellites or nuclear conductors in recent memory.

'Ooh! Ooh! Ooh! What about fillings?'

'Never had a cavity. Just lucky, I guess. That reminds me …' Brian counts his teeth in his mouth with his tongue. 'I should really go to the dentisht. It'sh been about five yearsh …'

Nik pinches the bridge of her nose and sighs. 'How many times have I told you about the hidden dangers of gum disease?'

'Too many. Trust me, if we make it out of this. It'll be first on my list.' The gravity of this last statement takes the air out of the room. They all fall quiet.

'Jewelry!' says Nik, breaking the silence.

'Look at me,' Brian lifts his arm to show a three-inch wide tear in the armpit of his Velvet Underground T-shirt.

'Fine. What about you, Darby? You've always got some bling. Is any of it real?'

Darby turns, drink in hand, and casts a withering stare that they've perfected from years of watching daytime soap operas. 'I resent the question and I will not be answering it.'

'I think you just did,' says Nik.

Brian interjects. 'Regardless, Tyler's coming in two days. We'll just have to do this the old-fashioned way. Aim for the head. I'm sure it'll be fine.' They fall silent again, the three of them staring at themselves in the mirror behind the bar, each of them trying not to think about the obvious question: but what if it's not fine?

Anyone who has worked in a restaurant is no longer fooled by the white linen tablecloths and the haughty French sommeliers – even the very best ones are filthy. It changes you. Whenever they go somewhere new, Darby checks the state of the bathroom before ordering. It serves as a proxy indicator for general cleanliness, but one can never know for sure. Each kitchen vent is a grease trap that calcifies at the end of each night. When the kitchen heats up, deposits of marbled fat liquify, drip-dropping into each dish and on every kitchen work surface. If left untreated, and if the fat drips onto the naked flames of the cooker, the entire place can go up. Nik gravely detailed all of this to the owner of The Romanesco. His approach to management has always been laissez-faire; he's content to have the place run itself so long as the checks keep coming, but when Nik cautioned him about fire risks and extensive, expensive damage, he reluctantly allowed her to close early for a deep clean.

When Brian arrives the afternoon of the full moon, Nik has posted signs all around the restaurant informing customers of an early closure. It still doesn't keep people from complaining, though. Brian is already testy, on the precipice of his monthly transition. Even though he ran and meditated beforehand to prepare for tonight, he is still on edge. He resents the fact that he's spending what could be his final moments slinging potatoes for tips, and it doesn't help that Darby is on what appears to be a farewell tour with each of their tables. They're hugging their regulars, ushering elderly couples from their table to the exit and lingering by the door for drawn-out final goodbyes.

'Darby, c'mon,' Brian hisses. 'Nik and I are in the weeds here.' They're trying to hustle everyone out as quickly as possible.

Darby glowers at him before kneeling down in front of a small child with pigtails and asking her to remember them in her prayers. Brian rolls his eyes.

Eventually, only Abe remains, sitting on his customary stool, drinking his customary glass of wine. Brian, Nik and Darby huddle around the cash register at the far end of the bar.

'Okay, one more to close out.' She prints out Abe's check and hands it to Darby. 'Take your time.'

Brian and Nik get to work stacking the tables and chairs against the windows, while Darby says goodbye to Abe.

Brian tries not to eavesdrop and to keep his eyes on his own paper, but at some point he thinks he hears Abe say, 'I love you.' Then there's the scraping of a bar stool, and Abe walks to the entrance. As he passes Brian, he stops.

'Those ... troubles you were having, with your business partner. Did you ever sort those out?'

'Umm ... partly. Nearly there. Just one final push.'

'Good, good ...' Abe takes off his glasses to polish them on his handkerchief. 'I wish you luck.'

'Thanks, Abe,' Brian says, offering an outstretched hand. Abe takes it, and surprisingly, pulls him in closer.

'I'm heading out, but could you be a friend and make sure Darby gets home safe tonight? I'm trusting you.'

Darby wasn't kidding; he is super protective. 'You've got it. Scout's honor.'

Abe leaves and Brian locks the door. When he makes his way back to the bar, he notices Darby has tears welling in their eyes. 'Hey,' he says, and hugs them. 'It's going to be okay. I promise.'

'Oh, it's not that. These are happy tears,' they lie. 'Now get back to work. We've got work to do.'

The barricade they make looked a lot different on their cocktail napkins. They thought it would give the feel of a medieval fortress fortified with treacherous wooden spikes, but the tables and chairs are too neat and flimsy. Nik suggests taking some of the kegs from downstairs to bolster defenses. Brian runs to fetch them and brings them up two at a time, and then Nik and Darby work together to shimmy them into place. When all is said and

227

done, their fortress looks like the preparations for a fight club at an IKEA, but it's the best they can do. Brian looks at them and shrugs.

'*You go to war with the army you have,*' he recites.

'Donald Rumsfeld?' Nik asks.

'Gross,' says Darby.

'It's nearly time,' Nik says, peering through the slatted blinds of the restaurant. 'The moon's nearly fully up.' She glances uncertainly at Brian. 'What … er … what happens now?'

Brian unbuckles his belt.

'Woah there, not so fast,' says Darby. 'You gotta warn folks before you just whip it out like that. Jesus, Brian, in this climate?'

He sighs. 'No, Darby. You know how expensive it is to burst out clothing once a month? We do this thing bareback.'

Brian strips down to his boxer briefs and then sits on the floor in the middle of their makeshift arena. Darby grabs the tray of silverware and checks the dishwasher, ensuring they have every last steak knife in the place. They bring them behind the bar where they wait with Nik.

'What are you doing?' Darby asks Nik, who is diligently restocking the bar. 'Brian, do you see this? Homegirl is fluffing pillows on the *Titanic.*'

'I don't know!' says Nik. 'I need something to do! Plus, if this goes well, I don't want to be yelled at by the day shift again.'

The minutes creep by. Then the hours. Brian sits on the polished concrete of the floor and scrolls through his phone. Nik and Darby watch him patiently as they laze atop the bar. 'When are you gonna do your thing?' asks Nik.

'Soon-ish – it's not always predictable,' he says, not taking his eyes off the *Love Island* Reddit on his phone. This could be his last night on Earth, and he needs to know if Millie finds love. Nik turns to Darby and rolls her eyes. Darby shrugs and lies across the counter.

'I know this is weird to say as we're about to fight for our lives, but this is really boring,' says Brian.

'I've got just the thing!' says Darby. They grab their phone and Bluetooth their music on the bar speakers. Darby's newest artistic outlet, a maximalist hyperpop mélange of distorted synthesizers and what appears to be cartoon sound effects will be the soundtrack to their werewolf vs. werewolf battle royal. 'Nik, Brian, dance with me!'

'Urgh, I'm not really in the mood, Darby,' Nik says.

'Wait! We could always …' Darby starts ferreting around in their pockets and pulls out a small baggie of powder. 'Molly, by moonlight,' they say huskily, as if narrating a perfume ad.

Nik snatches the bag away from them. 'Nope. Nuh-uh. Not on my watch. Fine, I'll dance with you, but we *cannot* pre-game this.'

They walk over to the half-naked Brian in the middle of the arena and pull him to his feet, then the three of them start to bop their shoulders. 'We look like idiots,' Brian grouches, but then throws out some surprise dad finger guns. Nik laughs and gives a little shimmy, and then they start to jump up and down, spin one another around, attempt the running man, then an ambitious three-way tango, and they're all laughing, because it's fun and death seems unthinkable in that moment and the situation is just Camus levels of absurd, but there they are, the three of them, side by side. They might not make it through the night; if they do, they likely won't have jobs; but right now, they have at least got each other.

Suddenly, Brian doubles over onto the floor, landing on all fours. Nik and Darby exchange a quick look of shock and jump behind the bar. Sitting under the counter, they hold on to one another as they hear Brian's retching and groaning grow louder and deeper over Darby's clap track, eventually culminating in a howl that will haunt even their grandchildren. There's a brief moment of silence from Brian until they hear the soft click-clacking of claws on the polished concrete floor. Darby can't fight their curiosity. They get to their knees and peer over the bar. Where Brian once stood, there is now a gigantic black wolf trotting around the restaurant. 'Aww … he's actually kind of cute.'

Brian stops and fixes his gaze on Darby.

'*I discover no kinship, no understanding, no mercy,*' Darby says in their best Werner Herzog impression. '*Only the overwhelming indifference of nature.*'

'Darby!' Nik warns.

Brian's ears pull close to his head as they hear a second long, descending howl in the distance. He leans back onto his hind legs and grumbles a low growl that can be felt through the floor.

'Get down,' Nik hisses, pulling Darby to the floor.

'It was miles away,' Darby says, waving their hand dismissively. 'We've got plenty of ti—'

There's a sudden dull thud against the door. It rattles against its lock as something paws at it, trying to work out how to open it, then there's a crash and the noise of splintering, but the barricade holds. Tyler's here. Nik and Darby slowly raise their eyes above the bar and see behind the window blinds the silhouette of a massive figure, circling the restaurant, searching for an entry point. Suddenly, a huge, amber lupine head ducks into view beneath the blinds and looks in. The glass fogs under its breath.

Brian leaps across the floor and snarls, the two wolves briefly snout to snout through the window. There's a huge roar from outside and then a thud as Tyler throws himself against the glass. The tables-and-chairs barricade wobbles alarmingly. Another thud, the window splinters. One more and then in a burst of glass and broken wood, an 8-foot werewolf lands in the restaurant.

'Okay, that one's less cute,' says Darby in a panicked voice, ducking for cover again while the two wolves begin circling one another. Tyler and Brian growl and snap, never breaking eye contact, looking for an opening. Tyler is much larger than Brian, the contours of his musculature still plainly visible beneath the thick pelt of fur. He roars again and snaps, ropes of drool hanging from his fangs. Brian keeps himself between Tyler and his friends, digging his heels in, waiting, waiting, then in the split second when Tyler blinks, Brian launches off his hind legs for an attack ... but Tyler is too fast. He dodges neatly to the side, like a matador letting a bull pass harmlessly by, then he clamps down on Brian's flank. Nik and Darby wince. Then Tyler bodily lifts Brian from the floor and hurls him through the pastry display case.

'Hey, HEY!' Nik shouts from behind the bar. 'Can you try and be a *little* careful? Do you know how much that costs?' In response, she hears the clunk-clunk and electrical sizzle of the point-of-sale system at the checkout being ripped out and driven down on Brian's head. 'Oh, God,' she says, as she hears the metallic jangle of coins from the register skitter across the floor. When Nik hears a gristly crunch and then a yelp, though, she stops her accounting.

Brian is on his side, his chest rising and falling rapidly. Tyler is standing over him, his lips pulled back and his giant canines exposed, ready for the kill. 'Brian!' screams Nik, but Tyler is already rearing up, aiming for Brian's exposed jugular ... when a knife cuts through the air in front of him and lands with a thud in the wall, quivering with reverberation, a hank of amber fur pinned to the plasterboard. Tyler and Nik both follow the trajectory of the knife back to its source and they see Darby, crouched on the counter, their one arm still extended from the throw, the other gripping a half-dozen steak knives. Darby whistles, 'Here boy! You hungry?'

Tyler growls and slowly lumbers forward. Darby whizzes knife after knife at him, the air filled with flashes of silver, but the wolf is fast. He ducks, dives and contorts his way past each projectile, until Darby's hands are empty. 'Oh, you're good,' Darby says, leaning down to scoop up another handful of knives from the silverware tray – but Tyler takes advantage of the opening and leaps onto the bar, sending Darby falling backwards, their knives scattering across the floor. Nik pushes herself off the wall and, with all the ease of a Saturday-night shift, glides the length of the bar, scoops up a bottle of vodka with one hand and then baseball-bat smashes it straight into the center of Tyler's face. While the wolf snarls with pain and surprise, Russia's finest export burning his eyes, Nik is already pulling Darby to their feet, the two of them spinning around to stand their ground. Tyler roars at them, his mouth bigger than Darby's head, revealing rows of razor-sharp teeth that slobber bands of bloody pink saliva onto the marble countertop.

'Tyler, stay!' Darby commands. 'Tyler … sit! Sit, boy!' Enraged, Tyler stalks forward, his claws clicking as he gets closer to Darby and Nik. Darby glances past Tyler, then looks him square in the eyes. 'I said *stay*. Who's a bad boy?' they say with a grin. Tyler hesitates, then turns to see over his shoulder, but it's too late – Brian has grabbed the back of Tyler's head and wrenched it back with an ugly snapping sound.

Nik and Darby take their cue: they sprint downstairs to the walk-in refrigerator and slam the door, listening to the muffled battle above them against the bumping of Darby's bass. Nik paces the length of the freezing room, her breath turning to mist as she speaks. 'We have to do something! He's hurt. He's not going to last much longer.'

Then, Darby remembers. 'Oh my God … I am such a ditz. I totally have a gun!'

Nik is confused. 'You, Darby, have a gun?'

'See, this judgment right here,' they say, circling Nik's face with their finger. 'This is why I didn't tell you. I *knew* you would freak out. It was a gift, okay, so spare me your little Second Amendment diatribe.'

Nik closes her eyes and taps her brow. 'We're fighting for our lives and you're just remembering this now?!'

'Honestly, I hardly use the thing,' says Darby. 'I mean, sure, whenever I'm switching bags from day to evening, I'll see it and then I'm like, "Oh yeah, this old thing" but—'

'Then go get it!' Nik shouts as she grabs Darby's wrist and pulls them out the door up the stairs to the dining room. They're just in time to see Brian sail through the air as Tyler hurls him against the back wall, cratering it in the process. 'Where is it?' Nik shouts, and Darby points back to the bar. They hunch over, trying to make themselves into smaller targets, and run behind Tyler as he starts kicking Brian's head like a soccer ball. Darby dives for their tote, while Nik grabs a broom, marches over to Tyler and breaks it over his broad, sandy back. The werewolf spins around from Brian and raises his paw to separate Nik's head from her shoulders when Darby fires. The piercing gunshot rings loudly in their ears. For a moment, everyone looks around, trying to see who's hit. Tyler checks his own body but seems to be fine. He looks up at Darby. They squeeze off two more shots in quick succession, but they miss again and hit the walls.

'I know you're new at this,' Nik yells, 'but it helps if you keep your eyes open.'

'Everyone's a critic. Do you want to do it?' they say, dangling the revolver on their finger as an offer.

'No, no, please, by all means, go ahead, no pressure.'

Tyler charges toward them. Darby fires again and again, each bullet missing its target by impressive margins, but then, as Tyler leaps onto the bar, Darby steadies themself and squints down the barrel of the gun.

'Play dead, you raggedy bitch.'

They squeeze off the last shot – and hit Tyler right between the eyes, taking out the back of his head and half his brain with it. The wolf looks stunned for half a second, then falls backward and hits the cement floor with a squelchy thud. As his final breath leaves his body, the patchwork amber pelt fades away, revealing a naked, blond thirty-something dead on the floor.

FOURTEEN

Brian's eyes flutter open and he adjusts to the brightness. He is laid out on an industrial metal table in the prep kitchen in the basement, an old black hoodie from lost and found politely draped around his waist like a fig leaf. Nik is sitting by his side, diligently dressing his wounds with the first aid kit she brought from home. 'Good morning,' she says, dabbing antibiotic ointment on the stitches along his sides.

He tries to sit up. 'Is ... is it over? Where's Darby?'

Nik puts a hand on his chest to ease him back down. 'Yes, it's over. Darby's upstairs cleaning up. You've just got to rest up and let me take care of these injuries. He really did some damage.'

'And Tyler?'

'Dead,' Nik says with a shrug.

Brian feels his whole body relax. That feeling he was searching for, of the weight being lifted off ... it's finally arrived.

'Now stay still, this one here on your chest is pretty deep. Let me stitch it up and then you're good to go. This may hurt a bit.' Nik grabs her needle and thread and gets

236

back to work. Brian does as he is told. The pinpricks feel like tiny bee stings. She'll never have another patient with a pain tolerance this high.

'I've been reading about wolves recently,' she says, focusing on her needlepoint. 'Did you know that the alpha male role was only found in wolves in captivity? Turns out wolf packs are actually matriarchal. Makes sense if you ask me.'

'Wait. Really? Tyler was so full of shit.'

'No, not entirely. He was right about one thing. All wolves need a pack to survive. A lone wolf is always searching for a pack. Everything in their nature tells them to belong to something greater than themselves. They succeed by forming relationships and life-long bonds. Aggression, domination, competition – all of that is destructive to pack dynamics. Cooperation, care and compassion do more to ensure their survival.' Nik ties and snips the thread and looks at him.

'I can't believe I fell for it all, Nik. I feel ... I'm such an idiot.'

'I don't think you're an idiot. Not about *that* at least. I think you were lonely and scared. You were searching for your pack. You just didn't realize that you already had one.'

Brian looks up at her and blinks back tears. Then he sits up and pulls her into a deep hug.

'No sudden movements, I don't want you to burst at the seams! These took a lot of time.'

'Hate to break it to you, but these will all be healed in a couple of hours. But I'm happy I can give you some applied learning experience. Getting you closer to those 10,000 hours.'

'Oh, if that's the case, then get your ass up. You've got time to lean, you've got time to clean!'

They break apart and Nik stashes her needle and thread back into her first aid box. 'I'll leave you to …' She nods at the hoodie, barely covering Brian's crotch, and then makes her way out, closing the door behind her. Brian hauls himself up and pulls on his clothes. He lumbers up the stairs just in time to catch Nik shaking her head, lecturing Darby.

'… and I just don't get what you've been doing this whole time!' The dining room is a mess. Darby stands in the middle of the room with a dustpan and broom amid a couple of neat piles of broken glass and splinters.

'I've been trying! I'm just not made for manual labor. Plus, I don't know what you want me to do about *that*,' they say, pointing the broom at Tyler's bloody corpse at the foot of the bar. 'It's heavy.'

They make plans to divide and conquer. Brian wraps Tyler up in a mat from the kitchen and ditches him unceremoniously in the dumpster out back. There is a chance it's trash day. The rest of the early hours are spent sweeping and cleaning as fast as they can before the morning shift shows up. They do the best they can, but surely the morning staff are going to notice that several of the windows are blown out, there are far fewer tables and chairs than there were yesterday, and there's a notable absence of a pastry case and a cash register. They rehearse their story: The Romanesco was vandalized. Police think it's the work of a former employee, disgruntled by the owner's attachment to zero-hours contracts and a reliance on tipping culture to underpay the staff. 'That's *very* specific,' Darby says, while Nik fires off a text to the bartender at their after-hours spot for a quick alibi.

Brian shrugs. 'Believable motive.' He suddenly notices a stray bullet in the wall, lodged in the plaster above Darby's head. Those have to go to keep their story straight. He grabs one of the steak knives, climbs onto a chair and levers the flattened bullet out from the wall. He holds it up with his thumb and pinky. 'Shit!' he says, dropping the bullet. It lands with a soft clink on the floor. Brian inspects his finger and thumb – the bullet burned like fire, and the skin is still scorched from where it came into contact. He instinctively puts his fingers in his mouth and sucks on them.

'Darby, didn't you say Abe gave you that gun?' he asks, coming down from the chair and glowering at the bullet.

'Yeah,' Darby shouts from the back of the restaurant.

'And the ammo too?'

'Obviously. Why?' Darby and Nik walk over to Brian.

'Oh, wow,' Nik says, crouching down and picking up the bullet. It's flat, like a coin, the metal soft and almost white. 'I guess now we know, silver is definitely *a thing.*'

'Wait. But that would mean that Abe ...' Darby's eyes go wide as the realization hits him. 'I never told him anything. I swear!'

Brian's just going into his inner cave so that he doesn't tackle Darby to the floor, when the door to the restaurant opens with a jingle. The trio turns to see none other than Abe darkening their doorstep. He wipes his feet on the doormat, takes off his hat and looks around at the wreckage.

'You'll want to get that fixed,' he says, casually pointing to one of the empty window frames.

Brian and Nik are frozen in place, but Darby strides straight toward him and pushes him.

'You knew?! Who the fuck are you?! Deep state? Do I know too much … oh my God. Where were you? We could have died!'

'Deep sta … ? What? Of course not,' says Abe. 'I can explain everything, but right now, time is of the essence.' He pulls out a pocketknife and walks in a straight line, swiftly plucking out each bullet from the walls and furniture until all but the one lodged in Tyler's head are accounted for. 'It's best we have this conversation away from an active crime scene. We need to leave.'

None of them move.

Abe walks over to Darby and touches his hand to their cheek. 'It's still me. You can trust me.'

Darby pouts. 'You swear you're not deep state?'

'Darby. I don't think deep state is a real thing.'

'Oh, like werewolves aren't a real thing?'

Abe half smiles. 'Touché. But listen, Darby. We need to go. Now.'

'Fiiiinne, then,' says Darby, relenting.

'Both of you, follow me,' Abe says, gesturing to Darby and Nik. 'You too, lycanthrope.'

Brian looks around the restaurant, puzzled, trying to figure out what Abe's just said and to whom. Then he notices that Abe's looking right at him.

Abe sighs. 'You too, werewolf,' he clarifies, and then walks out the door.

FIFTEEN

The early-morning sunlight crests above the buildings as they leave The Romanesco, Abe and Darby leading the way, bickering softly as they hurry across the parking lot.

'Hold on!' Nik suddenly shouts, then she turns on her heel and jogs back to the restaurant to lock up.

Brian looks at the splintered door, the busted-out frames, the holes in the masonry. 'Uh, Nik?' he calls. 'I don't think you need to do that.' Anyone who wanted to enter The Romanesco could just as easily step through one of the broken windows.

'We do!' Nik shouts back, dusting off her knees from locking the bolts on the bottom of the French doors and then jogging back over. 'For the alibi. There's no way I can afford to lose this job.'

They follow Abe and Darby through the streets, Nik still rehearsing their story. 'We cleaned. We left. We went to the bar. We don't know *anything* about this. Zip. Zilch. Nada.'

'You think that'll work?'

Nik shrugs. 'I hope?'

Brian is less confident. No matter how they leave the

242

place after closing, there's always something the morning staff admonish them for the next day. Nik bears the brunt of it, and she usually just handles it, but this is on a different level. If the morning shift can get that mad about the clean glassware left in the dishwasher, they're going to go nuclear when they see this level of carnage. In the back of his mind, Brian has already made peace with being fired in a matter of hours. But given how much Nik is fussing, she's mid-transition between the denial and the bargaining phases.

The city blocks of the peaceful neighborhood are still empty and quiet, everyone at home, asleep in their beds. A moment of stillness, like when a bomb goes off and there's nothing but bright dust and ringing. The only sounds are the chirping of birds and cab drivers passing them on their way home. They trudge behind Abe, unsure what to expect, while he leads them to a row of identical two-story shops with large rectangular windows. The one in the center is embossed with 'V. H. Flowers' in a flourish of calligraphy. The store is dark but for the purple glow of hydroponic lights in the back.

'We're here,' says Abe, jingling his keys into the lock and opening the door. 'After you.'

Brian takes the lead, with Nik and Darby in tow. He creeps through the 10-foot-high aisles of lush greenery, feeling his way toward the purple lights. Brian is on edge, unsure if this is a trap. He doesn't know what Abe's deal is, but he's definitely not just a mute guy who sits at the bar fawning over Darby. He hears refrigerators behind the

243

register hum and click like tiny robotic footsteps. As he inches closer to the greenhouse, a familiar acrid scent in the air thickens – he begins to feel nauseous. He pulls his shirt up to his nose and peers through the condensation on the glass of an indoor greenhouse to see rows of purple-hooded buttercup-type blossoms – the very same flowers Abe gifted Darby for their performance. Brian suddenly gags and loses his balance, but Nik catches him from behind and props him back up.

'What is that?' She scans each windowpane until she finds the handwritten label on the glass. 'Wolfsbane,' she breathes.

The lights turn on, startling them, and they spin around to see Abe behind the register with his hand on the light switch. 'Darby, could you take them out back? I'm sure you'd appreciate the fresh air,' he says, nodding deliberately at Brian. 'You've all had a rough night. I'll bring you some tea. It should help calm the nerves.'

Darby leads them through the back door of the flower shop to reveal a sizeable garden that would put Tyler's to shame – a hidden oasis surrounded by a latticework of ensnared ivy and botanicals, filled with dozens of color-blocked flower boxes in neatly labeled rows. All of the plants are in bloom in an explosion of color, each stem and root dripped and misted with bespoke irrigation rigs. They take a seat at a wrought-iron patio table underneath an ivy-covered pergola in the center of the garden. Brian puts his head between his knees and breathes deeply until the stench from the shop is replaced with the aroma of sweet, wet earth.

Nik's eyes dart around the garden, briefly considering each new bloom until another catches her interest. 'This is gorgeous. Have you been here before?'

'Of course,' says Darby. 'Isn't it cute? We had one of our first dates right here.' They run their hand wistfully over the surface of the table. They turn their face up to the sun, the light breaking through the ivy and catching flecks of glitter across their face. 'The place has been in his family for generations. He lives in the apartment above it. Developers have tried to get him to sell, but he's turned them all down.'

Brian hears the door open and the clinking of plates. He risks removing his head from between his knees and sees Abe making his way through the garden with a matching porcelain chinoiserie tea set and a selection of breakfast pastries on a tray. He places it at the head of the table and pours everyone a cup before finding his seat. Nik and Darby sip their tea, but Brian waits. He locks eyes with Abe and brings his cup to his nose to make a show of smelling it first.

'It's safe. I promise,' says Abe.

Brian looks to Darby, who makes a face that reads like a plea. He looks back at Abe and sips.

'It's good, right?' Abe says.

Fuck, it's delicious, Brian thinks. But he's determined to play it cool. 'It's all right,' he says dismissively. He shifts in his seat and clears his throat. 'This tea party is great and everything, but you still owe us some answers.'

Abe delicately places his teacup on its saucer. 'Ah, yes.' He removes his glasses and wipes the lenses. 'Where should I start?'

'I'll go first,' chirps Darby. 'Who are you?'

'It's still me, Darby. I swear. None of this changes us.'

Darby's face shows a glimmer of hope, but they catch themself before doubling back. 'All right, but why are you loading guns with silver bullets? And are you even a florist? Or is this place a front? God, you're not cartel, are you?'

'No, no, I am a florist. But a botanist would be a more apt classification. One of a range of disciplines that I have been immersed in over the years. Physiology, psychology, anthropology, all of them have their hidden corners of arcane knowledge. You see, I come from a lineage of investigators and scientists charged with keeping order and protecting any spillovers from the mythical world and, more recently, vice versa. It's been my life's pursuit, my duty, and the duty of every Van Helsing.'

Nik throws her hands up to silence him. 'Wait, wait, wait … Abe *Van Helsing*? As in *Abraham* Van Helsing?'

'Well, Abraham was my father,' Abe says, sipping his tea and returning it to its saucer. 'Everyone just calls me Abe.'

'Wait, who's Abraham Van Helsing?' asks Brian.

Nik closes her eyes and taps her brow while she sidebars with Brian. 'I say this with love, truly, but I am *begging* you to open a book sometime. Literally any book will do. You probably read the equivalent number of words doomscrolling Twitter every day.'

'So, you've heard of my family?' Abe is now keenly interested in Nik.

'I Wikipedia-d some things in preparation for last

246

night,' Nik demurs, eager to shift his attention away from her. 'But there's not a lot out there.'

'Yes, that is by design. Very curious …'

'Wait!' says Darby, the light of comprehension dawning. 'Van Helsing like the Hugh Jackman movie?'

Abe shifts uncomfortably. 'Ahem … oh, yes, well, there's *that*. But we sued Universal. It's so far beyond defamation that you just wouldn't … but let's not get into that.'

Brian looks from Nik, to Darby, back to Abe. 'Okay, great, now that we have all the details to find your Facebook profile, can you just get on with it? I'm tired, traumatized and soon to be unemployed. So, please, speed this up.'

Abe frowns at Darby. 'Is he always like this?'

'Unfortunately,' they shrug.

'Very well. It was about a year ago now when I received a tip from a colleague. There was a werewolf in my parish by the name of Tyler Gainsborough. Now, the odd lone wolf was never something to sound the alarm bells. They are social creatures, you see. Strongest in packs. But I was told that this one had the means and the ambition to consolidate power. He had already turned another and apparently, he had acquired quite a taste for it. His pursuit had to be stopped lest it muddy the separation between the two worlds. I began tracking his movements, following him from city to city on his fruitless recruitment trips, until eventually he found another right here in his hometown.' Abe looks meaningfully at Brian, who grimaces and tries to avoid everyone's eye contact.

'I was there the night he came to the restaurant. A lone wolf like Brian was suitable bait to see what Tyler had planned; I had to observe, to see how it played out, understand his true intentions, see if there were more of you that I hadn't yet tracked. Little did I know that following him into the diner that night would change everything.' Abe stops and reaches out for Darby's hand. They make a show of sulky reluctance, not wanting Abe to think they're won over so easily, but it's obvious that the revelation that their lover is a steampunk werewolf-hunter turns them to butter. 'It's a solitary existence doing what I do,' Abe continues. 'I never thought I would be able to find someone. After I met Darby, I had to do everything in my power to protect them.'

'Everything including trying to kill me?' asks Brian.

'Please, I never tried to kill you. I told you, you were bait. Besides, you seemed pretty harmless,' Abe says dismissively.

'Harmless?! I've killed at least two guys, maybe three if you count Mark!'

'Are you actually bragging about that?' Nik asks flatly.

'Okay, I admit. I had my reservations about you, Brian. Darby told me how great you were, but, as the old adage goes, you're only as good as the company you keep. So I still took precautions. I spent my nights at The Romanesco. I walked Darby home whenever I was in town. When you started showing signs of aggression, I sent wolfsbane to Darby to keep you at bay. But as Tyler grew desperate and started traveling more and more, I couldn't always be there. That's when I gave them the gun.'

'You said that was a six-month anniversary present!' says Darby.

'A happy coincidence, my love,' he says, squeezing their hand.

Brian looks at Nik to deliver an exaggerated eyeroll, but she cuffs him around the head and folds her arms. 'Three!' she mutters, not yet ready to forgive Brian for his body count.

'Where was I?' says Abe. 'Ah, yes. Well, after you and Tyler had that little quarrel at The Romanesco, I knew treachery was afoot. I had to probe you on it, see what your true intentions were. You told me all I needed to hear – I just gave you the little push you needed to make the right decision.'

'You *inceptioned* me?!'

'Please, I merely offered you a suggestion. From what Darby tells me, you need a little help undoing yourself from all the knots you tie yourself up in.'

'Ooh, burn ...' says Darby, snorting into their teacup.

'After you left, all I had to do was wait outside Tyler's home that full moon. And sure enough, what do I see but a large black wolf bounding down the street. I saw you, Brian, clawing at the walls, desperate for a way in. You were there to stop him. It was then I knew I had an ally. When you peeled off toward the park, I followed as fast as I could. But you were fast, too fast. When I arrived, the battle was nearly over and you were losing ... badly. As I saw the other wolf going in for the kill, I fired an arrow from the tree line. A silver-tipped arrow infused with a wolfsbane concoction I developed here. You're welcome, by the way.'

'Welcome? What if you'd missed? You could have killed me!'

Abe sets down his teacup carefully on the saucer and plucks a croissant from the tray, pausing until all eyes are on him. He tosses it into the air, which catches all of them off guard, and in one sudden movement, he shifts in his seat to hip-fire the handheld crossbow concealed in his jacket. The arrow cuts across the table, pinning the flaky pastry to the pergola column with a thud.

Darby instinctively erupts in an applause that peters out when they catch Brian's stare.

'I don't miss. And, I will have you know, I made sure you were still breathing before I absconded with my arrow.'

'Well, what about last night?' asks Nik.

'Yeah, for someone who's always hanging around, you sure did pick an odd night to be absent!' adds Brian.

'It was a tough decision, but I was watching, Tyler always in my crosshairs. I assure you I would have intervened if needed. But I am duty bound not to reveal aspects of the mystical world. It chooses when and how to reveal itself through these fated encounters. But the timing was quite propitious. Keeping all these secrets from Darby was weighing on me. Not intervening presented an opportunity to test your mettle. It was an audition of sorts.'

'Audition?' asks Darby, alerted after hearing one of their trigger words.

Abe pushes back his chair and stands up. 'Follow me.'

The three of them get up from the table as Abe disappears back into the flower shop.

'Treachery is afoot!' Brian mutters like a Victorian gentleman in imitation of Abe. Darby glares at him.

'*Three!*' hisses Nik, while they follow inside.

Behind the register, flanked by refrigerators filled with buckets of tulips, roses and lilies, there is a thick wooden door with multiple locks. It must have been there the entire time and they are just now seeing it. Doors don't just appear. Abe has a ring of keys and he inspects each one as he unlocks the series. 'I don't know if you all intend on going back to the restaurant after last night. But I could always use some help around the flower shop,' he says, unlocking the final lock and slipping the ring back into his leather jacket. 'And as for the extracurricular activities ...'

Abe opens the door to reveal a spiraling stone staircase that leads to the basement. 'After you.'

'Are these real flaming torches?' Darby asks, as they follow the stairs down for what seems like forever.

'No, they make the passage too smoky. They're faux flame but incredibly convincing, right?'

Suddenly, the staircase opens out into a vast library, much bigger than the floorplan of V. H. Flowers above. It's filled with rows of floor-to-ceiling wooden bookshelves, neatly stacked with volumes in varying sizes and colors, each etched with delicate lettering as faint as a whisper. The largest, leather-bound tomes are placed on the highest shelves, as if Abe keeps them out of reach intentionally. While there are no windows, presumably to keep out prying eyes, pendant lamps punctuate the ceiling in neat rows, bathing the library in soft light.

Nik clasps her hand over her mouth. Brian and Abe follow her as she ambles through the stacks, running her finger over the spines and reading out their titles. She pulls out a book on parapsychology and thumbs through the pages.

'What is this? Is this real?'

Abe smiles and pats her on the shoulder. 'My dear, you have been taught that science and magic are in opposition. But rather they are points on the same spectrum of knowledge.'

'Oh my God!' shouts Darby from across the room. Nik slams the book shut and looks up in alarm. In the far corner of the library sits a stately wood carved desk, more ornamental than Abe's asceticism would suggest, with stacks of Abe's journals throughout the years clearly labeled and in sequential order. Behind the desk there's a large cork-board diagram with photos of high-net-worth individuals linked with red yarn. Darby pores over the photos and traces the yarn with their finger.

'I loved her in *Mamma Mia!*' they say. 'And so many of the *Real Housewives* … ?'

'Yes, Tyler wasn't the first to try and consolidate power in the mystical world,' says Abe, firmly taking a steampunk crossbow out of Brian's hands and coming over to Darby. 'But luckily, his myopia about what he thought being a werewolf was – masculinity, power, aggression – made him incapable of finding the others who were right under his nose.'

'Wolves are matriarchal,' says Brian, looking over to Nik, who's still clutching the book in her hands. She winks.

'They are,' Abe says, nodding. 'Valkyrie *aren't* though, interestingly, and they're much smarter than werewolves and therefore harder to kill. Oh, yes, there's much more than werewolves out there, I'm afraid. Plenty of work to be done, and it's about time I got myself some help. So, what do you say?'

They look at each other in shock. Is he really asking this? 'Hang on,' says Brian, and the three of them go into a huddle. They've just survived mortal battle with a werewolf, they haven't slept in about twenty-four hours and they're almost certainly all fired.

'And, honestly, I'm on *such* a bad comedown,' complains Darby, who somehow managed to retrieve their molly from Nik's purse.

They all agree that now is *not* the time to be making major life decisions. Then again, whatever terrifying genocidal fantasy hell-beasts they might have in front of them if they accept Abe's offer could never be as stressful or demoralizing as working a Sunday brunch shift with the post-church crowd …

They all take a deep breath, then they straighten up and turn back to Abe. 'Sure,' says Brian. 'We're in. At least it won't be the same taste over and over again …'

ACKNOWLEDGEMENTS

Deep in my COVID malaise and desperate for something to break-up the monotony, I booked a virtual reading with The Witch of Salem. As a Massachusetts boy born and raised, my family had seen her for years and told me all the stories of her predictions that came true. I expected she would tell me it was time to switch jobs or move house, but instead, she said that I was going to write a book. I thought it was absurd, but two years later, well, this is that book.

Mystical backing aside, I could not have done this without my amazing editors at Atlantic Books. A huge thanks to James Roxburgh, I couldn't have had a more thoughtful, witty, and empathetic editor to finetune both the pathos and the profanity. And thank you to Bobby Mostyn-Owen for all their advice, punch-ups, and insights throughout the Atlantic Workshop.

In a book about coming of age and finding your chosen family, I have to thank my dear friends and enablers who have been with me through it all, who laugh at my jokes, and continue to put up with my recurring bouts of imposter syndrome: Cecilia Campbell-Westlind, Jen

Turner, Darlene Cayabyab, Cecilia Paredes, Nic Sera-Leyva, Nicole Fernandez, and Matt Swaim.

Thank you to my husband, Robert Henson, for everything, for all the ways you love me. I know I owe you a poem, but I hope a book acknowledgment will hold you over. To my sister, Jessy Sauchuk, thank you for always supporting me and giving me the courage to take risks. I am who I am because of you. And finally, to Freddie Mac, my co-author and thought partner who would jump onto my desk to lick the condensation from my cold brew. I hope you're sleeping in a sunbeam up there in kitty heaven.

NOTE ON THE AUTHOR

Tony Santorella was born and raised in Danvers, Massachusetts, site of the Salem Witch Trials and related hauntings. He moved to Washington, DC in 2005, where he waited tables until beginning his decade-long career in international development. When he's not writing, he's spending time with his husband Robert and their cat, Fannie Mae.